MUSLIN
MYSTERY

MUSLIN MYSTERY

VERA DODGE

Guideposts
New York, New York

www.guideposts.com
(800) 932-2145
Guideposts Books & Inspirational Media

Cover design by Wendy Bass
Cover illustration by Joyce Patti
Interior design by Lorie Pagnozzi
Typeset by Aptara

Printed and bound in the United States of America
10 9 8 7 6 5 4 3 2 1

MUSLIN
MYSTERY

Family Patterns
Time to Share
Muslin Mystery

CHAPTER ONE

When the phone rang, Sarah was standing knee-deep in bright red maple leaves. She'd raked them into a neat pile on her front lawn and had started to sweep them onto a tarp to drag them to the curb. Each arc of her rake sent a cloud of bright leaves swirling in the crisp fall air. But now she leaned on the rake to listen.

The cordless phone rang again from the porch where she'd set it.

It never fails, she thought. But excitement pricked the back of her neck as well. A phone call always held a hint of adventure for her. It could be anything: a new quilt waiting to be restored, one of her granddaughters with some crazy scheme, a friend who needed to talk or just wanted to go get a cup of coffee.

She hurried up the steps of her pretty Queen Anne home, dropped her gardening gloves by the door, and picked up the receiver.

"Hello," she said. "This is Sarah." Her son Jason always told her she should be more careful about giving her name out over the phone, but she couldn't seem to break the habit. Making callers guess who they were speaking to just didn't feel friendly.

From the other end of the line, she heard nothing but silence.

Sarah frowned and waited for the telltale clicks and hiss that would indicate she'd just interrupted her day for a telemarketer. "Hello?" she said again.

"Sarah," a girl said. "I need your help."

She sounded frightened, and she spoke so low that it took Sarah a moment to realize that she recognized the voice. It was Emily Price, who had boarded with her last fall. No, Emily Collins, Sarah corrected herself. Emily had married Tad Collins, who ran the local maple sugar plant with his father, that summer. Sarah had helped her remake her wedding dress, an antique that had belonged to Tad's grandmother, but she still wasn't used to the change in Emily's name.

"Emily!" she said. "It's so good to hear from you! Is everything all right?"

"I'm sorry," Emily said, her voice still strained. "I don't have much time. Could you come meet me?"

Sarah looked at the pile of leaves. The light wind had already begun to blow a few of them back out across the lawn. If she didn't get them down to the curb now, half her work might be undone by the time she got home. But she'd known

Emily for almost a year, and she'd never heard her speak like this.

"Sure," she said. "When were you thinking?"

"Could you come now?" Emily said.

In the background, Sarah could hear a man's voice. She couldn't hear what he was saying, but he sounded agitated.

"Just a minute," Emily said. She muffled the phone and said a few words. Then she came back on the line. "Sarah?" she said.

Now there was no question in Sarah's mind. "I'll be there in a few minutes," she said. "Are you at home?" Emily and Tad had bought a sweet bungalow a few blocks from the town square as their first house. Sarah could walk to it easily, but it would be even faster if she drove.

"No," Emily said. "The Collins place. Do you know it?"

Everybody in town knew the Collins place. Tad's grandfather had built it for his bride as a wedding gift sixty years ago. He'd already begun to make his fortune from his thriving maple syrup business, and he'd spared no expense in the building project. The home was on the outskirts of town, on land that adjoined the maple groves that sustained his business. It sat some distance from the road, but it was so big and so unusual that it had become a landmark of sorts for Maple Hill. Families out for country drives often stopped to linger near the gate, gazing up at the mansion's stained glass and turrets, and local kids liked to scare each other by driving out there at night and swapping stories about how the place was haunted. If it was haunted, the ghosts had to share. Tad's grandfather still lived there and so did Tad's father. Tad had grown up there as well. He and his father had moved in with his grandfather after Tad's mother passed away when he was a boy. This bit of Maple Hill lore had always struck Sarah as sad: three lonely men rattling around together in that big house that had been built to welcome a bride.

"I sure do," Sarah said. But she'd never been there. Almost nobody in Maple Hill had. And somehow, the idea of popping over to the Collins place felt different from making a quick visit to Emily's cozy bungalow. "It's all right if I come now?" she asked.

"Please," Emily said. For the first time, she sounded grateful instead of scared. "Thank you so much."

This was more like the girl Sarah knew. "Emily?" she said. "Do you want to tell me what this is all about?"

In the background, a man started to speak again. He didn't sound angry, Sarah realized. But he was clearly upset.

"It's a quilt," Emily said, her voice worried and low again. "Please come as soon as you can."

The line went dead.

Sarah stared at the phone. The Emily she knew would never have hung up on anyone. In Sarah's years as an expert quilt restorer, she'd seen a lot of passion for quilts. People stayed up late to make them. They went to great lengths to preserve them. But she'd never heard anyone sound so scared over one before.

A few minutes later, Sarah was driving down the country road that led to the Collins place, her travel bag of quilter's tools on the seat beside her: ruler, gloves, magnifying glass, pins, needles, archival quality thread, trimming scissors, tracing paper, and a jumble of other odds and ends. They'd be enough to tackle any quilting project. But Sarah wondered if she had what she needed to help Emily face whatever had frightened her. In any case, Sarah was glad that Emily had called. She'd always been a curious, sunny girl, and it had been a joy to share the house with her as she fell in love with Tad. Sarah might not understand the problem, but at least she knew there was one. Now she could try to help.

Dear Lord, she prayed. *I don't know what Emily's worried about, but you do. Please be with her, and please show me what you want me to do.*

It felt strange to slow and turn into the Collins drive. The wide yard had always seemed mysterious and forbidding, but now she saw that the gravel drive was just like any other in town—maybe even a little bit more overgrown. *That was bizarre,* Sarah thought. Maple Hill still had its share of dirt roads, but the Collins family wasn't hurting for money. She would have guessed that they might have paved the long, winding road to make it easier to navigate in the Berkshire winters. And it was clear that no one had pruned the trees that lined the drive for years. *The place needed a woman's touch,* she thought.

When she reached the house, she discovered a wide paved parking area, set to the side so that it didn't mar the lawn rolling down from the big home. She recognized Emily's small blue sedan, and pulled up next to it. Theirs were the only two cars in the small lot. Sarah collected her travel bag and stepped out. It hardly seemed real, being this close to the old house that she had only ever seen from afar. The stained glass insets between the clear windows glimmered in the morning sun, but the grass in the yard was sun-beaten and thin, and the bushes that fronted the porch were wild and twisted.

Sarah climbed the steps to the door and hesitated on the porch. *Dear Lord,* she prayed again. *I know you're with me. Help me not to be afraid. Help me to love Emily, and give me your peace.*

Just as she opened her eyes, and before she raised her hand to knock, the door clicked open.

Emily stood inside. Her thick brown hair was pulled back in a loose ponytail, and her blue eyes were worried. Sarah gave her a warm smile, but Emily only glanced at her. "Come in," she said, and pulled Sarah inside. Then Emily peered past Sarah, out the door. Sarah looked with her, but she didn't see anything unusual: only the long slope of the lawn and the gray thread of the country road winding through the low hills below.

After a minute, Emily pulled the door closed. "Thank you so much for coming," she said. They stood in a wide hallway, carpeted with lush oriental rugs and furnished with an ornate mirror and an extravagant chandelier.

Sarah could hardly take in the rich details. She was too concerned about Emily. Sarah looked at her questioningly, but Emily avoided her gaze. "I'm sorry for all the mystery," she said. "I just want this to be a surprise for Tad."

"Why don't you show me what you have?" Sarah said gently. Something in Emily's manner didn't ring true to her. A surprise might explain the rush and the secrecy, but it didn't explain the real worry in Emily's eyes.

For the first time, a smile played across Emily's lips. "Okay," she said, almost shyly. She put her hand on the knob of the door to the next room, then hesitated.

"I'm here to take care of Mr. Collins," she said. "His nurse has the day off."

"Tad's father?" Sarah asked. She didn't know Samuel Collins well, but she remembered him vaguely as a quiet boy who was in the same class as Martha and Sarah.

Emily shook her head. "His grandfather," she said, and opened the door.

The old man sat in a red leather chair beside an empty fireplace. When Emily stepped into the room, his face lit up as if he hadn't seen her for hours.

"Genie!" he said. "Where have you been?"

"I'm Emily, Grandpa," Emily said. "This is my friend Sarah Hart. Sarah, this is Ward Collins."

"It's good to see you," Sarah said, hiding her shock at the change in Ward Collins. She remembered him from her girlhood as a vibrant man, driving through town in the latest Cadillac. But after his wife's death he'd retired to the house he'd built for her, and he'd rarely been seen in town again. Now his thick dark hair had turned white, and his broad frame had grown thin and bony.

Sarah didn't need to disguise her emotions. Ward Collins didn't even glance at her. He frowned up at Emily in confusion. "Where's Genie?" he asked.

Emily bit her lip. "She's gone, Grandpa," she said.

Ward Collins gazed up at a portrait of a somewhat melancholy-looking young woman. "When is she coming back?" he asked.

Emily picked up an old comic book from a stack on a nearby table. "Have you read this one?" she asked. On the cover, Superman lifted a building from its foundations while a woman in the window looked down in surprise.

Ward squinted at it, then shook his head.

Emily took it to him. "I think you'll like it," she said.

Ward Collins set the comic book on his lap. He let it fall open somewhere in the middle. Emily stood beside him, her hand resting on his shoulder, until he turned to the next page. Then she opened a small chest beside the fireplace, took out a paper grocery bag, and carried it over to a large round oak table near where Sarah waited. Sarah could see an unfinished fabric edge peeking out of the bag.

So there really was a quilt, Sarah thought. Her heart quickened as it always did at the prospect of a new project. Even though she'd handled hundreds of quilts, she learned something new with each one. Every quilt was full of history and secrets. The fabrics the quilter had picked told the story of what life was like at the time the quilt was made. The pattern she chose was a reflection of her hopes and dreams.

Often, quilters left clues about themselves sewn into the intricate designs. There was nothing like the thrill of seeing an antique quilt for the first time.

Emily reached into the bag and pulled out a rumpled wad of fabric and batting, about twelve inches by twelve inches. She set it on the table and tried to smooth it out. Then she pushed it toward Sarah.

Sarah's brow furrowed. She smoothed the small square herself. It was a complicated collection of fabrics that seemed to be sewn almost at random, except that half of the square was green, divided sharply from the other half, which was composed of dark browns.

"This is your quilt?" Sarah asked.

"No," Emily said. "There are more." She pulled several other rumpled pieces out of the bag and laid them on the table. These were mostly browns and greens, but they weren't evenly divided like the first square. Curves and waves crossed the new squares. Some were almost striped, as if a river of brown ran through a green field. One square was almost entirely blue.

Sarah picked up the first square. Below the quilted face was a layer of batting and newspaper. Under it all was a faded brown backing. Sarah turned the piece over. Although the quilt hadn't been sewn together yet, this individual piece had been quilted, a task that is usually left to the end of the quilting process. Precise stitches had been sewn through all the layers of the fabric, holding the front, lining, and backing together.

"Tad's grandmother made it," Emily said. "I haven't shown it to him because it won't look like much to him until it's put together. But I want him to have something of hers."

Sarah nodded. When Emily had boarded at Sarah's house, Emily had shared that she had lost both her parents when she was in college. Maybe this was the reason for Emily's strange behavior. Anyone might have a hard time thinking about lost family members, especially if they had Emily's history.

"Have you ever seen anything like it?" Emily asked.

Sarah shook her head. "Not in person," she said. "I think it's quilt-as-you-go."

"What's that?" Emily asked.

"Normally you assemble the quilt pieces first," Sarah explained. "Then you lay them down on the backing and batting, and quilt through all the layers to hold them together. But in quilt-as-you-go, you quilt each piece individually. It's complicated, because you need to make sure the quilting lines up even though the pieces aren't sewn together yet. But it makes your project much more portable."

"Or easier to hide," Emily said thoughtfully.

Sarah's brow furrowed again. "I hadn't thought of it that way," she said. "But yes."

In the hall, a door slammed shut.

"Emily?" Tad called.

Emily froze. Her eyes locked with Sarah's. "I didn't hear his car come up!" Emily whispered, as if she were talking about a burglar, not her husband.

Sarah sprang into action, collecting the quilt pieces into a neat stack. She'd just stashed them away in the paper bag when Tad came in from the hall.

Tad made a beeline for Emily and gave her an enthusiastic kiss. For the first time since Sarah had arrived, Emily's face broke into a genuine smile. Then she pulled away.

"You remember Sarah," she said.

"Of course!" Tad said. He grinned and gave Sarah a warm hug. "You took care of my girl until I could talk her into marrying me! What brings you here?"

"Oh, just a little sewing project," Sarah said, rattling the bag. Unless Tad was a very unusual man, the finely made quilt squares wouldn't look like much more than scraps to him.

"Well that's great!" Tad said. "What is it?"

Sarah glanced at Emily. She didn't mind telling Tad the quilt was just a sewing project, but she didn't want to give away Emily's secret—or tell Tad a lie.

Tad turned to Emily, as well. Under his open gaze, she seemed to find the will to tell a piece of the truth. "It's just something your grandmother was working on," she said. "I thought Sarah could finish it for us."

Suddenly, Tad's smile vanished. "Emily," he said, his voice tight. "You know how Dad feels about that."

"I know," Emily began. "I just thought that—"

"I understood about the wedding dress," Tad interrupted. "I could see how you might want to wear something of Grandma Genie's, since you didn't have any family. And

I would have married you if you were wearing a gunnysack. But that wasn't easy to get past Dad. He's not rational about Grandma Genie."

By the fireplace, Ward looked up from his comic book. "Genie?" he said. "Is Genie coming?"

"Hey Grandpa," Tad said. He walked over and bent down to kiss the old man's cheek. "Grandma Genie isn't coming. She passed away a long time ago." Tad turned to Emily. "You see?" he said, nodding down at his grandfather. "Why would you want to stir this up?"

"I visit Genie every Saturday," Ward Collins said wistfully.

"That's right, Grandpa," Tad said, then turning to Sarah and Emily, "Dad and Grandpa make a trip to her grave every weekend."

Sarah took a step back from the bag, preparing to make a graceful exit. But to her surprise, Emily shook her head stubbornly. "I promised Sarah the work already," she said.

"Well, I certainly don't need—" Sarah began, but Emily picked up the bag of quilt squares and pushed it into Sarah's hands.

"This is important to me," Emily told Tad.

Tad looked at her, frustration struggling on his face with tenderness for his new bride. Finally, his shoulders slumped. He raised his hands in surrender. "All right," he said. "Whatever you want."

Emily crossed the room and stood on her tiptoes to kiss his cheek. "Thank you," she said, her voice suddenly soft again.

Sarah began to edge toward the door. "I'll just let you know how it goes, then," she said.

"Oh, Sarah," Emily said. "I'll walk you out."

Tad flashed his familiar grin. "Thank you, Sarah," he said. "Don't mind me. It was just hard on the family to lose Mom and Grandma Genie."

"I understand," Sarah said. She did. She had been only a young girl when Genie died, but the whole town had felt for Ward Collins and his young son as they grieved Genie's loss. A generation later, the whole town had reeled with disbelief when they heard that Tad's mother had passed away of cancer when Tad was only a boy himself. And Sarah knew the pain of losing a loved one personally. Her husband Gerry had been gone for almost five years, but the smell of his cologne on an old blanket or the sight of his favorite morning glories coming up in the spring could still bring tears to her eyes.

Emily opened the door, and Sarah followed her out into the hall.

"Thank you so much for coming," Emily told her. "And I'm sorry about all that."

"There are adjustments with joining any family," Sarah said. "Hang in there. You two will work it out."

"Especially this family," Emily said.

Sarah nodded. "All these men, used to living alone, without any women," she said. "I can see how it would take some adjusting."

But now Emily was avoiding her eyes again. "Yeah," Emily said. But Sarah could see that wasn't what she had meant.

CHAPTER TWO

The bell over the door of the Wild Goose Chase rang as Sarah walked in. Vanessa, the shop's owner, looked up from the wide table where she cut fabric and rang up orders. She had a historical romance in her hand, as she often did when business was slow. But at the sight of Sarah, she quickly laid it aside.

"Well, hello stranger," she said. "How long has it been since I saw you?"

Sarah grinned over the paper bag full of quilt pieces she carried. She'd just seen Vanessa the morning before, when she'd stopped by the store to pick up a few fat quarters for a new quilt. "A whole twenty-four hours," she said.

"Twenty-four?" Vanessa said. "I thought it was more like twenty-six."

"But who's counting?" Sarah joked.

"It's a shame," Vanessa said. "I wish we could see each other more often."

"That's nothing!" came a voice from the far side of the counter, where skeins and skeins of yarn were displayed in bright rows. "I was here twice yesterday, and I've already been here for an hour."

"Martha?" Sarah said, and circled around the corner. Her best friend sat cross-legged on the carpet, surrounded by varying shades of pink, green, and lavender yarn.

"It's true," Vanessa said. "She's been here so often I'm wondering if I should start charging her rent."

"Except my yarn purchases pay your rent!" Martha protested.

Vanessa tilted her head to acknowledge this was a fair point. "That might be true," she said.

Sarah crouched beside her friend, shifting the paper bag to one knee. She lifted a skein of pale green cotton. "What are you making?" she asked.

"Mile-a-minute baby afghans," Martha answered. "I think I'm actually going to make three of them."

Sarah did a quick search of her memory. One of the young couples at church was about to have a baby, but she didn't know of anyone else who was expecting. "For the Pittards?" she asked.

Martha nodded.

"And who else?" Sarah said. "Do you have any more grandchildren on the way you haven't told me about?" Martha's daughter-in-law was due with her second child in the spring.

A shadow seemed to pass over Martha's face. She shook her head.

"Nope," she said. "I'll give the other two to Project Linus. I've been trying to decide between pink, green, and lavender all morning. I can't bring myself to choose among them. So I'm going to make them all."

This logic might not make sense outside a fabric shop, but Sarah knew exactly what Martha was doing. And she knew something else: what it was like to feel helpless while a loved one was in poor health. Martha's husband Ernie had recently been diagnosed with Parkinson's disease, and ever since then she'd gone through creative projects faster than Sarah could count. Sarah recognized the impulse. She'd done the same thing when her husband Gerry got sick. While he was getting treatments, she'd appliquéd in the doctor's waiting room, and she'd quilted during his long naps. Doing any kind of project had felt better than sitting helplessly with idle hands. At first she had worried that she might not be able to use the things she made during that time. She wondered if they would bring up painful memories of losing her husband. But as she grieved and healed, she found that they were wonderful reminders of her love for him. When she thought back on the difficult days she had spent making them, she remembered how close God had been to her then. And that memory stayed strong, even after the grief had faded.

"I think that's a great idea," Sarah said.

Martha glanced curiously at the bag on Sarah's knee. "What have you got there?" she asked.

Sarah straightened up and set the bag on Vanessa's cutting counter. "A quilt," she said, and pulled a square from the bag.

Martha stood beside her. "That doesn't look like much of a quilt to me," she said.

"That's only one piece," Sarah told her. She laid a few more on the table.

"It's not pieced yet!" Martha exclaimed.

Sarah nodded. "Right."

"Then why sew the batting and backing together?" Martha asked. She turned a piece over. "These have already been quilted!" Martha was a knitter, not a quilter, but even she recognized how unusual the mysterious quilt pieces were.

"Quilt-as-you-go," Vanessa said.

"That's my guess," said Sarah.

Vanessa began to pull pieces out of the bag in earnest. A few moments later several dozen squares were scattered over the cutting counter.

"No two of these are the same, either," Martha said.

"That's what I suspected," Sarah said. "I haven't had a chance to look at them all before, but they don't look like any design I've ever seen."

"Was there a pattern?" Martha asked. "How will you know which pieces go together?"

"I don't know," Sarah said. "You see this piecing here?" She pointed at a swath of green made from various small scraps of fabric, all different shades of green.

Martha nodded.

"It looks like a mosaic to me," Sarah told her.

"That's what I was thinking," Vanessa agreed.

"Mosaic?" Martha repeated.

"It's a technique quilters developed when fabric was more expensive," Sarah said. "Quilters sewed together scraps of similar shades to make a new piece of fabric: several blues together or several pinks. Then they'd cut shapes from that new piece. People still do it today because it creates such interesting variations in shade."

"Almost like a watercolor painting," Vanessa said, smoothing down another piece, which mixed pale blues with more greens. "But I can't understand why someone would use quilt-as-you-go for a mosaic. You cut mosaic pieces freehand, then sew them down to a single large backing. Doing it in pieces this way is incredibly complicated."

"Exactly," Sarah said. "The only thing I could think of is that there might be some kind of pattern. And I thought you might recognize something I don't."

Vanessa was African-American and had grown up in the South, so she had a different background in quilting than Sarah did. Both of them loved the famous standards like Around the World and Sunshine and Shadow, but Vanessa had also introduced Sarah to variations on the tradition, like the bold patterns of the quilters of Gee's Bend, which were so original they were collected by major art museums. Sometimes patterns that seemed totally unfamiliar to Sarah were old friends to Vanessa, and vice versa. Together, they guessed there weren't many patterns or styles one of them hadn't seen.

Vanessa turned all the pieces right side up, counting silently. "Forty-two," she said.

"So it's probably six by seven," Sarah calculated.

Vanessa nodded. "Although with a quilt this unusual, you never know," she said. "It could be three by fourteen."

"Or two by twenty-one," Martha chimed in. "A quilt scarf."

Sarah smiled. "Does it look familiar to you?" she asked Vanessa.

Vanessa frowned in concentration. She tilted her head this way and that. She pushed several of the squares around on the table into different configurations. Then she shook her head. "No," she said. "It doesn't."

Martha's phone rang, a tiny choir singing one of the barbershop quartet tunes she loved. Martha scrambled to answer it. "Hello?" she said.

Vanessa turned a few of the pieces over to study the stitching on the back. Sarah flipped the piece closest to her. Green quilting stitches rambled across the fabric like a twisting stream. Pale tan stitches were jumbled among them, seemingly at random. They curved in arcs that ran out before they reached the edge of the fabric to join with another quilting line. They met at points, then opened up at strange angles. Sarah turned back the edge of the backing fabric. Her hunch was correct: The tan stitches didn't hold the pieces together as the green quilting stitches did. They seemed to be some kind of embroidery or decoration. But what kind of shape were they supposed to create?

"Oh, honey," Martha said. "I'm so sorry."

Sarah glanced up at her friend. Martha's face was drawn. She stared past Sarah at the soft rows of yarn, her mind clearly elsewhere.

"Me?" Martha said. "But do you really think I—" She broke off when the person on the other line began to speak again.

"Of course I will," she said. "Anything I can do...I love you too."

"Is everything all right?" Vanessa asked as Martha ended the call.

"I'm sorry," Martha said. "I have to go." She looked down at the pile of yarn on the floor.

"Don't you worry about that," Vanessa said. "I'll just pack up all of it and hold it until you have time to come back."

"Thank you," Martha said.

Sarah knew better than to press Martha if Martha didn't want to talk, but she wrapped her friend in a long hug. "You know you can call me anytime," she said.

"I know," said Martha. She slipped her phone back into her purse and hurried out.

Vanessa and Sarah watched her go. "Dear Jesus, please go with Martha," Vanessa said.

"Amen," Sarah said. When she looked back down at the piece in front of her on the table, the strange angle of the tan thread, crossed by a random line, resolved in her mind into the letter A. Sarah was used to this. Her mind was always picking out patterns in the clouds, or in the swirls of quilting. She was probably just trying to make sense out of nonsense again. She flipped over the piece beside it. This time her eyes quickly picked out another letter in tan thread: P. Was it another coincidence?

Quickly, Sarah flipped over another three squares. The letter M. The letter H. The letter R.

"Vanessa," Sarah said.

Vanessa looked over at the upside-down squares. Sarah traced the shape of the A with her finger. "Do you see a letter here?" she asked.

"Look at that," Vanessa said. She turned over a pair of the pieces she had been investigating: another M and an S. "Are they all like this?"

Moments later, Sarah and Vanessa had turned all the remaining pieces. Most had a letter sewed in faint stitching on the back. About a dozen were blank.

"It must spell something," Vanessa said. She pulled a pair of Ls, an H, an O, and an E together to spell HELLO.

Sarah pulled an H, an L, an E, and a P, to spell HELP.

Vanessa laughed. "I wish I could," she said. "I just don't know what to tell you. With this many letters there must be thousands of combinations."

"And why are some of the squares blank?" Sarah asked.

"Spaces," Vanessa said. "Between words."

"Of course!" Sarah said. "How could I have missed that?"

"You wouldn't have missed it for long," Vanessa said.

"Do you see anything else I don't?" Sarah asked.

Vanessa shook her head, still surveying the blocks. "One thing I can tell you, though," she said. "This isn't anything like any pattern I've ever seen. I think you must be right that it's a one-of-a-kind mosaic. And for some reason, someone decided to quilt in pieces."

Sarah sighed and began to stack the squares back up again. "Well, thank you," she said.

"Any time," Vanessa told her. "It looks like you've got more than one puzzle,"

"Yes," Sarah said. "But I only have to solve one of them to solve the other."

CHAPTER THREE

S
arah!" Liam boomed from behind the counter of The Spotted Dog. Laugh lines crinkled around his green eyes as he smiled in greeting. Murphy, Liam's faithful Corgi, burst from his post by the nearest bookshelf and galloped over, his long body quivering with glee. Sarah cradled the bag of quilt squares she carried in one arm and bent down to scratch his ears while the happy dog tried to decide whether to wriggle in ecstasy or lick her hand in thanks. When Sarah straightened up Murphy looked up at her mournfully for a moment. Then he sat down at her feet.

Liam laughed. "He likes you," he said. "He's got an idea that if he blocks your way, you'll never leave."

Sarah looked down. She couldn't see her shoes. They were pretty much hidden by the determined Corgi's spotted torso. "I'm not sure how that would be for business," she said.

"I think we could get used to it," said Liam.

Sarah gave him a quick searching look. Liam was a great businessman who offered the best service to his customers. But every now and then, she found herself wondering if he treated every customer with as much care as he treated her. Sometimes, she even hoped he didn't.

"Well," Liam said. "To what do I owe this pleasant surprise?"

"Would you call this a surprise?" Sarah smiled. She went to the Wild Goose Chase several times a week, but she was at The Spotted Dog almost every day for her beloved chai lattes.

"I try not to take my good luck for granted," he said.

Gently, Sarah extricated her feet from Murphy. He looked up at her with reproach in his big brown eyes. Liam pulled a treat from under the counter and handed it to Sarah. She offered it to the dog, who took it with an air of resignation, then trotted off to the bookshelves to enjoy his prize.

"I'm looking for a book," Sarah told Liam.

"A quilt book?" Liam asked. He stepped out from behind the counter to lead her into the bookstore. Outside of Vanessa's shop, The Spotted Dog had become the best source of information on quilts in town. When it first opened, the bookstore attached to the café had only a few random books on quilting, but in the past few years the quilt book selection had become substantial. "What are you looking for?" he asked.

"Mosaics," Sarah said.

Liam came to a stop at the well-stocked quilting shelf. "I thought those were made from rock or shards of glass," he said. Sarah shook her head. "They're pieced like that," she explained. "Only with different scraps of fabric."

"*Hmm*," Liam said. "I don't know if we have anything like that." He ran his finger along the bright-colored spines, and stopped at a thick encyclopedia of quilts. "Maybe this one," he said.

He seemed to be unusually well acquainted with the contents of the section, even for a bookstore owner.

"You seem to be fairly interested in quilts," Sarah said.

Liam flipped the book open and glanced at her over its pages. "You could say that," he said, looking through the index. "Marble fabric, mountain heritage...mosaic quilts. Here."

He passed her the book, which was open to a full-page photograph of a garden, each flower cut from pieced mosaic scraps. The effect gave each bloom breathtaking variety and depth. "Is this what you're looking for?" he asked.

"Exactly," Sarah said.

Liam handed her the book and retreated behind his counter to tap at his computer. "Ah, here we go," he said. "I don't have anything else in stock, but it looks like I could order you a few titles on mosaic quilts if you're interested."

"You don't need to go to any trouble," Sarah said.

"It's not trouble," Liam told her. He began to tap at the computer again. Sarah idly paged through a few more titles but found no more references to mosaics. It was a rare quilting technique, and so was quilt-as-you-go. And one quilter deciding to use both techniques on the same project still baffled her. Quilt-as-you-go was designed to make a project easier, but the technique would actually make a mosaic quilt more complicated. What kind of quilter would set out to deliberately make a project more difficult than it needed to be?

Sarah replaced the last volume on the shelf, stepped back to the café side of The Spotted Dog, and took a seat at one of the small tables near the register. Liam always kept fresh flowers in small vases, changing them out each week. This week they were carnations, white tipped with red. She pushed the small vase to the side, and checked to make sure the table was clean. Of course it was. Liam's place was always spotless.

She flipped open the small notebook she carried with her, and wrote the alphabet in two even rows down the page. Then she pulled a handful of quilt squares from the crumpled paper bag and began to count. E. She made a hatch mark beside the letter on her notebook page. P. M. H. U. When she had finished counting, she carefully replaced the quilt squares in their bag. The coffee machines sputtered and squealed behind the counter, but she was too absorbed to pay much attention to anything else.

Two A's. One C. Six E's. Two each of H, L, and M. One N. Three O's and three P's. One each of R, S, and U. Three Y's. And one with three letters, probably a monogram: EPC. That was strange, Sarah thought. The C could stand for

"Collins," but Genie's name didn't start with E. Was it possible that Emily was wrong about who had made the quilt? Had it been made by someone in an earlier generation? And the C didn't have to stand for Collins, Sarah supposed. It could have been made by someone outside of the family. That was, if it was even a monogram. It might stand for something else altogether. The C could stand for "club," or "church." Sarah turned over the piece but found no other clues. For the time being, it was just one more mystery in a quilt full of them.

Thirteen of the blocks had no letters on them at all— probably spaces between words, as Vanessa had suggested, but perhaps some kind of border. If the quilt was six by seven, six might go at the top and six at the bottom.

Sarah frowned at the page. A boy in her high school class had been crazy for anagrams years ago, and he had spent a day creating word combinations from her name: Sarah Jane Drayton. There had been dozens of them, none of which made much sense, although one, "Hosanna Trader Jay," had always stuck in Sarah's mind. But if her own brief name had so many possibilities in it, this many letters must have thousands. Where should she begin?

Liam set a hot chai latte, complete with a generous dollop of whipped cream, down on her table. Sarah looked up, surprised.

He grinned. "I got your order right, didn't I?" he said.

Sarah nodded. The chai lattes were her favorite, and despite her other efforts to stay healthy, she always ordered them with whipped cream.

"I didn't want to bring it until you'd finished with the quilt," Liam said, slipping into the chair across from her. "I know those old pieces are precious."

"Thank you," Sarah said.

"What are you working on?" Liam said, nodding at the pad. "It looks like some kind of secret code."

"I don't know," Sarah said. "Maybe it is. There are letters sewn into the backs of some of these quilt squares." She pulled the top one from the paper bag and turned it over on the table to show him the faint stitching.

Liam nodded.

"I don't have a pattern for this, so I'm not sure how it all fits together," she told him. She replaced the square in the bag and took a sip of the latte. The taste of the warm, sweet drink seemed to lift a weight from her shoulders. "I was hoping I could make out a message that might help me put it all in order."

"Do you mind?" Liam said, reaching for the notebook.

Sarah shook her head.

Liam studied the letters and hatch marks, his expression serious. "With this many characters, you'd have thousands of options," he said.

"Thousands?" Sarah repeated. "How do you know that?"

"My father was with British Intelligence during the war," Liam told her and grinned. "My birthday cards used to be in code, and I had to crack them to get my presents."

Sarah smiled back. "So how would you solve this one?" she said.

Liam rose and picked up the notebook. "Well," he said. "We have some tools these days we didn't have back when I was a lad."

He slipped back behind the counter and began typing at his computer again. A moment later, he nodded.

"Thirty-five thousand," he said.

"Thirty-five thousand what?" Sarah asked.

"Combinations," Liam told her. "I'm using an Internet anagram generator. It finds every combination of genuine words that can be made from any group of letters. Of course, then it takes a real live human being to decide which ones make any sense. Not every combination means something, even if the words are genuine."

Sarah carried her latte with her to the register. Liam turned the screen so she could see.

"A Ace Eyeopeners Phloem Phylum Yo," Sarah read from the first line.

"You see what I mean," Liam said.

"And there are thirty-five thousand of these?"

"Thirty-five thousand and change," Liam said.

Sarah glanced down the list. The computer's other suggestions didn't seem much more intelligible. "A Ace Eyeopeners Hue Lymph Pool My," she read from a later line. "None of these seem to make any sense."

Liam shook his head. "A few will," he said. "But a very few. It just takes time to go through them. Tell you what," he said, clicking at the top of the page to make it a favorite. "I'll keep looking through this as I have time, and let you know what I find."

"Thank you," Sarah said, and read another line: A Ace Eyeopener He Oomph Lumpy Sly. "That's a real favor."

"Glad to do it," Liam said.

The bell over the door rang. A pair of local teenagers came in, the first harbingers of the after-school rush that would crowd the little shop for the next several hours. Of course, Liam knew them by name. "Annie!" he bellowed. "Katie! Have you been behaving?"

The girls grinned with delight and hurried up to the counter to order. The bell rang again and a trio of boys tumbled in.

Liam glanced at Sarah in apology.

Sarah nodded and stepped away from the counter to let the girls order.

Back at the table, she let the letters swim before her eyes while she finished her latte, half-hoping the right answer would jump out at her in one bright flash of intuition. But nothing did. By now the shop was packed with teenagers, chattering loudly, teasing each other, laughing.

Sarah collected her purse and the crumpled paper bag of mysterious quilt squares. She hadn't had a chance to just lay everything out at home, where it was quiet. Maybe if she did she'd be able to see something she hadn't yet.

When she stopped by the register, Liam was setting a pair of Italian sodas on the counter for a pair of elementary school girls. They accepted their drinks with serious expressions, obviously feeling very grown-up to be ordering at the coffee shop for themselves.

"How much do I owe you?" Sarah asked.

"For what?" he said.

"The latte," Sarah said, and pulled her wallet from her purse.

"I don't remember any latte," Liam said, his eyes twinkling.

"Liam," Sarah said.

"That'll be four dollars and forty cents," he told the elementary school girls. One of them began to pull dollar bills carefully from a bright pink wallet. Then he looked back at Sarah.

"I'll let you know if I find anything," he said.

 CHAPTER FOUR

arah never got tired of laying out a new quilt in her sewing room. There was nothing like getting to handle fabric pieces that other hands had lovingly cut and sewn, sometimes as much as a hundred years ago. She loved learning the old and unusual antique fabrics, and sleuthing through books of patterns to find out where they might have been purchased. She loved tracing the old lines of quilting and stitching, and the delicate work of preserving every stitch she could even as she replaced quilt pieces that were tattered beyond recognition. She loved adding stitching to restore the quilt's structural integrity. And she also loved the silence, the time to organize her thoughts, both about the quilt and about other things in her life—and the time to dream. Who had made the quilt? What old dresses and new fabrics had been carefully cut to create the vivid patterns? What warm feelings had been stitched down the troughs of the seams? Who had it kept warm through cold winter nights? Where had it traveled? What had it seen? She enjoyed the role of historian as well: keeping close track of the work she was doing and the discoveries she made while returning the quilt to its former glory.

But this quilt had never been whole. It was Sarah's job to make it complete, for the first time.

When she returned home from The Spotted Dog, she went straight to her sewing room, where she laid the quilt pieces out on the wide fabric surface of her sewing table. Then she pulled a fresh spiral notebook from her supply shelf, flipped it open, and began to write. She recorded the quilt's current owners, Emily and Tad Collins. She guessed at the time of the quilt's creation, likely forty or fifty years ago, although as she thought about it, she couldn't pinpoint the time of Genie Collins' death. She described the quilt's condition, in separate blocks, and the manner in which it had been stored.

Then she began to measure the blocks. On average, they were between twelve and one-eighth inches to twelve and three-eighths inches square. She made a note of this, and also noted the letters stitched on the backs, and wrote them in the notebook. For a long minute, she sat staring at them, but even written neatly in the new notebook, they didn't mean anything more to her than they ever had.

Finally, she swung her quilter's lamp over the table, donned her magnifying eyeglasses, and settled in to the long task of cataloging each of the forty-two individual squares. For each piece, she counted every small mosaic scrap, noted the general layouts and colors, described the quilting stitches, and recorded the letter on the back. The dominant colors remained brown, blue, and green, but there were also vivid flashes of orange and red. When she finally looked up from her task, night had fallen.

She turned to a new page, and wrote "Quilter's Label" at the top. Whenever she restored a quilt, she sewed a small tag to it, containing all the history she could discover, so that the quilt's story wouldn't be a mystery to future generations. She didn't have much to go on with this quilt, but she did know the quilter's name, and the town and state. She made a note to ask Emily for some other details: the year it was made, and Genie's birth and death dates.

Then the doorbell rang.

Who could that be? Sarah wondered. Her cousin Rita French had moved out a few weeks ago, so she didn't have any current boarders, and she wasn't expecting company.

When she opened the door, her daughter-in-law Maggie stood under the warm light on her front porch with her twin daughters, Amy and Audrey. The two girls were both carrying backpacks. Clothes and schoolbooks poked out of them.

"Sarah, you're a lifesaver," Maggie breathed. "Thank you so much." She gave the girls a gentle push toward the house and turned to go.

"Maggie?" Sarah asked. "What's going on?"

Maggie turned around, recognition dawning in her harried eyes. "Didn't Jason call you?" she said.

Sarah shook her head.

Maggie pushed her auburn hair back. Some of it fell back down around her face. A few curls continued to stick straight up, adding to her general air of dishevelment. She came back up the porch's low steps.

"Oh, I'm so sorry," she said. "A pipe broke in our basement. Jason had to turn the water off so it wouldn't flood, but we can't get a plumber out till morning. He suggested we bring the girls over here so they can have running water for showers in the morning. He was going to call and ask if it was alright."

"Well, of course," Sarah said. She stepped aside to shoo the girls in.

"Are there cookies, Grandma?" Audrey asked over her shoulder.

"In the cookie jar," Sarah said.

"Not too many before bed!" Maggie called after her.

"I don't have any boarders right now," Sarah said as the girls disappeared into the kitchen. "Would you and Jason like to stay as well?"

"Thanks," Maggie said. "I think we'll probably be working a good part of the night to save what we can down there."

Sarah shook her head. "I'm so sorry to hear it," she said. "I hope it goes well. The girls will be fine here."

"I know that," Maggie said, and smiled. "My only worry will be getting them to agree to come home. But I'll see you for lunch this week?"

Sarah nodded. "Absolutely." Sarah had been making a point of trying to get together with Maggie for lunch every few weeks. Maggie's schedule was sometimes tricky, but

Sarah was determined to seize the opportunity to get to know her daughter-in-law better.

"See you then," Maggie said.

The two women gave each other a quick hug, and then Maggie jogged back down the steps to her car. Sarah pulled the door closed and paused for a moment before she went back down the hall. Having the girls for a night was a great surprise, but she also felt just a little bit shy. The girls had lived in another state since they were born, so Sarah had never really had a chance to spend much time with them outside of brief visits on holidays. In the few months since Jason and his family had moved back to town, Sarah and the girls had gotten to know each other better, but Sarah was still learning to negotiate what it meant to be an active part of their daily lives. In some ways, Sarah had known the girls all their lives, and she loved them as much as she loved anyone. But in other ways, they were still new friends.

Lord, please bless this time, she prayed. *Help me to be the grandmother they need.*

She went back to the kitchen, expecting to find them crowded around the cookie jar, but the kitchen was empty. A rustle from her sewing room gave them away.

"Grandma, what's this?" Audrey asked, pointing to the squares spread over the sewing table.

"It's a quilt," Sarah said. "At least, it's going to be when I'm done with it."

"I've never seen a quilt like this before," Amy said. "Usually each square has a similar pattern. These squares don't seem to have *any* pattern." Both girls leaned over the quilt squares eagerly, but neither of them reached out to touch anything. Sarah smiled. They were definitely her granddaughters. They'd already learned not to handle an antique quilt without taking precautions.

"I think that's because it all makes one big pattern," Sarah said.

"Of what?" Audrey asked.

"That's what I'm trying to find out," Sarah told her.

"It'd be easier if the squares weren't all so crumpled up," Amy said, frowning at the severely wrinkled piece in front of her.

"That's just what I was thinking," Sarah said. "Are you girls up for a project?"

"Can we do it instead of our homework?" Audrey asked.

"How much homework do you have?" Sarah asked.

"About half an hour of math," Audrey said.

"Mine's done already," Amy said.

"Good for you!" said Sarah.

"That's because she doesn't do anything else," said Audrey.

"I do too," said Amy. "I just don't spend all my time talking on the phone is all."

"How about this," Sarah said. "We'll do the project, and *then* you can do your homework. Wash your hands and then bring those quilt squares to the kitchen. I'm going to put some water on."

"Are we making quilt soup?" Audrey called as Sarah went out.

A few minutes later, steam poured from the mouth of a big black pot, with all forty-two wrinkled quilt squares stacked on the counter near it, beside a pile of acid-free paper. Audrey struggled into the kitchen, her arms full of thick quilting books. Amy followed behind her with an equally large load.

"I don't get it," Audrey said. "What are all the books for?"

Sarah took the stack from her and set it on the counter. Then she piled Amy's load on top of it. "Gather round," she said.

As the girls jostled on either side of her, she took the top quilt square from the pile and held it over the steam. Slowly, the wrinkles relaxed and the fabric went flat.

"Wow," Amy breathed.

"Now watch this," Sarah said.

She pulled a book from the stack, laid a piece of acid-free paper on it, and set the flattened quilt square on the paper. Then she topped it off with another piece of paper, and laid a second book on it, making a kind of strange sandwich. "This way it dries flat," she explained. "Who wants to try it?"

An hour later, the pile of quilt squares had vanished and the kitchen was littered with stacks of book and quilt piece sandwiches.

"We did it!" Audrey said.

"You girls did a great job," Sarah said. "Now for the homework, Audrey."

"Do I really have to?" Audrey said. "I don't even get to sleep in my own bed tonight. It's almost like having a vacation day."

Sarah shook her head. "Off you go," she said.

Reluctantly, Audrey padded out of the kitchen. Amy sat down in one of the kitchen chairs by the window.

Sarah took the pot from the stove and poured the hot water into the sink. "It's so nice to have you girls nearby," she told Amy.

Amy nodded politely, but she didn't look convinced.

Sarah soaped the pot and rinsed it. "How do you like it here?" she asked.

"It's all right," Amy said. "I miss California."

"I guess it's pretty different here," Sarah said.

"The people are nice," Amy said. "But they're not the people I know."

Sarah set the pot in the dish drainer and sat down across from Amy. "Well, you can get to know them," she said. "People around here are pretty friendly." Her heart went out to her granddaughter. Sarah had lived her whole life in Maple Hill. She didn't know what it would be like to leave behind everything she'd ever known and start again, but she could imagine it would be hard.

"That's the problem," Amy said.

"What do you mean?" Sarah asked.

"People are really nice here," Amy said. "I like them. Other kids invite me to do stuff, and it's really fun. I went on a hayride with Pru and Lexie this weekend, and we drove all over this farmer's property and into the woods near his fields." Sarah recognized the names of Martha's granddaughters. "When we came back they had hot cider and doughnuts in his barn, and I got to pet the horses noses and play with some rabbits they had in hutches in the back."

"I used to love going on hayrides," Sarah said.

Amy nodded. "And I have new friends too," she said. Her voice rose a little bit as she said it, as if the thought caused her some sort of distress. Sarah's brows drew together in concern as she watched her granddaughter. She didn't say anything just yet. She wanted to give Amy a chance to explain herself.

"Brita Durden and Pam Holleman ask me over almost every weekend. We don't always do anything special. A lot of times we just watch a movie and paint our nails. One time Brita's mom bought us pizza crusts and toppings and we made our own pizzas, with whatever we wanted on them. It was fun." It sounded like fun to Sarah, too, but when Amy told the story, her voice was still strained with some kind of unease.

"Well, honey," Sarah tried. "Those are all good things."

"But then I forget about my friends at home!" Amy exclaimed. "I want to do everything with the kids here. I start telling them all my secrets. It makes me feel like I'm betraying my friends in California."

"Oh, honey," Sarah said. She put her hand over Amy's on the table. *Help me know what to say, Lord,* she prayed.

"I don't know what to do," Amy said. "I don't want to forget my friends in California. But they aren't here. And I don't want to be alone."

"It must be hard to move from place to place," Sarah said.

"It's awful!" Amy exclaimed, her voice breaking.

Sarah struggled to think of something to say. She'd never been through this experience herself. What did she have to offer? Then a light went on. "You know what?" she said. "I've lived in Maple Hill my whole life."

Amy looked at her grandmother, tears in her eyes.

"But I've had friends who moved away," Sarah said. "And your dad and Aunt Jenna moved away too. That was pretty hard for me, to raise them and get to see all the different parts of their life all those years, and then have them go so far away."

Amy nodded.

"But wherever they went, the only thing I wanted was for them to be happy," Sarah said. "I didn't want them to sit around and miss me. I wanted them to go out and have a good life, and make friends who I knew would take care of them the way I wanted to."

Amy's brow was furrowed, taking this in.

"And you know what else?" Sarah said. "I found other things to do besides being a mother, like restoring these quilts. And your dad and aunt made friends and got married, and started their own families. But we never forgot each other. We loved each other too much."

"I never forgot you," Amy said. "Even though you lived far away."

"That's right," Sarah said, nodding. "And I loved you more than anything else in the world, even though I didn't get to see you very often."

"Huh," Amy said, taking this thought in. "Do you think it's like that with my friends in California?"

"If they're real friends, I know it is," Sarah said.

"But still," Amy said. "I loved you, but I didn't really *know* you. I don't want it to be like that with my friends. I used to know everything about them. I don't want to forget them. And I don't want them to forget me!"

Sarah laid a hand on her granddaughter's shoulder. Amy's feelings were real and raw, and she knew better than to argue with her about them. She'd just do her best to love her through this time.

Amy dropped her gaze to one of the books they'd set on the table. Idly, she lifted it from the paper and fingered the quilt square underneath. Then she looked up in surprise.

"Grandma," she said. "What's this?" She pulled back the quilted fabric and batting to reveal a piece of old newspaper.

"Paper," Sarah said. She picked up another "quilt sandwich," removed the book from the top and pulled the fabric back to reveal a similar piece of paper inside. "Back in the old days, they used newspapers to make quilt patterns. And sometimes they just put in a layer of newsprint because it made it easier to stitch straight."

"And they left it in?" Amy said, her voice registering disbelief.

"People back then didn't have as much as we have now," Sarah said. "They used everything they had, including newspaper. It helped make the sewing easier, but it also gave the quilt another layer for extra warmth."

"That's crazy," Amy said, shaking her head.

"It might seem crazy now," Sarah said. "Back then, it was simple common sense. I actually like to work on quilts with the old newspapers in them. You can learn all kinds of things about the time the quilt was made, and what life was like back then."

Amy peeled back the batting on her quilt square and peered down at the yellowing, smudged newsprint. "This article's about ... " she scanned a few lines. "Maple syrup!" she said.

Sarah pulled the batting back from her own piece to reveal her square of paper. Then she looked from her paper to Amy's in surprise. "So is this," she said.

"Maple syrup must have been pretty important back then," Amy said.

"Maybe," Sarah said. She lifted another book to reach another flattened quilt square. Could it be coincidence? She pulled back the fabric and batting of the third piece. The text of the new article mentioned maple syrup too—as well as a land dispute over the maple grove that had laid the foundation for Tad Collins' family fortune.

"Grandma?" Amy said. "Is something wrong?"

Sarah looked up into her granddaughter's worried eyes. "No, honey," she said. She dropped the still-damp quilt square back into place and laid the book on top of it. "We should let these dry. I'll look at them in the morning. Let's go get you ready for bed."

CHAPTER FIVE

It's impossible!" Audrey moaned. "I can't go to school looking like this!"

She had forgotten her special diffusion hair dryer, and although she looked just like her normal pretty self to Sarah, Audrey was convinced that having to use her grandmother's basic-model hair dryer was worse than death.

"We can tell Dad I'm sick," Audrey said as Sarah cleared the breakfast plates. "I'll stay here and help you with your quilt. I'll do anything you want. I just can't go to school like this."

"Honey," Sarah said. "You look just beautiful."

"I look like a poodle!" Audrey moaned.

"You look fine," Amy said.

"Maybe I can stuff it all in a baseball cap," Audrey said. "And wear sunglasses. Nobody will recognize me and everyone will think I skipped school until I go back tomorrow."

"No teacher is going to let you wear sunglasses in class," Amy said.

"It's just one day, honey," Sarah said. "Do you really think anyone is going to notice?"

"I'm the new girl," Audrey said. "Everyone notices everything about me. And it's not just one day. These kids have all known each other all their lives. I've only been here for two months. So every day matters a lot more. I haven't known them for years. I've only *known* them for days."

Suddenly Audrey's dramatics didn't seem so silly. But Sarah wasn't sure how to help.

At the front of the house, the doorbell rang, probably Jason arriving to take the girls to school.

"Dad!" Amy said, and shot out of the kitchen.

Audrey looked up at Sarah miserably. Sarah didn't know what it felt like to move across the country, but she remembered worrying about what the other kids thought about her.

"Honey," she said. "I know exactly how you feel, and I've lived here all my life. You know what that means?"

"What?" Audrey asked.

"It means that everyone has the same worries about what people think of them, whether they're the new girl or they've been here for years. And you know what else it means?"

Audrey shook her head.

"Everyone is too busy worrying about what everyone else thinks about them to notice that your hair is a little bit different."

Audrey frowned and shook her head. "Maybe you worried about that too, Grandma," she said. "But you weren't ever the new girl. It really is different."

"Audrey!" Amy called from the front of the house. "Dad's here! Hurry up!"

Audrey jumped out of her chair. At first Sarah thought she was about to dart out of the kitchen, but then Audrey caught Sarah around the waist in a tight hug. "I love you, Grandma," she said.

"I love you too, honey," Sarah said. "So much."

Audrey kissed her on the cheek and scampered out of the kitchen.

Sarah went to the door to meet Jason. Amy was already waiting in the car. Jason's face looked pale and his eyes were bright with exhaustion.

"How did it go last night?" Sarah asked.

Jason shook his head. "It was tough," he said. "We were up till almost three moving things out of the way and drying out the stuff that got wet. A lot of it was inventory for Maggie's store. She works hard to find those antiques, and she doesn't choose just any one to take home. I know how much they mean to her. I'll feel awful if any of them are ruined."

Sarah laid her hand on his shoulder. "It's not your fault the pipe broke," she said.

"I know," Jason said, pushing his hair back off his forehead. "But you want to protect the people you love."

He glanced at her as if he were explaining something she might not know much about. Sarah gave him a knowing smile. Jason smiled back, sheepishly. "I guess you might know something about that too," he said.

Sarah gave him a quick hug. "I do," she said. "And it can be one of the hardest feelings in the world. But you did your best. And Maggie knows you love her. That's the most important thing."

"I guess you're right," Jason said.

Audrey came rattling down the stairs, her book bag dangling from one hand. "Are you finally ready?" she joked as she flew out the door.

Jason grinned and swatted at her but missed.

"Thanks so much for taking care of them," he said.

"They're welcome any time," Sarah said. "You all are."

Jason kissed her on the cheek and trotted down the steps. Sarah stood in the door and waved until the car pulled away. Then she closed the door and made a beeline for the sewing room.

The book and quilt piece sandwiches stood on her sewing table, where she'd stacked them that morning in order to make room for breakfast. Now she carefully lifted books and set aside papers, sorting them into new stacks: quilt squares, paper, books. She reshelved the books to make room to work. Then she flipped on her quilter's light, put on her magnifying glasses, and began to examine the newspaper articles sewn into the quilt in earnest.

Every single one, she quickly realized, concerned the Collins family in some way. The stories were sometimes hard to read, with columns cut in half or sewn through, or sliced off before they ended. But eventually a handful of facts emerged. The Collins family hadn't always owned the maple grove that was the foundation of their fortune, it seemed. It had once belonged to a man named John Peters. Sarah couldn't make out all of the details, but it seemed there had been a dispute concerning the circumstances under which the land had transferred to the Collins family. In fact, it seemed as though there were several articles, over several months, that mentioned different challenges John Peters had made about the legality of the exchange. The articles weren't just brief notes. They were full features, complete with pictures. The black shapes of maple trees spread across the yellowing paper. A young couple in dark clothing held hands at some kind of public ceremony, but their faces were hidden in the stitching.

Sarah racked her brain. In a town the size of Maple Hill, most people knew each other or at least knew of each other, but she'd never heard of a John Peters. In fact, she didn't know of any Peters family at all. That was odd. Usually Maple Hill families stayed put, especially families that had owned land in the area since the old days.

What were the dates on these articles? They looked like they must be from the local paper, and she couldn't imagine a regional or national concern paying so much attention to Maple Hill news. If she could find a date, looking up full copies of the articles in the library or the historical society would be a simple task. She could find all the facts she wanted, and begin to put the story in some kind of order.

But the *Maple Hill Monitor* collection on the historical society's microfilm hadn't been indexed by topic yet, and in the library it was just gathered into big bound books. Without a date, finding the articles would be a serious search.

Sarah searched through the pieces, then searched again. But none of the articles she was able to read contained a date. In a few places, she found corners of the paper that might have contained the standard day, month, and year stamps, but the numbers disappeared tantalizingly into the original quilting. Sarah was a bit of a detective, but she was a quilt restorer first. Nothing could entice her to rip out the original quilting, not even a mystery this puzzling. But were there any other clues that might help her find the original articles in the library files? Without an approximate date, she'd be swimming in information. She'd have to start reading the *Maple Hill Monitor* from the time it began publishing until she came across something that matched.

Painstakingly, she sorted through the pieces a third time, looking through the maddeningly brief fragments she could read for anything she might have missed. Finally, she turned over an advertisement for Electric Static Liniment to check the printing on the back. She pulled back the batting to read a line higher than she had before. It was the end of a sentence, just a single name. But it was a name she knew: Ward Collins.

So whatever the story of the maple syrup company land, it wasn't buried too far back in history. In fact, it sounded like some of the major players were still living.

A minute later, Sarah sat in front of her own computer, typing names into a search engine. She started with "John Peters" and "Maple Hill." The first two hits were a real estate agent in Nevada and a cattle farmer in Alabama. She scrolled down the page. None of the other hits were anywhere near the Berkshires.

That's what she'd been afraid of. From investigating other quilts, she knew that modern people leave a lot of traces on the Internet, but people from previous generations often didn't show up at all, unless someone had put them on a genealogy site. And to search those effectively, she'd need to know a few relatives. But no relatives of John Peters had been mentioned in the fragmentary articles she'd just looked through.

She returned to the search engine landing page. Searching "Ward Collins" wouldn't do her any good. Even if she did manage to find articles on Maple Hill's Ward Collins, the vast majority of the information would be official releases from the maple syrup company. His name was probably mentioned in the local and regional press every time a news outlet wrote anything about the factory. To find the originals of the articles she'd been poring over in the quilt, she'd need a date.

She leaned back in her chair and crossed her arms to think. The syrup factory had been in operation since before she was born. She didn't ever remember a time when it hadn't existed. But it hadn't been in operation forever. It must have started sometime. And from what she could gather from the articles, the dispute over the land seemed to have erupted around the time the business opened. Maybe that was a date she could work with, the opening of the business.

She tapped a few keys, brought up the maple syrup company's Web site, and scanned through the company history until she found the date it was founded: 1936. It wasn't a very solid date, but it was a date. She could start there, and move forward—and back, if necessary.

It was worth a try.

A minute later, she had her bag on her shoulder and her keys in her hand, heading for the library. The historical society was open only a few mornings a week, but the library was always open.

Maple Hill was a beautiful town in any season, but Sarah was especially fond of the fall. The town was true to its name: maples lined almost every street in town and stood in the yards of most houses. And unlike ginkgos or birches, whose leaves turned a uniform bright yellow in autumn, or oaks, whose leaves tended to simply fade to brown and fall, maples burst out in a whole carnival of color as soon as they felt the frost. Every tree down the block was a different color: bright red, rich orange, joyful gold. Sometimes a single tree boasted more than one color: amber nearest the ground, building to crimson at the top. When Jenna and Jason had been children, they'd always been delighted to find maple leaves on the sidewalk, because of all the variety of colors they could find in a single leaf.

As she turned into the downtown area, Sarah smiled to see harvest decorations beginning to dot the streets. The crystal and gift shop near The Spotted Dog had a pair of giant purple mums on either side of the door, and two giant bundles of cornstalks with pumpkins at their feet seemed to stand watch at the foot of the steps to the library.

As Sarah climbed the steps of the Maple Hill Library, the door opened and Emily Collins stepped out.

"Emily!" Sarah exclaimed. "I'm so glad to see you. I've been working on your quilt, and—"

"That's wonderful," Emily interrupted, hurrying down the stairs. "But I don't have time to talk."

Sarah turned to watch as Emily brushed past her. She'd never known Emily to interrupt her before. And the girl didn't look like she was in a hurry. She looked frightened.

"Is everything all right?" she asked.

"It's just fine!" Emily said, a little too loudly.

Sarah glanced around the street to see who Emily might be trying to convince. The block they stood on was empty except for a few kids playing in the park across the way. Sarah was confused, but mostly she felt for the worried girl. *Lord,* she prayed. *Show me how to help her.*

"Well, I'll let you go then," Sarah said. "But I'm doing some research on the quilt now, and there are a couple of facts I'll need from you. Genie's birthday and death date. Do you know them? Or could you look them up and call me?"

"Her death date?" Emily repeated, looking even more agitated.

Sarah nodded.

"I'm sorry, I really have to go," Emily said.

"All right, dear," Sarah said. Something strange was going on with Emily, but she didn't want to pry. "I'll let you know how the research goes."

Emily was already striding down the sidewalk toward her little blue sedan.

Sarah stood on the steps, watching her until she got into her car and pulled away from the curb. She had hoped that Emily's strange behavior when she gave Sarah the quilt was just some kind of passing mood, but if anything, this new encounter was even stranger. Emily had seemed worried before, but this time she had been almost rude. And in all the time Emily had lived with Sarah as a boarder, Sarah had never known her to be brusque like this. What could be wrong with her?

Emily's sedan reached the corner and turned, slipping out of sight beyond a row of downtown buildings. Sarah shook her head and went into the library.

Inside, a middle-aged man sat at one of the long reading tables that lined the library's main atrium. He wore a crisp gray suit, unusual on weekdays in Maple Hill, and his fingers flew over the face of his phone, tapping out a text. Sarah recognized him at once: Alex Crane, Samuel Collins' second-in-command at the syrup company. She'd met him when Emily first moved to town to work at Genie Maple Syrup. He'd actually brought her by to see Sarah's place. It was during the weekend Emily had spent visiting the town to make the decision about taking the job she'd been offered at the syrup company. Alex was Emily's boss when she did join the company, so Sarah had heard about him from time to time in Emily's stories of little events that happened at work. And of course, Alex had been involved with the festivities surrounding Tad and Emily's wedding.

"Alex!" Sarah exclaimed. "It's nice to see you!"

Alex looked up from his fancy phone with fright in his eyes. When he recognized her, his expression changed quickly to irritation. Sarah's smile of greeting faded. She didn't like the feeling that she would frighten anybody, and she liked Alex's attitude even less. Maybe he had some idea that he shouldn't be interrupted while tapping away at his cell phone, but she thought the basic rules of politeness still applied, no matter what gadgets you had. Or maybe, she thought more charitably, he didn't recognize her. Finally, it was curiosity that spurred her on. It couldn't be a coincidence that Sarah had found Alex here after Emily's hurried exit. Maybe he could shed some light on the situation for her.

"I'm Sarah Hart," she said. "Emily Collins lived with me before she married Tad. I recognized you from the wedding."

Now Alex's face broke into a broad smile. He pocketed his phone and rose from the table. "Oh, Sarah!" he said. "Great to see you!"

The quick change in his attitude bothered Sarah more than his original irritation. It hadn't been pleasant, but it at least felt honest. The sudden warmth of his greeting, however, felt strange and insincere. But maybe she could still get some useful information from him.

"I just saw Emily too," Sarah said. "She was going out as I came in. She seemed worried to me. Did she seem worried to you?" This was a gamble. She knew that Emily and Alex must have seen each other if they'd both been in the small library. Emily hadn't been forthcoming about why she was there, and maybe Alex wouldn't be either, but chances were they'd spoken together. Maybe by pretending she knew they had, she could find out what was going on.

"Emily?" Alex said, taken aback.

Sarah nodded. "I thought you must have been meeting with her," she said. "She just left, this instant." But now that Sarah came to think of it, why would Alex and Emily meet away from the Genie Maple Syrup Company in the middle of a weekday? Surely there were enough conference rooms out at the sprawling new plant for them to find a meeting place.

"No," Alex said, and paused, as though stalling for time. "I can't say she seemed any different to me."

Sarah watched him, keeping quiet. When people were nervous, like Alex was, sometimes the best strategy was just to wait in silence. Eventually they'd come up with something to say to fill the space. And often that something was more revealing than anything Sarah could think to ask directly.

"We were just working on some historical research," Alex explained after a moment. "And she remembered she had another meeting. Maybe that's why she seemed nervous. She may have been running a little late."

Sarah nodded. "Historical research?" she said.

Again, Alex looked trapped. He nodded.

"I was just looking up the company history this morning," Sarah said. "The material you already have on the Web site is impressive."

"Oh well," Alex said. "Thanks. Our history is a big part of our brand, you know." Then his eyes narrowed slightly. "What took you to the site today?"

"I'm restoring a family quilt for Emily," Sarah said. "I like to do a little research into the history of all my projects."

"A quilt?" Alex said. "She never mentioned that to me."

"Well, it's a family heirloom," Sarah said. "Not a business matter."

Alex nodded, his expression dark. "Of course not," he said. "Well, if you'll excuse me, Sarah, I've got to be getting back to the office as well."

"Of course," Sarah said, standing aside to let him pass. "Nice to see you."

"You too," Alex said over his shoulder. The front doors of the library swung open, letting in a flash of morning light, and then thudded shut. Sarah looked at them thoughtfully. Nothing in Alex's story added up. She couldn't imagine that the second in command at a big local company would be doing library research in the middle of the day, especially not with Emily, the company accountant, in tow. And she couldn't imagine either of them being secretive about the history of a sleepy maple syrup company in a small town. The newspapers sewn into the quilt did hint that there was more to the company's history than met the eye, but whether or not Emily and Alex had really been researching the company's history that morning, perhaps Sarah could find some answers by investigating its early days herself.

When she strode up to the circulation desk, Spencer Hewitt, the handsome young librarian, flashed her a smile as his hands flew over the covers of a pile of books, busily swiping their bar codes to check them out for the young girl who had brought them up. Sarah recognized Evie Gibbons from church.

"Elephants, huh?" he said. "I thought you were into crocodiles?"

"I read all the books about crocodiles already," Evie said. She glanced up at Sarah. "Hello, Mrs. Hart."

"Hi, Evie," Sarah said.

"You read all the crocodile books already?" Spencer said. "Well, maybe we'll just have to do something about that. I'll see what I can dig up by interlibrary loan."

Evie's eyes widened. "Really?" she said. "Thank you!"

Spencer set the last book on top of her stack and pushed it toward her. "Due back next week," he said.

Evie collected them in her thin arms. "I know," she said, and carried them away.

"Friendly guy, Alex Crane," Spencer said in greeting.

"Do you know him?" Sarah asked.

"Yep," Spencer said. "Every now and then he comes in here and uses the public computers, just like the kids. Which is strange, because with his salary, you'd think he could afford one of his own. Or ten of them."

"You would," Sarah agreed.

"This morning he was talking with Emily, though," Spencer said. "It was the first time I'd seen her in here with him."

Gossip might be a sin, but it was amazing how much you could learn in a small town just by listening, Sarah thought.

"Neither of them seemed happy," Spencer added.

Sarah nodded. It was reassuring to hear she wasn't the only person who had thought Emily and Alex's behavior was unusual. And it didn't sound as if they'd been doing much research, either, so her instinct that Alex hadn't been telling the truth was confirmed.

Spencer spread his hands over the circulation desk. "But that's not what you came here to talk about," he said. "What can I do for you?"

"I'm looking for a few articles," Sarah told him. "On the old Collins land. I think they were in the *Maple Hill Monitor*."

Spencer stepped out from behind the counter. "It sounds like you've seen them somewhere already," he said.

"Only parts of them," Sarah said.

"In a scrapbook?" Spencer guessed.

"In a quilt," Sarah told him.

Spencer raised his eyebrows. "That's an interesting place to preserve a document," he said.

"Well, that's what's funny about it," Sarah said. "Newspapers are used for warmth in quilts, not to protect the documents. But in this one, it seems like the quilter actually selected the articles by topic."

"Interesting," Spencer said. He slipped out from behind the counter and made his way up to the archive room. Sarah followed behind. "Have you got a date for me?" he asked as he unlocked the door.

"Not a very solid one, I'm afraid," Sarah said. "All the dates were hidden in the stitching."

"Another interesting problem," Spencer said, ushering her into the room.

"But the articles did seem to concern the opening of the business," Sarah said. "And according to the company Web site, that was 1936."

"Nineteen thirty-six it is," Spencer said. He pulled out a heavy bound volume. "Here we are."

"This is the first half of nineteen thirty-six" he said. "I'm afraid it's going to take you a while."

Sarah took the book and flipped open the cover. She recognized the front page of the *Maple Hill Monitor*, with the familiar masthead it still published under today. Sarah leaned forward to scan the text.

"I see I've lost you already," Spencer laughed.

Sarah glanced back and smiled at him. "Thanks so much for your help," she said.

Nineteen thirty-six had been a year of change in Maple Hill, as it had been in so many places, but the news was still hopeful. The paper printed wedding pictures of young brides in homemade dresses, smiling with delight. Birth announcements welcomed the town's newest members. Among them were the names of many people who still lived in town today. Doctor McLean, who'd just retired last year. Jessie Givens, who ran the gardening club that planted tulips and hyacinths in the park each year. Adelaide Harper, who directed the bell choir at church. The town had celebrated a winter carnival in February, with roasted chestnuts and ice carvings. They'd thrown a big May Day parade, with floats made from wagons decorated with the branches of flowering trees.

And in early June, Sarah found an article announcing the opening of the maple syrup factory. The first photograph featured a wooden building Sarah didn't recognize, surrounded by the shapes of tall maple trees and draped with bunting. A brass band stood to one side. Their hands and faces were blurry because they'd been playing while the photographer took the picture. On the next page was another photograph. This one Sarah recognized right away. It was the young couple in dark clothes from her quilt. But in this version she could see their faces. She didn't even need to check the caption to know their names: Ward Collins and Tad's grandmother Genie.

Quickly, she read the caption, which confirmed her deduction. *Ward Collins, owner of the new concern, with fiancée Genie Woltherstorf.* Sarah flipped back to the previous page and read the article from the beginning, but it was mostly concerned with the brass band, the various speeches made, and the watermelon that had been served. There was no mention of any land dispute, or of John Peters. *Had the dispute not been made public yet?* Sarah wondered. Or had the paper delicately left mention of the scandal out of its coverage of the celebration?

There was something else Sarah recognized in the picture: the expression on Genie's face. In this image, it was just as melancholy as the expression Sarah remembered from Genie's portrait at the Collinses' magnificent house.

"Genie," Sarah whispered. "Why are you so sad?"

CHAPTER SIX

J ust as Sarah was about to turn into The Spotted Dog to order a sandwich and think, she glimpsed a familiar figure half a block down the street. Martha, her best friend, was coming down the steps of the police station.

"Martha!" Sarah called. She passed The Spotted Dog and hurried to catch up.

But for some reason, Martha didn't turn to greet her. Instead, she seemed to hesitate.

Sarah hesitated as well. Was that really Martha? Maybe it was just someone who looked like her. It was just after one o'clock, and the downtown streets were busy with people stepping out of restaurants or returning from their lunch breaks. *But I'd recognize Martha anywhere,* Sarah thought. "Martha!" she called again.

Sarah doubled her stride. As she did, Martha turned around. Her smile seemed strained, but Sarah knew her friend better than to ask why right away. Martha was almost always upbeat, but if something was wrong, she needed to take her own time to share the things that mattered to her. She was almost like a quilt, revealing herself little by little. Maybe that's why they were such good friends. Other people enjoyed Martha's high spirits, but Sarah was willing to keep uncovering layers until Martha felt comfortable to really share her heart.

She caught up with Martha halfway between The Spotted Dog and the police station, near the gift shop that sold wind chimes, crystals, and New Age books.

"It's good to see you," Sarah said. The wind chimes clinked and rang beside them.

"You too," Martha said. "Have you made any progress on that Collins quilt?"

"Some," Sarah said. "But everything I learn seems to lead to a new mystery."

"Do you know how all those pieces fit together yet?"

"I'm still working on that," Sarah said. "What about you? Are you here to pay another ticket for parking your car in a tree?"

When they were just girls and learning how to drive, Martha had forgotten to put the parking brake on in her father's car. During the night, it had slowly rolled down the bluff the family home stood on, and dropped gently into the upper branches of a big oak that grew at the foot of the bluff several stories below. Her father's friends had rigged up an elaborate pulley system to pull the undamaged car from the leafy branches, but the police chief at the time had given her a five-dollar ticket, to teach her a lesson. Sarah still loved to tease her about it, and Martha usually responded by teasing Sarah about one of her youthful indiscretions, but today Martha just looked unhappy.

"I'm running an errand," she said.

Something really was wrong, Sarah realized. "Have you had lunch?" she asked.

Martha shook her head. "I think I'll just get something at home," she said.

"It's already one o'clock," Sarah said. "Why don't we get something now?"

"I don't know if I've got time," Martha said.

Sarah took her friend's arm and began to steer her back to The Spotted Dog. Martha didn't resist. "Liam's got a case full of beautiful sandwiches," Sarah said. "It'll be even faster than making lunch yourself."

Liam grinned when he saw them come in. "To what do I owe this pleasure?" he asked. Murphy trotted out from behind the counter, and then came bounding over. Sarah stooped to scratch under his neck. Liam craned over the counter to see them.

"I'm still working through those anagrams," he told her. "They're alphabetical. I got through to D and then I decided to start from the bottom for a change of pace."

Sarah straightened up. Murphy looked up at her, stricken that she might think anything in the world was more important than petting him.

"So far I'm up to 'Yo-ho-ho! Appease yummy repellence,'" Liam said.

"What is he talking about?" Martha asked.

"It's for the quilt," Sarah explained.

"Was the quilt made by pirates?" Martha said.

"We're in a bit of a hurry," Sarah told Liam. "Could we just get two chicken salad sandwiches and some lemonade?"

Moments later, two tall glasses of lemonade stood on the counter before them.

"You ladies take those and sit down," Liam said. "I'll bring the sandwiches out to you."

Sarah pulled her wallet from her purse. "And what do we owe you?"

"You can pay after you eat," Liam said. "You're in a hurry, aren't you?" Sarah might have had a salty retort for someone else, but somehow Liam's brogue made his suggestion seem perfectly sensible.

She and Martha settled into a window seat near the door. Martha took a sip of her lemonade. "This is good," she said.

"It always is," said Sarah. She watched as Martha stared silently out the window for a few moments, and then she decided it was time. You had to treat quilts as gently as possible, but sometimes there was no way to fix a problem without tearing out a few stitches. It was the same way in friendships.

"How are you doing?" she asked.

Martha looked at her, her blue eyes still unhappy. "Just fine," she said.

Sarah squeezed her hand. "No, you're not," she said softly.

Martha's eyes filled with tears. She bowed her head, and one of them rolled down her cheek and splashed on the table. She swiped at it and looked back at Sarah.

"It's Ian," she said.

Sarah's heart dropped. Ian was Martha's seventeen-year-old grandson, and although no grandmother is supposed to have favorites, he was the closest to Martha of any of her grandchildren. Martha knit beautiful designs into her various creations, and Ian wanted to be a painter. It might not have seemed like an ideal combination, but Martha and Ian recognized each other as artists. They were always talking about colors and shapes, and showing off their various projects to each other. And Ian had had a history of health problems. When he'd first started high school, doctors had removed a large tumor from his abdomen. It wasn't cancerous, and the doctors said he was going to be fine, but the family still worried.

"Is he sick?" Sarah asked.

Martha shook her head. "I guess I should thank God for that," she said. "But in some ways, this seems worse."

"What?" Sarah asked.

"He's in trouble with the law," Martha said.

"Ian?" Sarah said, surprised. Ian had never been anything but an obedient child and a polite young man. She couldn't even begin to guess what kind of trouble he could get in. "Are they sure it was him?"

Martha nodded. "He even signed his name," she said.

"To what?" Sarah asked.

"Graffiti," Martha said. "He's been going out at night and painting all kinds of things. The railroad trestle out toward Dillon, and that old barn at the back of the Percy property. And the old abandoned maple syrup factory."

Relief washed over Sarah. "At least he's not hurt," she said.

"I know I should be grateful for that," Martha said. "But it's still hard. I know I'm not his mother, but I love him so much. And I'm not sure what to do for him. I want to swoop in and make it all better, but he needs to learn his lesson."

"I know what you mean," Sarah said. "And I'm so sorry. If it were up to me, Amy and Audrey would never have a day of trouble in their whole lives. But then I think about how much I've learned through my problems."

Martha nodded unhappily. "That's right," she said. "But it's just so hard to watch them go through it.

"Tell me what happened," Sarah said.

"I got the call yesterday, while we were at the fabric shop," Martha said. "It was Ruth. They'd just gotten back from the police station. Nobody worries much about the railroad trestle, and old man Percy wasn't too upset about the barn, but somebody at the syrup factory saw what he'd done and wants to press charges. It wasn't hard to find him, since he signed his own name. But when Ruth and Tim brought him back from the station, he wouldn't talk with them about it. He only wanted to talk with me, because he said I'm an artist like him, so I'd understand."

Sarah squeezed her hand again. Martha had started to regain her composure as she spoke. Out of the corner of Sarah's eye, she caught sight of Liam's tall figure, carrying their two plates over. His timing was perfect: not too soon, and not even a second late. Had he been watching them? Was he sensitive enough to recognize how delicate their conversation was?

He set a plate down in front of each of them. He'd scattered strawberries and melon beside the sandwiches, along with a dollop of cole slaw and a thick wedge of pickle.

"Thanks so much," Sarah told him.

He didn't give one of his normal hearty greetings. He just nodded and faded back to the register.

"And so you talked with him?" Sarah asked as Martha picked up her sandwich.

Martha nodded, her eyes even sadder than they had been. "And it was awful, Sarah," she said. "I've never fought with that boy about anything. I've always been the one he could come to for support with any of his harebrained schemes. But he thought he didn't do anything wrong, because he didn't hurt anyone. And I couldn't tell him he was right about that. He needs to learn that he can't just go around in life doing anything he wants."

"That's right," Sarah said gently.

"But he was so disappointed in me," Martha said. "He thought he had made this beautiful art, and nobody in the world understood it."

"Does he understand how people might be upset about him painting their property?"

"He said they weren't using it," Martha said. "He said he specially chose things where nobody else went. He just wanted to try painting on a bigger canvas. I hate feeling like I let him down. And I hate that he can't see what's wrong with what he did."

"I'm so sorry," Sarah said.

"It's funny being a grandmother," Martha said. "Sometimes it's the best job in the world, because you only have to worry about making cookies and drawing with crayons, not about changing diapers or making them do homework. But when they get in trouble, you love them just as much as you love your own kids. And you feel so helpless."

"So what were you doing at the courthouse?" Sarah asked.

"We were talking with Chief Webber," Martha said. "Ian did the wrong thing, but I don't want him mixed up with the juvenile justice system. Chief Webber says an apology and some community service will do for the trestle and the barn, but there's someone at the syrup company who won't drop the charges. I can't believe they care about that old place so much. I bet nobody's been in it for years. Chief Webber has him there at the station right now, trying to work out some community service placement so we can let the people at the syrup company know he's serious about making this right. I'm supposed to pick him up again in a few minutes."

The image of the original maple syrup factory, covered with bunting on the day it was opened, flashed in Sarah's mind. "You know," she said. "That old factory might have something to do with the quilt I'm researching. And maybe you'll get some idea of what to say to Ian if you have a look at what he painted. What do you say we all take a drive out there after you pick him up, and see?"

 CHAPTER SEVEN

S arah squinted in the sun outside The Spotted Dog, her cell phone pressed against her ear so that she could hear over the intermittent Main Street traffic. Emily's voice mail message played, and then the signal beeped.

"Hi, Emily," Sarah said. "I've just been thinking of you and wanted to check in. I've made a little progress with your quilt, and I'd love to talk with you about it. Just give me a call when you're able."

When she hung up, Martha and Ian were coming down the block from the police station. Sarah smiled and waved. Ian, a gangly seventeen-year-old with a shock of strawberry blond hair and a generous dusting of freckles, gave her the same friendly smile he'd given her all his life. "Hello, Mrs. Hart!" he called.

Sarah smiled back. "Hello, Ian," she said. She walked down a few storefronts to meet them where her car was parked, just across from the library. She popped the locks, and the three of them got in, Martha beside Sarah in the front passenger seat, and Ian in the backseat, behind his grandmother. Sarah pulled out of the spot, onto the road.

"Maybe Martha told you I'm working on a quilt that has something to do with that old syrup factory," Sarah said, looking back at Ian in the rearview mirror. "I hope you can help us find it. I haven't been out there in ages."

Ian's face clouded. "What does it have to do with your quilt?" he asked.

Sarah made the turn onto the street that would turn into the narrow country road that led toward the maple grove. "I'm not sure yet," Sarah said. "But I found an article about it in the quilt."

"In the quilt?"

Sarah nodded, and explained the old-fashioned technique of using newspaper for stabilizing and warmth. "But it's strange," Sarah said. "I've never seen another example where the quilter seemed to take such care in selecting the articles. Usually they just use whatever's at hand, because nobody will see the paper once the quilt is finished. But in this quilt it's almost as though the quilt maker thought she was sending a secret message."

"Genie Collins," Martha said, and shook her head. "She was a strange woman."

A light went on in Sarah's mind. "That's right!" she said. "You've met her! You dated Samuel for a while, didn't you?"

In the backseat, Ian leaned forward slightly to hear. "Well, I wouldn't call it dating, really," Martha said. "But he used to talk to me at school, and a few times we went to the drugstore and he bought me a soda. Everyone thought he was stuck-up, because of all that money, but I thought he was just very shy."

"I remember he never talked to me at all," Sarah said.

"He didn't talk to anyone," said Martha. "I only got to know him because we were lab partners in biology. And he wouldn't talk to me until halfway through the semester. But I kept trying to be nice to him, day after day, and then one day he opened up."

"So you knew his mother?" Sarah asked. "Genie?" Excitement pricked the back of her neck at the prospect of hearing a firsthand account of the woman whose quilt she was restoring. Emily and Tad had never met Genie, since she had died before they were born, and it sounded like Genie wasn't a topic that they could discuss even in their own family.

Martha nodded. "I only met her once," she said. "I remember Samuel had just gotten his license, and he wanted to take me out to the house. Of course, everyone wanted to go to the Collins house."

"Of course!" Sarah exclaimed, thinking of her own excitement about visiting the place, forty years later.

"So he picked me up in the parking lot after school and drove me out there. I just remember how beautiful all that stained glass in the entrance was in the afternoon light. There were patches of color scattered all down the hall and up the stairs. They had servants, but it was Genie who got us a snack. She served us lemonade, with mint in it, and ginger snaps."

"What was she like?" Sarah asked.

Martha was quiet for a minute. "Very sweet," she said finally. "But hard to talk with. Samuel didn't really seem to want me to ask her questions, so I only asked her a few. It was hard to understand her answers."

"What do you mean?" Ian asked.

Martha was quiet again. "I don't know," she said. "It's hard to explain. She spoke just like everyone else, as if she were making perfect sense, but sometimes I wondered if she'd really heard what I said. Or if maybe she'd misheard and was answering some other question. I can't explain it."

"No," Sarah said, curling her fingers around the steering wheel. "I think I understand."

"She was a good quilter," Martha offered. "I remember she had a very beautiful summer quilt on the back porch. It was a pattern she had made herself, garden flowers with some birds flying in the sky overhead. I'd never seen anything like it."

"It's strange to hear you say that," Sarah said. "The pieces of hers I have seem almost clumsy. And the quilting is very erratic."

"I don't know," Martha said. "It was a long time ago. But the colors she used were so vivid."

"She could probably afford the best materials," Sarah guessed. "The higher quality fabric has better dyes, with deeper colors."

"Well, these didn't seem to be made out of scraps of old dresses," Martha said. "So you might be right. I always hoped Samuel might take me out there again, but that was the end of the semester, and when class ended, he didn't really talk to me again. I'd see him in the halls and try to say hello, but he treated me just like I was anyone else. It wasn't long after that that Genie died. I tried to talk to him then, because I knew he didn't have many friends and I thought he must be so sad. But then he wouldn't talk to me at all. He just stared at me until I gave up and went away."

"It's hard to lose somebody," Sarah said, thinking back on the difficult days after she'd lost her husband Gerry. Some days she hadn't wanted to do anything but sit in the house and cry. Some days she wanted to go out and pretend that everything was normal, without everyone asking her how she was holding up. She could only imagine how hard it must have been for a teenage boy to lose his mother. Of course he might have seemed strange to the other kids in school. "Did you go to her funeral?"

"She didn't have one," Martha said.

"She didn't?" Sarah repeated.

"Unless they kept it very quiet," Martha said. "But I was paying pretty close attention. When I heard the news, I wanted to go to the funeral, even if Samuel wouldn't talk to me, so he'd know that somebody cared about him. I watched the paper for weeks for the announcement, but I never saw it. I even walked down by the funeral home a few times to see if her service was listed on their schedule. But it never was. I heard something about her dying while she was out of town, so maybe they held the service somewhere else. But I would have thought they would have had some kind of observance when they brought her back to bury her in the cemetery."

"When was this?" Sarah asked, hoping maybe it would help her pin down a death date for the quilt label.

"Our junior year in high school," Martha said. "Nineteen sixty-three. In the spring."

It wasn't a solid date, Sarah thought, but it was a start. She could get through the copies of the *Maple Hill Monitor* for spring 1963 in a single morning at the library.

The houses of town had run out long ago. They'd passed the rolling hills and fields outside town, and gone around the long curve of road below the Collins house. Now tall maple trees, their leaves bright yellow and red from the touch of fall, rose on both sides of the road. *The sap of these trees was the source of the wealth that had built the house on the hill,* Sarah thought. It was hard to believe that such a magnificent mansion had been drained from the trunks of these mighty trees, drop by drop.

Sarah slowed as they reached the wide drive for the new maple syrup factory, marked by a big sign with a modern icon of a genie escaping from a bottle, and the company's official name: Genie Maple Syrup Company.

"Genie," Sarah read thoughtfully. It was one of those things she'd seen all her life but never really connected before. "Ward must have named it after her."

"Don't turn here," Ian said. "The old factory is farther on."

"Just tell me when," Sarah said. People in town knew there was an abandoned factory somewhere on the syrup company's property, but the syrup company always had people out working among the trees, and they didn't take kindly to trespassing. Sarah had never seen the old factory except in the newspaper picture.

"Samuel took me there one day too," Martha said. "Just after they opened the new factory and closed the old one up. He showed me all the places where he used to play there as a boy."

"You never told me any of this before," Sarah said.

"Well, there's not much to tell," Martha said. "I didn't spend that much time with him, and it didn't seem like it mattered much, till now. And Samuel seemed to hate the idea that people might talk about his family. So I guess that probably kept me from mentioning anything too."

"Turn here," Ian said, pointing to a scraggly dirt path that led through a broken-down wire and railroad tie fence. Sarah nosed the car onto the drive, which quickly dove into the shade of the maple forest.

"It was so peaceful that I kept coming back now and then," Martha told her. "I even brought Ian once. So in a way this is all my fault. I'm the reason he even knew how to get here."

"It's not your fault, Grandma," Ian said. "And I didn't do anything bad. At least, that's not what I was trying to do."

"You might have shown him where it was," Sarah said. "But you didn't send him back out here with a can of paint."

"I guess not," Martha said, looking back at Ian.

"Just wait until you see," Ian said from the backseat.

Up ahead, they could see a break in the woods, a flash of green lawn, and a glimpse of aged planking.

"Almost there," Sarah said. In a strange way, she felt a little like she had when she went up to the Collins house for the first time. The old newspaper picture made the factory seem so far away in time that she could hardly believe she'd be looking right at it in another few moments.

Then the car pulled out into the clearing, and Martha gasped.

"Look at that!" she said.

Sarah turned the car off and the three of them got out.

"It's beautiful," Martha breathed.

Sarah nodded. She recognized the building from the pictures: the narrow windows, the rickety porch, the wide doors for loading and deliveries. But Ian's art had transformed it. All over the face of the old paneling, he'd painted beautiful maple trees, exactly like the ones that surrounded the building. Somehow he'd managed to paint all the way up the building, so that the painted trees stood two stories tall, broken only by the flashes of sun reflected in the windows.

"This isn't graffiti," Martha said.

"No, it isn't," Sarah agreed.

"You see?" Ian said.

His voice broke the spell his artwork had cast. Martha turned to give him a severe look. "I see you painted all over someone else's property without his permission," she said.

"But you said it was beautiful!" Ian protested.

Martha's face softened. "It is," she said. "I can see it's not just graffiti, sweetheart. But you've still got to learn you can't just start painting on anything you want to. Especially not when it belongs to someone else."

Ian looked down and scuffed his toe along the ground.

As Martha and Ian talked, Sarah gravitated toward the old factory. She was interested in something more than just the face of the building. She wanted to see what secrets it might be hiding inside. She marched up the stairs to the front door and tried it, but the old lock held fast. Inside, the shadows were too deep to make out any shapes among them. She glanced back at Martha, who was still deep in conversation with Ian.

Then Sarah went down the porch steps and tried the giant loading dock door at the far side of the building. It was securely locked as well. Sarah ducked around the corner of the building. It was overgrown with sumac and junk trees, but she walked along the back of the big building anyway, pushing the brush aside every few steps to see if there were any hidden entrances.

About halfway around the back, she found a narrow door, completely hidden by several trunks of sumac. She pushed the jagged-edged leaves out of the way and rattled the handle. To her surprise, the door opened.

An instant later, she stood inside. Light poured into the big room she'd entered from windows high in the walls. In the front of the building, the space was divided into two floors, but here the room was open clear up to the roof. It had probably been the main factory room, Sarah guessed, although it was almost completely empty now. The dusty floors showed the irregular imprints of what must have been giant machines, as well as round discolorations that she guessed came from the syrup vats. On the far side of the room, a wooden staircase led up to a door.

Sarah followed it up. The second floor was nothing more than a uniform set of empty offices. She could see that the move to the new buildings had been efficient, since there were no abandoned desks or chairs, and no stray papers scattered on the floor.

At the end of the hall, another staircase led down. Sarah followed it into the darker room below, which seemed to be some kind of receiving and shipping room, with big bay doors, as well as a kind of retail area, with a counter and shelves. Everything was dusty, but otherwise pristine.

In some ways, this felt stranger than the broken-down barns she'd explored as a young girl. This place hadn't been abandoned to return to nature. It was as if it had somehow gotten lost in time.

"Sarah?" Martha's voice came from outside. Sarah was surprised how clearly it carried into the old building.

"Martha!" she called. "Can you hear me? I'm in here. I'm all right!"

"How did you get in?" Ian shouted. Even muffled by the wood, Sarah could hear the surprise and admiration in his voice. She stifled a smile.

"I'll be out in a minute," she called.

Just as she turned to go, she caught the flash of some bright metal out of the corner of her eye. It came from behind the old retail counter. She moved toward it, and discovered a brand new safe of brushed gunmetal steel, about two feet by two feet. She crouched over and reached to touch it, but then pulled her hand back. A light blinked from the face of the safe, and a motion-sensitive device brought a glowing blue screen to life.

Password, please, it flashed.

Sarah stared down at the display, perplexed. What was this brand-new safe doing in this time capsule of a building? And how had they gotten it in? Not through the narrow, brush-choked door she had squeezed through. And all the other doors were securely locked. That meant that whoever had placed the safe there likely had a key to the building. Was it an employee at the syrup factory? Or a member of the Collins family, Tad or Samuel? Or even—Sarah thought of Emily's strange behavior over the past few days—Emily?

And what could they possibly be hiding in it?

"Sarah!" Martha shouted again. "Are you still all right?"

With a start, Sarah realized it had been more than the minute she had promised.

"Yes!" she shouted. "I'm coming!"

She got to her feet, took one last look at the safe, and then threaded her way back out of the building.

"I can't believe you got in there!" Ian said when she came around from the back. "I tried those doors over and over. They're locked tight! How did you do it?"

Sarah liked Ian, but she wasn't about to give him a clue about how to break into a building when he'd already painted the whole thing without permission. She smiled and shook her head.

Martha put her arm around her grandson and gave him a tight squeeze. "See, there are still some things we know that you haven't learned yet," she said.

Ian ducked his head bashfully. "I guess so," he said.

"But I learned something too," Martha said. "I can see you weren't trying to deface this building. You need to learn how to respect other people's property. But you've got some big ideas. And we need to help you find some bigger canvases to match them."

 CHAPTER EIGHT

I think this is your best bet," Jeff Purvis said, pointing to a thick roll of clear plastic for insulating windows. The weather had already turned cool, and Sarah knew it was about to get downright cold. Before that happened, she wanted to cover her old windows with the clear film. It kept the cold out and the heat in.

"These old houses sure are beautiful," Jeff added. "But the heating bills aren't pretty."

"You've got that right," Sarah said. "I'll take it."

Jeff bent down to pull out the heavy box, and Sarah followed him as he carried it to the counter. As he slipped behind the register he'd left to help her, the bell over the door rang merrily. Both Jeff and Sarah turned to see the new customer. To Sarah's surprise, it was Samuel Collins, dressed in a rich-looking wool coat and crisp flannel pants. He paused in the doorway and glanced around. He seemed ill at ease.

"Hey there," Jeff called out in a friendly voice. "Can I help you?"

Samuel walked down the narrow aisle to the counter. He nodded when he recognized Sarah. She smiled back.

"I hope so," Samuel said to Jeff. "I'm looking for some rope."

"Rope?" Jeff repeated. "Any particular kind?"

Samuel shook his head quickly. "No," he said. "Just something strong."

"You'll find spools of it on the back wall," Jeff said. "Just let me help Mrs. Hart here check out and I'll be right with you."

"I appreciate it," Samuel said.

Jeff rang up Sarah's purchase on the register while Sarah watched Samuel's large form retreat to the back of the store, questions crowding into her mind. Why did Samuel seem ill at ease? What did a man like him need rope for? And why was he shopping for it himself, instead of sending one of his many employees, or asking one of the servants they must have up at the big house?

"Will there be anything else?" Jeff asked.

Sarah returned quickly to herself. "Oh," she said. "No, this is perfect. That's it. Thank you."

Jeff named the price, and she pulled her wallet out to pay. As she gathered her bag into her arms, she glanced at the rear of the store again, but Samuel Collins was still hidden by the tall shelves of nails and paints.

When Sarah arrived home, she found a young woman sitting on her front porch. As Sarah came up the walk, the woman rose and smiled. She had short, curly blonde hair and her face was tanned.

"Hello!" the girl called, as if she were welcoming an old friend.

Despite herself, Sarah smiled back. "Can I help you?" she asked, climbing up the steps.

"I hope so," the girl said. "I'm Belle Silver. I'd like to rent a room from you."

Sarah liked the girl's open smile and easy manner. Her instinct was to throw the door open, invite the girl in, and make a pot of coffee for them. But her son Jason was always after her to be more careful about the people she rented her rooms to. "It's just you and them in that big old house, Mom," he told her. "You need to check them out before you let them move in."

"All right," Sarah said. "When were you thinking of?"

"Today," Belle said.

That was unusual, but there might be a good explanation. Sarah fumbled with her keys for a moment, then opened the front door, stepped in, and set her hardware store purchase down just inside. "Come in. I'll give you a little tour, and then we can see about the rental application. Are you new in town?"

Belle nodded as she stepped into the house. "I've been working as assistant manager at a bath products shop in Jefferson," she said. Jefferson was another small town about half an hour away from Maple Hill. "But my degree is in graphic design, and they've just hired me to start as a designer at the copy shop downtown."

"Oh, you'll love working there," Sarah said. She knew the little downtown storefront well. She'd been in there to get shower invitations made for new mothers in the church and to make copies of the church bulletin for Reverend Peabody. Once they'd even helped her make calendars with family pictures as presents for Jason and Jenna and their broods. The staff were always friendly and patient—and creative.

Belle nodded. "I'm really excited," she said. "But now I need a place to stay. And Sandy at the shop suggested your house."

Sandy had graduated with Jason, and was one of Sarah's favorites among his classmates. Now she was a young mom, and worked part-time at the copy shop while her kids were in school. Sarah loved to pass the time of day with her when she found her in the shop. Sandy's recommendation eased some of Sarah's wariness about her prospective tenant. "Isn't Sandy lovely?" Sarah said.

"She's so sweet!" Belle agreed. "And she's smart. She's created a whole inventory system there. It saves all kinds of money in wasted paper and ink orders."

"I'm not surprised," Sarah said. She set her purse down on the little table by the door, and gestured to the stairs. "Would you like to see the rooms?"

"Oh, I'm sure they'll be fine," Belle said.

"Well, let's take a look," Sarah said, leading her up. "This way you can choose which one you want." She paused at the top of the stairs, where she'd created a small sitting room, with a love seat, a few overstuffed chairs, a small television, and a little shelf of books—mostly Sarah's beloved mystery writers.

"This is so cozy." Belle said. "I think I might never leave if I lived here!"

"Have a look at the rooms," Sarah said.

The first room was the one Emily had lived in before she married Tad. Sarah had painted the walls soft yellow, and made blue gingham drapes.

"Pretty," Belle murmured.

"And then there's this," Sarah said, ushering her to the room across the hall. This one was more formal, with mulberry curtains, dark wood furnishings, and a white quilt with a pair of pieced peacocks in dark greens, blues, and reds facing each other on the bed.

"Oh my gosh!" Belle said. "This has to be mine. Peacocks are my favorite."

"All right," Sarah said. "Let's get you a rental application."

Belle followed her down the stairs and waited in the dining room while Sarah found a rental agreement in her office. When she returned, she set it down in front of Belle. "There are a few rules you'll want to look over, although I don't imagine they'll be any problem. I don't allow overnight guests of the opposite sex, or any kind of smoking, drinking, or drugs in the house. You're welcome to use the kitchen, and there's a shelf in the refrigerator for food. Do you have any pets?"

Belle shook her head.

Sarah nodded. "Well, if you'd like to get one, I'd need to have approval first, as long as you're living here."

"That makes sense," Belle said.

Sarah laid a pen down beside the rental application.

"Take your time," she said. "I'll just be in my sewing nook over here."

"You sew?" Belle said, excited.

"I do," Sarah said.

"My mother used to sew me the prettiest dresses when I was little," Belle said. "One time she made us both matching dresses. I thought that was the best thing in the world."

Sarah smiled. "I used to sew outfits for my son and daughter too," she said. "But now I focus on quilting. I restore antique quilts."

"That must be so much fun," Belle said. "All that history."

"Yes," Sarah said. "But sometimes there's not as much history as you hope."

"What do you mean?"

"Well," Sarah said. "A quilt can tell you a lot about itself, if you know how to look at it. Some fabrics were sold only in certain parts of the country, so often you can tell where a quilt was created just by identifying the materials. But what you really want to know is who made it, and what her life was like, when she was born and when she died. And that can be hard to find out."

"So what do you do?"

"Whatever it takes," Sarah laughed. "I spend a lot of time at the library and the historical society. And sometimes," she said, thinking of her excursion with Martha and Ian that afternoon, "I do my own investigating."

"You're like a detective!" Belle said.

Sarah smiled. "I guess maybe I am. Well, don't let me keep you from your application."

Belle smiled and ducked her head over the paper, and Sarah slipped into her sewing room.

The quilt pieces were waiting for her, just as she had left them, divided into neat stacks of brown and green and blue. Sarah laid out a row of five brown squares side by side to see if she could find any connection between them. After a good long minute of staring, nothing jumped out at her. But the pieced browns themselves began to intrigue her. Their pattern was irregular, but it gave the overall effect of something in nature, like the bark of a tree, or dirt overturned in the garden for planting.

Suddenly, Martha's words flashed through her mind. *It was a pattern she had made herself…garden flowers…the sky overhead.* Could the rich brown hues represent dirt? Were the patches of green actually leaves, the red and orange flowers, the swaths of blue sky? There was one way to find out. Quickly, Sarah scooped up all three stacks of quilt squares. She swept through the dining room, where Belle glanced up and smiled, and into the hall, where she began to lay the quilt squares down by color: a thick strip of brown soil, a layer of green leaves, and then blue along the upper edge. It didn't immediately resolve, but sometimes mosaics only made sense when seen from a distance.

Sarah climbed halfway up the stairs and looked down over the polished mahogany railing. If she squinted, she could see the outlines of a garden, but the edges of the piecing didn't really line up. Maybe some squares were out of place.

She went back down the stairs and rearranged the pieces. While she was trading a dark blue with a light one to make the gradation even more dramatic, Belle stuck her head through the doorway from the dining room. "I think I'm done," she said. Then she spied the quilt pieces scattered on the floor.

"Is this a part of the quilt restoration?" she asked.

"This is part of the 'whatever it takes' I was telling you about," Sarah said.

"It looks kind of like a field," Belle said. "With vegetables growing in it?"

This was another perspective, and one Sarah hadn't thought of. "You know what?" she said, gesturing to Belle to step around the old squares. "Come up and look at these with me. Maybe you can see something I don't see."

Dutifully, Belle followed her up the stairs. Both women leaned over the railing, looking down.

"Actually, it looks less like a field from up here," Belle said after a minute.

Sarah shook her head. It looked less like a garden than it had as well, despite her efforts to rearrange the blocks. For one thing, the spots of red and orange were in the wrong place; they showed up mostly in the brown patches, which she had thought might be dirt, rather than in the green. And the blue may have faded over time, but still, it was a strange color to pick for the sky—more purple than blue. Also, all the blue pieces seemed to be curved, with few pieces where the blue ran solid through the whole square, which is what she would expect if they were supposed to create a strip of sky at the top edge of a design. Maybe they represented a river? But no matter how Sarah rearranged the pieces in her mind, she couldn't see a pattern that made sense.

"Do you see anything?" Belle asked.

"I'm afraid I don't really," Sarah told her.

"I don't either," Belle said. "But I should probably be going. My shift starts in a few hours, and I have some other errands to run in town. But I'd love to stay here tonight, if my application looks all right to you."

Belle started down the stairs, and Sarah followed. She already knew she would be delighted to have the friendly young woman share her home. And Sandy's reference was as good as anybody's, in her book. "I think it'll be fine," she said.

Belle gave a delighted squeal and threw her arms around Sarah. "I'm so happy!" she said. "I know I'm going to love it here."

"I hope you will," Sarah said. "It'll be nice to have you."

"Okay," Belle said. "Well then, I'll see you tonight."

Sarah waved at her new boarder as Belle went down the walk. Then she turned back to the quilt pieces scattered over her hall. A river, a garden, a field: she had all the pieces of the puzzle, but she couldn't get them to fit together. She stared at them until the pieces began to swim in her vision, every bit as mysterious as they had always been. Then she shook her head and knelt down to begin to collect them.

Another dead end, Sarah thought. As she picked up the last pieces, she pictured Emily's frightened face on the steps of the library. *Lord, please be with that family,* she prayed. *If this quilt can help them, let me find the answers I need.*

CHAPTER NINE

S arah!" Irene Stuart exclaimed as Sarah stepped through the historical society doors. "What a great surprise! I just spent a little time with Nettie Draper this morning. She was married to the founder of Maple Hill, and it seems she's a bit of a quilter. I couldn't help but think of you."

Sarah smiled. The historical figures Irene studied were so real to her that she spoke about them as if they were old friends. The habit confused some people, but it had always held a certain charm for Sarah. She laid her notebook, with the few slim facts she'd been able to collect about Genie Collins' quilt, down on the counter.

"How can I help you?" Irene asked.

"Well," Sarah said. "I'm looking for information about a quilt I'm trying to restore. It seems to have some connection with a land dispute between Ward Collins and a man named John Peters. I've never heard of him. Does the name ring any bells for you?"

Irene was nodding vigorously. "The Peters family!" she said. "Of course. They were some of our most outstanding citizens."

This was a surprise to Sarah. Maybe the Peters family had been important to the town in its earlier days. But in that case, why were there no Peters left in town?

"Abe Peters was one of the very first settlers in the area," Irene told her, coming around from behind the counter. "In fact, I think he arrived just a few years after Ben Draper. The two of them owned most of what we know of as Maple Hill today at one point. Ben Draper had what we think of as our downtown now. Most of Abe Peters's land was to the east of town."

"Where the maple factory is now?" Sarah guessed.

Irene nodded, looking at her quizzically. "Yes," she said. "How did you know?"

"Did you ever hear of any questions about how that land passed from the Peters to the Collins family?" Sarah asked.

Irene pursed her lips. "I'm not sure about that. It would have happened sometime after nineteen hundred, right?"

Sarah nodded.

"I spend most of my time in the century before that," Irene said. "But I've got some files that might be interesting for you to go through. Tim?" she called.

A skinny teenager in a black T-shirt and wire-rimmed glasses appeared in the doorway to the historical society's back room. "Did you call me?" he said.

"Hello, Tim." Sarah smiled at the gangly high schooler. Tim interned at the historical society for school credit.

"Tim's a miracle worker with the filing system. Sarah's looking for information on the Peters and the Collins families," she told him. "I thought she might find something in Daisy Anderson's files."

Tim nodded. "I think she did get started on the Peters family," he said.

"Daisy Anderson?" Sarah repeated.

Tim gestured for Sarah to follow him into the back room. "She was an amateur historian of Maple Hill," he said. "When she passed away in the nineteen eighties, she left almost twenty boxes of her research to the historical society. Nobody's ever been through it before. It's one of my projects for the fall."

On the large wooden table in the back room sat a collection of mismatched boxes: file boxes, book boxes—even one advertising fresh Florida oranges. Papers, handwritten and typed, poked out of the boxes from equally mismatched file folders, with an occasional newspaper clipping thrown in for good measure.

"I just started," Tim said apologetically. "I can tell she had some kind of filing system, but I haven't really figured out what it is yet. But if you can find it, the information is good. She was incredibly thorough."

Irene appeared in the doorway behind them. "When Tim gets it sorted out, it'll be a godsend," she said. "Especially for more recent history. Most of the early details I can give off the top of my head, but as the town grows and more families move in, even I start to get fuzzy."

Sarah let her purse slip off her shoulder and looked over the jumble of boxes and papers. "How does it seem to be organized?" she asked.

Tim pulled a folder from a nearby box. "She seemed to arrange things mostly by two topics: family or property. Like this one," he said, letting the file drop open, and scanning the contents. "It's about the McRitchie house. But she's gone all the way back to the original deed—" he held up the photocopy to show Sarah. "—and up to the real estate listing for the last time it was sold." He flipped through the rest of the papers in the folder, shaking his head. "It's amazing," he said. "Then she's also got some history she wrote herself after interviewing members of the family. Apparently the McRitchies weren't the original owners. Somebody built the house just after the Civil War, but his wife wasn't healthy enough to live in a northern climate. He was traveling on a train and met someone from Virginia who wanted to come north, so they traded houses sight unseen. That's how the McRitchies first came to this town. And then they owned the place for a hundred and ten years."

"Does it have information on the McRitchie family too?" Sarah asked, curious.

Tim shook his head. "No. Nothing that doesn't have to do with the house itself. That's one of the little quirks of her filing system. If she did do research on the McRitchie family, it'll be in another file completely."

Sarah nodded. "And these are all the files?" she asked.

Tim grinned and shook his head again. He pointed to several stacks of boxes piled neatly against the far wall, another fifteen or so in total. "And those," he said. "What families are you looking for?"

"Peters," Sarah said. "And Collins."

"Well, I've gone through about five of these boxes so far," Tim said. "And I haven't found those families in them. That means there are only about fifteen for you to look through. You're welcome to dig in."

"It won't disturb your filing project?" Sarah said.

"There's plenty for me to work on. Don't worry about that," Tim said.

"All right," Sarah said. She pulled the nearest box toward her, and flipped the top folder open. On the top was a studio photograph of a dour old man with a woolly white beard. She checked his name, Stifflemire, then flipped to the next item in the file. It was a newspaper clipping of a young couple on the steps outside a church. Sarah checked the caption. The girl's name was Laura Stifflemire. Not a Peters or a Collins file, then. Sarah laid it aside, and pulled the next one from the box.

"I think we've lost her," Irene said dryly.

"I'm sorry," Sarah said. "I'm just so curious."

"Don't be sorry," Irene said. "This is what we're here for." She patted Sarah on the shoulder and slipped back into the next room.

Six boxes and almost an hour later, Sarah opened a manila file to find a photocopy of a *Maple Hill Monitor* article about the fiftieth anniversary of the town's founding. In the first paragraph, side by side with the name of the town founder, Ben Draper, she saw the name *Peters*. Her heart skipped a beat. She sank down in one of the chairs that surrounded the work table to read.

Irene was right: Abe Peters and his wife, Dolly, had moved to town shortly after Ben Draper, the town founder, had claimed the first land. Five years later, in 1786, the two of them and three other families had applied to the state for the town's incorporation papers. Abe Peters, it seemed, was something of a land speculator, and in the great migration from the coasts into the heart of the country, that bent served him well. From sale announcements in the *Maple Hill Monitor*, she could see that his holdings grew steadily until the town's population began to grow, when his property began to shrink again as he sold it to newcomers, probably at a tidy profit. His son, David, appeared to have financed some of the construction of Maple Hill's best-known downtown buildings. She loved thinking of a time when everything she knew in town was still just a dream in someone's mind. It gave her a sense of possibility, that maybe some of the things she did with her life would still mean something to future generations.

David's grandson, Frederick, was born a few years before the Civil War. He must have had every advantage, but he didn't seem to have a job or a trade. He had married late, and his youngest son was born in the early years of the new century, in 1911, and christened Jonathan Abraham Peters.

Sarah's heart skipped a beat again. This was the first appearance of the man who figured so prominently in the papers Genie Collins had sewn into her quilt.

Jonathan's mother had died in childbirth, and her son had grown up troubled. When he was nineteen, the police blotter recorded that he'd spent a night in the local jail after an incident at the local tavern. Two years later, when he was twenty-one, his father passed away. A few years after that, in 1936, the paper printed a long column on the second page detailing the suit John Peters had brought against the maple syrup company. The suit alleged improper dealings in the sale of his family land. The final item in the file was a brief note a few months later, reporting that the suit had been dismissed. Then the file ended.

It was as if John Peters, and the entire Peters family, vanished from Maple Hill's history.

"John Peters," Sarah whispered. "Where did you go?"

"I'm sorry?" Tim said. As Sarah searched through the boxes, he had been quietly organizing files, making notes, and creating indexes.

Sarah shook her head. "It's nothing," she said. "I'm just thinking out loud." She set the Peters file down on the table. Where had John Peters gone? And why would the wife of the man he accused of fraud sew pieces of the unpleasant story into the quilt she'd made?

Then another thought struck her. Whenever the Peters family bought or sold land, there had been an announcement of the transaction in the paper. But she didn't remember a *Monitor* article about the sale of the land by John Peters to Ward Collins. She thumbed through the papers again to confirm it. No article. Perhaps Daisy had overlooked it. But she didn't seem to have overlooked any other detail of the Peters family history. Maybe, she thought, the answer lay in the history of the Collins family—if Daisy Anderson had chosen to compile it.

"You said you hadn't found anything on the Collins family in the boxes you've indexed?" she asked Tim.

"Nope," he said.

Sarah did a quick count. Tim had been through half a dozen of the boxes already. She'd gone through six herself. That left about eight more boxes, and if there was a Collins file, it ought to be easy to find. The maple syrup company had been so important in the town's history that the file would have to be one of the thickest in the pile. And there was only one way to find it.

With renewed vigor, Sarah dug into the boxes. But another hour later, she'd come up empty. None of the files she'd checked in any of the boxes mentioned the Collins family, except in passing. She let the last file drop to the table, leaned back, and sighed.

"No luck?" Tim said. Then his eyes widened. "Did you go through *all* of those?"

Sarah nodded. "Yep," she said. "But she doesn't seem to have made a file on the Collins family."

"Daisy's funny like that," Tim said. Sarah suppressed a smile. He was starting to sound like Irene, talking about historical figures as if they were still alive. In a way, though, she guessed they were. "Sometimes she'll collect all kinds of details on something that doesn't seem important. But some things she ignores completely. I'm still not sure why."

Sarah rose and slung her purse over her shoulder. "Well, thanks for letting me look at the files," she said.

"Daisy would be glad you did," Tim said.

Sarah smiled and went out into the historical society's main room.

"Did you find what you needed?" asked Irene.

"Some of it," Sarah said. "She did have a file on the Peters family. It's strange. They were so prominent in the last century, but the family seems to have disappeared when John Peters left town."

"Remind me what else were you looking for?" Irene asked.

"It should have been easy," Sarah said. "The Collins family."

Irene's face broke out in a broad grin. "That may still be easy," she said. She turned away, pulled open a drawer in one of the file cabinets behind her, and rifled through it. When she turned back, she had a bulging file in her hand, almost three inches thick. She laid it down on the counter between them. "The Collins family," she said, as if she were introducing them to Sarah at a party.

Sarah flipped the file open. The top item was an article about Ward Collins' arrival in Maple Hill, when he was just eleven years old. His aunt and uncle, Sam and Andrea Thompson, had adopted him after the untimely death of his parents.

"What is this?" Sarah asked.

"A few years ago, someone in communications at the syrup factory called me up and asked me to do a historical search on the family. They were thinking of doing a book about their history, in conjunction with the company's six-tieth anniversary. So I spent a week digging all this up. They never did the project, but I kept this file on hand. Every now and then I think maybe I'll go ahead and write the book my-self. The factory's been such an important part of the town's history."

Sarah scanned down the first article. The Thompsons who had adopted Ward Collins farmed land to the east of town, and the paper listed an address Sarah recognized. It was on the same road where the Collins place and the syrup factory now stood.

"Irene," Sarah said. "Could I look at one of those plat maps?" Irene's most prized item in the historical society archive was a set of beautiful original maps that showed how land ownership had changed from decade to decade. They were worth looking at simply for their dark ink lines and beautiful hand tinting, but they were also full of invaluable information for anyone interested in the town's history.

"Sure," Irene said, stepping back out from behind the counter. "What years are you interested in?"

Sarah checked the article, grateful to be able to find the date in the uppermost corner after her struggles with the frustrating pages sewn into Genie's quilt. "The nineteen twenties," she said.

"Coming right up," Irene said, and pulled out one of the wide flat archival drawers the maps were stored in. "Here we go. You looking for anything in particular?"

"I don't know," Sarah said. She walked over to look at the map. It took her a minute to find the center of town, because some of the streets she knew hadn't been built yet, but after she did, it was a simple matter to find Old Maple Hill Road and follow it out toward the syrup company's maple grove. There, in the telltale bend near the Collins house, was a vast tract of land, all tinted pale pink, marked "Peters." She scanned the nearby plots, a rich patchwork of pale yellows, greens, and blues. Finally, she found what she was looking for: a small triangle of about forty acres, sharing a border with the Peters land near where the maple grove stood. It was labeled "Thompson." So Ward had grown up in sight of the land he eventually built his fortune on. But the scrap of land his family owned seemed so small compared to the vast Peters tract. And Ward had been so young when he bought it and opened the syrup company. How had he ever managed to earn enough to buy the Peters land? Especially *before* he made his fortune from the Peters maple grove?

Irene saw Sarah's quizzical expression. "Did you find what you need?" she asked, glancing down at the map.

Sarah sighed. "I wish I knew," she said. She went back to the fat file on the counter. Maybe it contained more answers. "Do you mind if I—?"

"Please!" Irene said. "You'll be the first person who's looked at it besides me!"

Sarah collected the file and settled down into one of the historical society's comfortable wing chairs. If anything, Irene was even more thorough than Daisy Anderson. The next item in the Collins file was an announcement that Ward Collins had gathered a group of investors to open a syrup company to tap the Peters family's vast maple grove. After that came the announcement of Ward's engagement to Genie Woltherstorf, the daughter of one of the town's most prominent businessmen. It included a photograph of the young couple, but for some reason, Genie looked different in this picture than she did in other pictures Sarah had seen. It took Sarah a minute to recognize the reason: In this picture, Genie seemed genuinely happy.

The next item was one Sarah recognized: the two-page spread on the opening of the syrup company, complete with brass band, that Genie had sewn into her quilt. The article after that was familiar to Sarah as well, from the Peters file: a copy of the item repeating Peters' claims of fraud. The next few items heralded the growth of the syrup company as it found customers nationwide and began to hire more and more local men to keep up with production demands. By this time, the country was in an upheaval over the war in Europe. Ward Collins donated an entire tanker full of maple syrup to the war effort, and consulted with the government as an expert in food production and logistics. By now, he was also featured in public events, along with the town's other important men. Sarah found several photographs of him sitting on makeshift platforms in front of towering images of bald eagles. Sometimes Genie stood beside him, but despite the fact that her husband's arm often circled her protectively, in these pictures she again had the sad expression Sarah knew so well.

Just after the war ended, Ward and Genie's son Samuel was born. A daughter was born a few years later, but she apparently didn't live long. Her obituary appeared in the paper just eighteen months after her birth announcement. After that, the news became more familiar to Sarah, because she had also lived through it. When she and Samuel were in elementary school, Ward had closed the original syrup factory and opened the modern facility that still operated today. After that, Ward's name mainly appeared in connection with news at the factory. Scattered in between were a few articles that traced the arc of Samuel's life: a winning time at a regional track meet, the name of the college he would be attending on a list of graduating high school students, and his return to the town to take a position at the family business. Sarah fingered the announcement of his marriage to Lydia Beckett, whom he'd met at college, with sadness. Given what Martha had said about him, he must have really loved Lydia to overcome his shyness and build a relationship with her. Both Samuel's and Lydia's faces were open and hopeful in their engagement picture. But she'd lived so briefly after their marriage: less than ten years, according to the obituary. Beside it, slightly out of order, was the announcement of Tad's birth. Then the company's fiftieth anniversary celebration and Ward's retirement. Its sixtieth, under Samuel's leadership, brought her up to the present day.

But the file didn't end there. When Sarah turned over the article on the sixtieth anniversary, she found another small stack of newspaper clippings and copies. The first was an announcement of Genie Woltherstorf's birth. Sarah picked it up with the same tingling feeling of excitement she'd had when Martha began to tell her about having met Genie before she died.

Unlike most of the birth announcements Sarah had seen in her research on various quilts, Genie's birth wasn't shared with a simple note. Instead, the paper ran a full-page article describing her baptism and the reception at the hotel that followed. The hotel restaurant had been closed for the afternoon, and her father Jack Woltherstorf had put out the word that he would buy any white flowers anyone in the town would bring him, until the room was filled with thousands of blossoms: white rose and lilies, white lilacs, tall stalks of white stock. He'd imported a string quartet from Boston for the occasion, and Genie's baptismal dress had been made from lace all the way from Holland.

Sarah thought of Ward Collins' introduction to the town, as an orphan helping his aunt and uncle eke out a living on a small plot of land. It couldn't have been more different from Genie's. How did a boy like that wind up marrying a girl like Genie? And how would Genie's proud parents have felt about that?

She thumbed through a few more articles. From the time she was born, Genie, it appeared, had been included in every social event that mattered in the town. She went to ice-skating parties, church picnics, and ice cream socials.

But Sarah noticed something at all these events. Whenever Genie was pictured, she wore the same sad expression. Everyone around her might be smiling with delight, lost in the music, or holding up big dishes of ice cream, but Genie always seemed melancholy and lost in thought. The only time Sarah had ever seen her look truly happy was in the announcement of her engagement to Ward. The final item in the file was Genie's daughter Maude's obituary, at age eighteen months. It included a mention of the longtime family maid who had helped nurse Maude through her last weeks: Ava Harper. Sarah knew that name. The family was still in town. In fact, it was Ava's daughter Annie who owned the gift store near The Spotted Dog. It was interesting, Sarah thought, that a family as prominent as the Peters family had been could vanish from town completely, but the maid's daughter was now a successful businesswoman.

But where was Genie Collins' death date, for the quilt label? There should be an obituary somewhere in the file for her, as well. Sarah flipped through the last few articles, then flipped through them again. She hadn't missed anything. Genie Collins' obituary simply wasn't there.

"Irene?" Sarah asked.

Irene bustled out from behind the counter.

"Is someone giving you trouble?" she asked.

"Not exactly," Sarah said. "It's just that I'm looking for a death date for Genie Collins, to put on the label of the quilt I'm restoring, and I can't seem to find her obituary."

Irene leaned in and glanced down at the file. Then she straightened up. "Oh," she said briskly. "I guess I must not have pulled it. Let me go back and check our obituaries file." She disappeared into the back room.

Sarah fingered one of the last items about Genie Woltherstorf. It was a photograph of a group of girls in bright white dresses with high collars, sitting around a table that had been set for tea as part of an afternoon event to celebrate their upcoming graduation. One of the girls flirted coyly with the camera over the lip of her teacup. Another brandished her cup and saucer at the photographer with a wide grin. But Genie sat back in her chair, gazing at the fancy silver teapot with its elaborate scrollwork with a sad expression.

Sarah's brow knit in concentration. It seemed that whatever shadow had crossed over Genie and made her seem so melancholy and pensive had been part of her life before she married Ward. This made her think of another bride she knew, who suddenly seemed so unhappy after her marriage: Emily. Did Emily's problem really have to do with her marriage to Tad? Sarah wondered. Or did it have to do with something in her past?

"Well, this is strange," Irene said, coming out of the back room with a pair of leather-bound volumes. She set them down on the desk beside Sarah and flipped one open. Strips of obituaries, arranged by alphabet, lined the yellowing pages.

"Look at this," she said.

She flipped the book open to Collins, then turned pages until she reached the page where Genie's should have been. There was only one entry: for Genie Collins' baby daughter. None for Genie herself.

"Let's see," Irene said. "She passed away in 1962?"

"Nineteen sixty-three," Sarah said, remembering her conversation with Martha. "In the spring."

"Well, they didn't stop keeping this obituary index until 1975. So if she had one in the local paper, it should be here. I even looked under W, just to be sure."

Irene flipped open the second book, found the Woltherstorf family, and ran her finger down the page. Obituaries for Genie's parents and grandparents were all pasted carefully in even rows. But the book went on to "Wyckoff" without including Genie.

"How unusual is it," Sarah asked, "not to have an obituary?"

"Very unusual," Irene said. "In this town? I've never seen it."

CHAPTER TEN

The sound of Sarah's name was so faint, it almost seemed as if a ghost was calling to her. She turned around on the sidewalk at the foot of the historical society steps. Halfway down the street, Liam stood outside his shop, waving his arms. Murphy sat back on his haunches, watching his master with bemused tolerance, as if he'd long since become accustomed to the strange ways of human beings.

How had Liam spotted her all the way down here? How had he even *recognized* her at this distance?

Sarah shook her head. Liam called her name again. If he kept it up, the whole town would hear him. She headed off down the block toward him. Liam waved one more time, then let his arms fall to his sides.

Murphy glanced down the street to see what might have occasioned this sudden change in his master's behavior. When he saw Sarah approaching he lost all composure. He barreled down the sidewalk, his long torso swinging behind him like a train car that hadn't been coupled tight enough. When he reached her, he gamboled with delight until she reached down to scratch his ears. Then, satisfied, he sat down in front of her feet.

"Well, Murphy," she said. "This is a problem, you see. How am I supposed to get down to the store if you're in my way?"

Murphy gazed up at her serenely. All was well in his world. He couldn't be distracted by her worries.

"Murphy!" Liam called, and followed it up with a sharp whistle. Immediately, Murphy was on his feet, giving his master all the attention an eager cadet might give his commanding officer.

"Come!" Liam called, and the ball of energy was off again, returning to his master.

Sarah followed Murphy down the sidewalk, laughing. When she got to The Spotted Dog, Liam had knelt down to reward Murphy's good behavior with a bit of affection. Murphy had rolled over on his back, and was squirming from side to side to make the most of it as Liam rubbed his belly. When Sarah's shadow crossed them, Liam gave Murphy's barrel chest two good pats, and stood up.

"I'm glad I saw you," he said. "I got that book you wanted."

"Oh!" Sarah said, surprised. Had she asked for a book? Then she remembered the mosaic book he had looked up for her the other day. But she hadn't exactly ordered it.

"It's a beauty," Liam said. "Let me show you."

Sarah followed him into the store, doing a quick calculation in her head. They had talked about the book only two days before. How had he gotten it so fast?

"Look at this," Liam said. He pulled a book out from underneath his register and laid it on the counter, facing her. On the cover was a beautiful image of a sunflower, its petals pieced from different scraps of yellow fabric, its round face a mix of browns that gave it unusual variation and depth.

"This is beautiful," Sarah said, opening it.

"Didn't I tell you?" Liam said.

Sarah turned the pages, looking over images of snowmen, butterflies, birds, country homes, all pieced together from tiny scraps of similar-colored fabrics. There was even a quilt of Elvis, with his famous swoop of hair cut out of various shades of black. The book finished with a beautiful landscape of a mountain overlooking a lake made from different shades of blue.

"It's really something," Liam said.

Sarah closed the book. "Thank you so much for ordering this," she said.

Liam grinned.

"But how did you get it so fast? Do your suppliers normally ship so quickly?"

Liam avoided her gaze. "I told them it was for one of my best customers," he said.

"We only talked about this two days ago," Sarah said. "Did you pay for overnight shipping?"

Liam looked back at her, his eyes twinkling. "Not everything's a mystery you have to solve, Sarah Hart," he said. "Don't you have a more important one on your plate right now? With the anagram quilt?"

Sarah's mind flashed back to the quilt, still in pieces on her sewing table. She'd been researching it all morning, but it hardly seemed important compared to her questions about what was bothering Emily, or what had happened to Genie Collins. "I guess so," Sarah said.

Liam studied her face for a moment. "Why do you look so worried?" he asked.

"Well, Emily hasn't been herself since she gave me the quilt," Sarah said. "Whenever I try to reach out to her, she acts as though she doesn't want to talk with me. And then I found there was newspaper in the quilt squares."

Liam's brow furrowed.

"That's not the strange part," Sarah said. "Quilters often used newspaper in the past to stabilize the stitching, and give the quilt more weight. But I discovered that all of these papers contained articles about the Collins family."

"Almost like someone chose them," Liam said.

"*Exactly* like someone chose them," Sarah said. "When I went to the historical society, I discovered there was no way they could all have been included by chance. They were from different papers, over a period of years. Someone must have been collecting them all that time, and then sewed them into the quilt." She decided not to tell Liam what the articles were about. They could be damaging to the Collins family name, and she didn't want to repeat the old claims of fraud if there was nothing to them.

"That *is* strange," Liam said.

"That's not even the strangest thing," Sarah went on. "While I was researching them, I started looking for Genie Collins' obituary. Even if nothing else gets written about a person during her lifetime, you can always find an obituary. But Genie Collins doesn't seem to have one."

"Maybe she never died," Liam said, making a gentle joke.

"Well," Sarah said, "I'm starting to wonder. And I'm just not sure what to do next. I guess I haven't looked through the actual newspapers at the library. There's a small chance the historical society made an error when they were collecting obituaries and omitted Genie's, although I doubt it. But I've already spent the whole morning combing through documents, and found nothing but dead ends."

"It's funny you should say dead ends," Liam said. "I'll tell you what I'd do."

"What?" Sarah asked.

"I'd check the cemetery," he said. "It's the first place to look for someone who's dead. Newspapers print all kinds of things. But graves don't lie. At least, not as often."

He was right. The cemetery was the obvious place to check on the facts of Genie's death. "Now, why didn't I think of that?" Sarah asked.

"It sounds like you've had some other things on your mind," Liam said.

"I guess I have," Sarah said. She looked down at the book on the counter, and dropped her purse from her shoulder to reach for her wallet. "How much do I owe you for this?"

"Oh," Liam said. "I know you weren't making an official order when we talked about it. Why don't you take it home, look it over. Make sure it's something you really like. If you don't want it, just bring it back. If you do, we'll work it out later."

"Well, all right," Sarah said, still slightly reluctant. "Thank you."

"Anytime," Liam said.

The cemetery was hardly worth driving to, just a ten minute walk from the center of town, a wide, quiet plot of land shaded by the giant maples the town was named after, along with a few dignified oaks. Sarah left her car by the historical society and walked over, letting her mind drift. She was a logical thinker, but sometimes her best ideas came to her when she wasn't trying too hard to think. And sometimes she just needed a good rest, even if no thoughts came to her in those moments.

She was glad to see that the small booth at the front entrance was manned. Maple Hill Cemetery wasn't a big business concern, but on Tuesday and Thursday there was usually somebody on duty to help people look up the graves of loved ones or ancestors in the cemetery records. Today it was Alana Marquez, who usually worked at the cemetery offices downtown. Sarah had gotten to know Alana after Gerry's death. Jason and Jenna had tried to be there for her, but there were still so many details to take care of and decide about. It was especially hard for her to make decisions about the gravestone and burial plot, but Alana had been kind and patient with her even when she struggled to make up her mind. Sarah had had warm feelings for her ever since.

Alana caught sight of Sarah before she even reached the booth, and swung the door open.

"Well, this brightens my afternoon," she called.

"Mine too," Sarah said.

When she got to the booth, they gave each other a quick hug.

"How are you doing?" Alana asked.

Since Alana knew Sarah through Gerry's funeral, whenever Alana asked that simple question, Sarah had a sense that she was asking about how Sarah was doing with Gerry's loss. And Sarah was grateful for the question. Even though it had been years now, and she had a rich life and good friends and family, she still felt his absence every day. That feeling was one that would never go away, and Sarah had actually started to think of the enduring sense of loss as a way of never really losing him. In a strange way, the fact that she had never stopped missing him was a way of always having him with her. "I'm doing all right," Sarah said. "Thank you for asking. How are you?"

"Oh, you know," said Alana. "Some good, some bad. But I do like working out here in the afternoons. The trees are a lot prettier to look at than the office walls."

"I bet," Sarah said.

Alana nodded and glanced in at the cemetery's shaded, rolling lawns, studded with intricately carved headstones. "Are you here to visit Gerry?" she asked.

Sarah shook her head. "Not this time," she said. "I'm looking for the Collins family plot. Genie Collins."

"Let me look for you," Alana said. She flipped a binder open to the letter C, ran her finger partway down the list of names, and then opened another notebook. This one was full of maps that Sarah could see mirrored the plots and curving lanes of the cemetery. "Here," she said. "I've got a Maude Collins, and Lydia Collins…"

"Samuel's baby sister. And his mother," Sarah said.

Alana nodded. "… but no Genie," she said.

"Maybe it's under another name?"

Alana shook her head. "I don't think so," she said. "They've got eight plots there, but according to this only two of them are occupied."

Sarah shook her head. She had come this far. She might as well go see the plot for herself. "Where is it?" she asked.

Alana pointed on the map. "Here," she said. "Just past the Great War memorial."

"I know where that is," Sarah said. "I'll probably see you on the way back."

"Good luck!" Alana called after her.

Sarah reached the Great War memorial a few minutes later. From there, finding the Collins family plot wasn't hard: it was graced by a pair of twin white angels, both of which stood as tall as Sarah. In the center was a shiny black granite headstone, with Ward's and Genie Collins' names and birthdates cut into the slick surface. Beside it was a slightly smaller stone carved with Samuel's and Lydia's names and birthdates. But only Lydia's had a year of death as well. A smaller angel looked down over a small black stone, set flat in the earth. It read "Maude Collins," and the birth and death dates were heartbreakingly close. Alana seemed to be right. As far as the Collins family headstones were concerned, Genie Collins was not buried in the family plot.

"Then where are you, Genie?" Sarah wondered aloud.

She took the long way back, which looped by the plot where Gerry had been laid to rest, in a slightly more modern area of the cemetery. His headstone was nothing fancy, just a simple grey arch, with his birthday and date of death carved above the line "beloved husband." There was a spot for her there as well, but he had been insistent that she not order her headstone along with his. "You've still got a lot of life to live," he'd told her. "Let someone else worry about that later. And by then, you won't be worried about it at all." Gerry always had been able to see clear to the heart of things, Sarah remembered. It was one of the many things she missed about him.

"Hello, stranger," she said, stopping before his headstone.

She didn't have much more she wanted to say to him. Just a simple greeting, that was all, to let him know she was there. They hadn't ever needed too many words between them, anyway. But as she stood by his stone, she could feel all the worry and frustration of the past several days begin to lift from her shoulders. None of the details she'd been fussing over mattered much compared to her love for Gerry and his love for her. In fact, as things fell into perspective, the importance of the quilt and its many mysteries began to fade. Only a few things still really seemed to matter: Genie's happy expression in her engagement photograph. Emily's love for Tad, and her desire to help him appreciate his family.

Lord, Sarah prayed. *Please don't let me forget what really matters.*

"Did you find what you were looking for?" Alana asked when Sarah returned to the little booth.

"I did and I didn't," Sarah told her.

"Sometimes that's the way it goes," Alana said, and smiled.

Sarah smiled and turned to go. But then another thought caught her up short. She'd found less information on Genie in the Collins section of the file than she had in the Woltherstorf material. What if the same were true in the cemetery? Maybe, for some reason, she'd wanted to be buried with her parents.

"Would you be willing to look up another name for me?" Sarah asked.

"Of course." Alana said. She opened the book of names again. "Go ahead."

"Woltherstorf," Sarah said.

Alana searched quickly through the W section.

"Got it," she said, and flapped the map book open. "See?" she said again, and pointed.

Sarah nodded. The Woltherstorf family site was on the other side of the cemetery, near a grove of tall pines.

"Thank you," she said.

"That's why I'm here," said Alana.

When Sarah got in sight of the tight cluster of pines, she saw that the Woltherstorf plot also wouldn't be hard to find. Like the Collins plot, it was dominated by a statue, this time of a tree trunk cast in sand-colored cement, with a small bird perched on one branch. Like the Collins plot, it was composed of several graves, with the patriarch and his wife in the center, and Genie's parents nearby. And like the Collins plot, there was no sign of Genie Collins anywhere.

Sarah took a quick turn around the other side of the stone tree, but that plot was devoted to the resting places of another family. Sarah returned to the Woltherstorf side, and gazed down at the matching gravestones that told the story of their births and their passage from this world.

Her discovery brought up even more questions than it answered. But at least now she knew for sure.

If Genie Collins was buried anywhere, it wasn't in Maple Hill.

CHAPTER ELEVEN

||||||||||||||||||||||||||||||||||||||||||||||||||||||||||||||||||||||||||||||||||||||||||||||||||||||||||||||||||||||||||||||||||||||||||||||||||||||||||||||||||||

S arah checked her watch as she walked back downtown to where her car was parked. One o'clock. She still had time to meet up with Maggie at two thirty for lunch. Maggie tended to get a rush of noon shoppers at her antique store, so Sarah usually visited her early in the afternoon for a late lunch. Often Maggie took something to the shop from home, but it might be nice for Sarah to take something over today. Maybe she'd stop into The Spotted Dog again and pick up some sandwiches and drinks.

Sarah's thoughts were interrupted by movement in the park across the street. When she glanced across the way, she recognized Emily, deep in conversation with two men.

Wonderful! She'd been wanting to talk to Emily to share her progress and see if she could get some more facts about the quilt, but even more important, Sarah wanted to see how Emily was doing. She couldn't shake the look of fear she'd seen on Emily's face at the library the previous morning. Coupled with Emily's strange behavior when she went to pick up the quilt, it all made Sarah uneasy. If Emily was in trouble, she wanted to know about it, so she could help. Maybe God had arranged this little appointment to help her move forward with the quilt project and reach out to Emily.

Thank you, Lord, Sarah prayed as she crossed the street to the park.

But as she got closer, she slowed to a crawl. The conversation Emily was having with the two men didn't look friendly. The men's backs were turned, so Sarah couldn't see who they were, but Emily's face was twisted as if she were trying not to cry, and she kept shaking her head every time either man said anything.

Carefully, Sarah made her way around the perimeter of the park, staying outside the screen of lilac bushes that shielded the skirt of the park from the courtyard and fountain, where Emily stood with the men. Sarah tried to move slowly, so she wouldn't attract any attention. The lilacs were thick enough for her to see through, but unless she moved too suddenly, it was unlikely anyone in the little group would catch a glimpse of her. They were too engrossed in their conversation.

As she got closer, Emily's voice rose. "You don't understand!" she cried. One of the men stepped forward, pointing his finger at her face. Their voices dropped down again below the level Sarah could hear.

By then, Sarah had worked her way halfway around the park. Now Emily's back was almost turned to her, and Sarah began to get a glimpse of the men. When she saw the first man's face, she felt a shock of recognition. It was Alex Crane, the lawyer over at the syrup company, who she'd just talked with in the library the morning before. His eyes were narrowed and hard as flint. Emily shook her head steadily while he spoke, as if she were trying to deny something.

A few more steps, and Sarah would be able to see the face of the other man. Already she could tell that he was older than Alex Crane by his wavy, graying hair. Sarah moved incredibly carefully now. She was only a few yards from the little group, and she didn't know how she'd explain herself if they saw her. But Emily was clearly in trouble, and there was no chance Sarah was going to leave her alone with the two men.

One more step, and the second man's face became visible. Sarah stopped short in surprise.

It was Samuel Collins. Unlike Alex Crane, he didn't look angry. He just looked tired, and sad, and strangely helpless. When Alex stopped berating Emily, Samuel started to talk to her, but he seemed to be pleading with her, not telling her what to do. As Sarah watched, he pulled a thick manila envelope from his expensive blazer, and held it out to Emily.

At this, Emily burst into tears. She shook her head, at a loss for words.

Now Alex Crane's voice rose in the crisp fall air. "You'll be sorry for this!" he threatened. Then he took Samuel Collins by the arm and began to steer him out of the park to a black Lincoln parked on the corner. Samuel allowed himself to be led, but he kept checking back over his shoulder, stealing glances at Emily. Emily watched them, tears running down her face, until the car pulled away from the curb. Then she sank down on one of the little benches that surrounded the fountain and buried her face in her hands.

Sarah ducked through one of the cuts that led through the lilac hedge into the heart of the park and walked over to Emily. The girl was so upset that she didn't even notice Sarah's approach.

Lord, Sarah prayed. *This isn't the meeting I expected. But help me to show your love to Emily.* She put her hand on the girl's shoulder.

Emily jumped as if she'd been hit.

Sarah pulled her hand back.

"I'm so sorry," she said. "I didn't mean to scare you. I just saw you here and wanted to make sure you're all right."

"Oh, Sarah," Emily said. For a moment, she looked up at Sarah with the same open expression Sarah remembered from their months sharing the house together. But then Emily dropped her gaze. "Everything's fine," she said. "I'm just a little upset."

Sarah sat down next to her on the bench. "About what?" she asked.

"Oh," Emily said. "It's nothing you can do anything about."

"Maybe not," said Sarah. "But sometimes it helps to talk. Are you having trouble with Tad's family?"

At this, Emily made a strangled sound somewhere between a laugh and a sob. "You could say that," she said.

Sarah squeezed her arm. "Getting married is a big adjustment," she said. "And it's an even bigger adjustment when you realize you don't just get to live with your husband for the rest of your life. You have to live with his whole family."

A tear dropped from Emily's downcast face onto her jeans, leaving a little round mark.

"Why does it have to be like this?" she said. "Why can't it just be between me and Tad? We love each other. Shouldn't that be enough?"

"Well," Sarah said, "It's certainly the best place to start."

Sarah pulled a tissue from her purse and handed it to Emily. Emily took it gratefully and wiped her nose and face. She looked into Sarah's eyes, clearly yearning to tell her something.

"Whatever you have to say won't shock me," Sarah said. "I've been around a long time, and I've seen a lot of things. Chances are, what you're going through isn't too different from what everybody else goes through at one time or another."

Emily nodded and took a deep breath. Then she glanced at the street and shrank against Sarah. The black Lincoln had come back, and was circling the block. As it passed the two of them, it slowed down, then sped off again with a roar of its engine.

Tears sprang into Emily's eyes again. She shook her head. "Thank you so much, Sarah," she said, her voice breaking. "I know you want to help. But you don't understand. I could lose everything."

Before Sarah could say anything, Emily was on her feet, rushing back to her blue sedan, which was parked on the street near where the Lincoln had been.

"Emily!" Sarah called after her, but she didn't turn back.

Lord, Sarah prayed. *Wherever she's going, don't leave her alone.*

She watched as Emily climbed into her car and drove off, replaying the events she'd just seen in her mind in hopes that she might see something she'd missed the first time. But she couldn't make any more out of it than what she already knew. For some reason, Emily was in trouble with Samuel Collins and Alex Crane. Crane seemed dangerously angry, and Emily seemed deeply afraid. But why would they be angry at a sweet girl like Emily? And what did Emily have to fear from Sarah's old classmate and his lawyer?

It wasn't until she'd thought through all the events again that Sarah realized something else. The passengers in the black Lincoln must have seen her on the bench with Emily as they passed by the second time. Now they might think that Sarah was somehow involved with Emily's problem too.

CHAPTER TWELVE

As Sarah unlocked her car door, she looked up, and paused. She was parked just a few doors down from The Spotted Dog, directly in front of the gift shop owned by Annie Harper. It had never been her favorite place in town, since a lot of the gifts had to do with astrology and crystals, and there was a section in the back of New Age books about recognizing your potential through chants and positive thinking. None of these things were bad in and of themselves, but to Sarah the whole idea of using crystals and astrology to deal with life felt sad. She had a God who she could talk with anytime. She believed he answered her prayers and guided her when she needed direction. She generally avoided the gift shop, but now she pulled her key out of the lock and went back around the car.

According to the articles she'd just read at the historical society, Annie's mother had worked with the Collins family for years. Maybe Annie would remember something about the circumstances surrounding Genie's death—or her disappearance. Sarah pocketed her keys, and went into the shop.

Annie sat behind the counter, reading a book. A row of wind chimes and charms hung from the ceiling above her. She looked up as the door thudded shut behind Sarah.

"Can I help you?"

The sweet and spicy smell of incense was heavy in the air. "Hello," Sarah said. "I hope so. I'm working on a project for the Collins family."

Annie's face darkened. "My family doesn't work for them anymore," she said.

Sarah came to a stop on the other side of the register and hesitated. Obviously, she'd hit some kind of a nerve. But she was here now. "I didn't know they had," she said. "but I just discovered that your mother was connected with the family while I was doing some research at the historical society. Emily Collins has asked me to help her restore an old family quilt, and I'm trying to find information to help me with the project." Sometimes mentioning a quilt opened doors for her, Sarah had found. People often had fond memories of quilts their grandmothers had sewn, or favorite blankets from their childhood.

Annie did seem to soften at this. "Emily Collins?" she asked. "That young girl?"

Sarah nodded. "Apparently it's a quilt that Genie Collins started, but never finished. She's asked me to help put it together."

Annie shook her head almost sadly. "The Collins family," she said. "There's been a curse on them for generations."

Sarah stiffened. Had Annie seen the scene with Emily and Samuel and Alex play out too? Did she also think Sarah was somehow involved? And what did she mean by "curse"?

"I'm sorry," Sarah said. "I'm not sure I understand."

"There's a curse on that family," Annie repeated. "There has been for years. It comes through the men. But it destroys the women. That little Emily is just the last in a line of them."

"What do you mean?" Sarah said.

"Well, if you've been looking at the family history, you ought to know," Annie said. "Genie Collins' little girl baby, who never lived to see her second birthday. Lydia Collins, who died before her son turned ten."

Sarah didn't believe in this so-called curse, but it did seem as though Annie was well acquainted with the family history. Maybe if Sarah played along, she could learn more about what had happened to Genie Collins. "And Genie," she added, offering another link in the pattern Annie was talking about. "She died when her son was young as well."

Annie raised her eyebrows, but she didn't offer anything else.

"That's what I'm most interested in," Sarah pressed on. "I like to put some information about the original quilter on a label, and I haven't been able to find any records about Genie's death. I thought you might know something about that time, since your mother worked with the family. Would you be willing to answer a few questions?"

"I wouldn't get mixed up with the Collins family if I were you," Annie said.

"I won't take much of your time," Sarah promised.

Annie shrugged. Sarah couldn't tell if this was meant as a yes or no, yet she tried a question anyway. But she didn't start immediately with Genie's death. Maybe she'd get farther by coming at it from another angle.

"Did your mother ever tell you anything about a dispute between Ward Collins and a man named John Peters?" Sarah asked. "Does that name sound familiar to you?"

Annie shook her head decisively. "Nope," she said.

Well, thought Sarah. That would hardly be a topic Ward Collins would be likely to talk over with his servants.

"What about Genie's quilting?" Sarah asked. "I hear she was an excellent quilter."

Annie nodded. "She always seemed to have a needle in her hand."

"The quilt I'm working on seems to be a mosaic pattern," Sarah told her. "That means all kinds of small pieces of varying shades of a color, stitched together to make a bigger piece. It's mainly browns, blues, and greens. Did you ever see her working on anything like that? Or did your mother ever mention anything along those lines? It would have been near the end of Genie's life. She never finished it."

Annie shook her head again just as decisively. "Never did," she said. "She favored the brighter colors when I knew her. A lot of flowers and gardens."

Sarah's excitement was slowly turning to disappointment. Well, maybe Annie could help her with at least one detail. "Do you happen to remember the date of Genie's death?" she asked. "I haven't been able to find the obituary at the historical society."

"That doesn't surprise me," Annie said.

Sarah paused. Annie's answers had been so clear and decisive up to now. But just like the records at the historical society, when it came to Genie's death, Annie's answers turned suddenly mysterious.

"Why do you say that?" Sarah asked.

Annie gave another one of her cryptic shrugs.

Maybe priming the pump with the information Sarah already had would help. "Samuel was around my age in school," she said. "So I remember when Genie died. In 1963."

"Do you?" Annie asked.

Sarah thought back. She remembered the season she'd heard the news that Genie had died, and remembered her heart going out to Samuel, and wondering how it must feel to lose your mother at such a young age. He was only sixteen at the time. In some ways, that was very grown-up. In some ways, it wasn't grown-up at all.

"Did you go to the funeral?" Annie asked.

Sarah shook her head. Martha's comments about looking for the funeral announcement flashed through her mind. "The family was so private," she said. "They probably had closed services of some kind."

"That's one way to put it," Annie said.

Sarah folded her arms, suddenly impatient with Annie's knowing expression. "What are you trying to say?" she asked.

"People said Genie was real shy," Annie said. "You heard that?"

Sarah thought back to Martha's story of Samuel's reluctance to introduce her to his mother. And Sarah had lived in the same town as Genie most of her life and only seen her a handful of times. Sarah nodded.

"She wasn't just shy," Annie said. "She was different."

"Different?" Sarah repeated. "What do you mean by that?"

Annie shrugged again.

Scanning back over their conversation for a clue, Sarah realized that Annie hadn't answered her original question. "But what does that have to do with her death?" she asked.

Again, Annie's eyebrows went up. "Have you ever seen a dead woman buried with trunks of all her clothes and things?"

Slowly, Sarah shook her head.

Annie nodded. "They did that back in Egypt," she said, nodding at a stack of books by the register that featured a picture of a pyramid on the cover. "But not so much around here."

"What do you mean?"

"My mother never talked to me about a funeral for Genie Collins," Annie said. "And if anyone would have gone, it would have been my mom. She worked for those people for four decades of her life." A momentary shadow crossed her face again. Then she leaned forward. "But I'll tell you what she did tell me about. Packing up every last thing Genie Collins owned the week before they announced her death. And not in an organized fashion, either. They just told her one day, pack all of this up. We don't want you going home until you're done. She didn't come home that day till after midnight. She called to tell me she'd be late, but there was a thunderstorm that night, and I was scared to death. I never forgot that feeling, waiting for my mom to come back from the big house, while I was there in our place, all alone. When she got back that night, I was still wide awake. That's when she told me what she'd been doing, so I'd forgive her for leaving me alone in the storm."

Annie's story was fantastic, but even as Sarah listened, pieces she hadn't been able to explain before dropped into place in her mind. Genie's missing obituary. Martha's sense that Genie wasn't having quite the same conversation that everyone else was. What did Annie mean by "different?" And how could that possibly have spurred the family to fake Genie's death?

"What are you saying?" Sarah asked. "You think they sent her away?"

Now Annie straightened up, her face half-shadowed by the uneven shapes of the chimes and charms that hung over the register.

"I'm saying I'd stay away from the Collins family if I were you. No one who gets mixed up with them comes out the better for it. There's a curse on them, especially the women. Your little friend Emily is just the next one in a long line of them."

CHAPTER THIRTEEN

You look like you've seen a ghost!" Maggie joked when Sarah stepped into the antique shop.

Sarah set her purse down on top of the glass counter full of beautiful antique brooches and earrings. "Maybe I have," she said.

"That sounds mysterious," Maggie said, laughing. "You'll have to tell me the whole story. But let me go get lunch from the back, first."

Lost in contemplation of Annie's story about Genie Collins, Sarah had forgotten all about lunch again. "I was thinking of bringing something," she said. "But I just didn't get that far."

"You'll be doing me a favor to share mine," Maggie called over her shoulder. She disappeared into the back and emerged again with a neat blue insulated lunch pack. "Jason and I have been trading off packing our lunches to help us save money," she explained as she returned to the front counter. "But I think the last time Jason packed lunch, he was a high school football player. When it's his turn, there's always twice as much as I could ever eat."

She unzipped the pack and pulled out a pair of sandwiches. "Honey and peanut butter?" she said, holding one out to Sarah.

"That sounds wonderful," Sarah said, accepting it gratefully.

Maggie set a plastic bag of nuts on the counter. "There must be half a pound of these pistachios," she said, then looked back in the bag. "And an apple," she nodded, setting it beside the nuts. "And an orange. You see what I mean?"

Sarah smiled and nodded, savoring the salty peanut butter with the sweet honey. For a few minutes, the two women ate in companionable silence. When Maggie was finished with her sandwich, she broke the orange apart and gave half to Sarah.

"So," Maggie said. "Are you going to tell me about this ghost you've seen?"

Sarah thought for a minute. The events of the day were still spinning in her head, and it would be a relief to tell someone. Maggie had a good head on her shoulders, and she might pick up on a clue Sarah hadn't. But something prevented Sarah from diving into the story. Maybe it was because it wasn't just a story, after all. Something really seemed to be wrong with the Collins family. She had seen it in Samuel's defeated face, and Emily's frightened expression. And from what she had gathered from Annie, something had been wrong there for a long time.

"I'd love to tell you," Sarah told her daughter-in-law sincerely. "But I'm afraid it's not my story to tell."

Maggie didn't press her. "You must run across a lot of ghosts," she said. "Restoring those old quilts."

"Well," Sarah said. "I do like to try to get a sense of the person who created the quilt I'm working on. Quilts take a lot of time to make, and a lot of thought. People can't help leaving something of themselves behind in them."

"I think that's what I like most about getting to live with these antiques," Maggie said, gesturing around the store. "Imagining the people who must have used them, and all the different places they've been. People leave clues about themselves behind in anything they've used. Sometimes it's just the way the varnish gets worn off a desk, so you can see that whoever used it was left-handed. Sometimes it's a note someone left in the pocket of an old morning dress. You never get all the facts, but you get enough to make up some interesting stories."

Sarah had always liked Maggie, though their relationship was sometimes strained. But this was something she shared with Maggie—a deep interest in the stories of the past. Maybe they had more in common than either of them really knew. "I know what you mean," Sarah said.

Maggie popped the last orange slice in her mouth and rose from her stool. "Well," she said. "Do you want to see my new discoveries? Jason's still getting used to the idea of this store, and he's never been crazy about antiques in the first place, so I'm always excited to have someone else to show them to."

"Sure," said Sarah. She was still getting used to the idea of the store, too, which Maggie had recently opened without first discussing it with Jason, but this was a chance to connect with Maggie, and whether she approved of everything Maggie did or not, family was forever. She wanted their relationship to be strong, despite any bumps along the way.

Sarah followed Maggie down the crowded aisle of delicate end tables, carved-back chairs, and glassed-in bookcases, to the storeroom at the back. When Sarah stepped in, Maggie was pulling a sheet away from a low round table. In the dimness of the back room, it took Sarah a minute to see that the simple glass circle was an incredibly delicate shade of pale blue, supported by ironwork filigree.

"Oh, Maggie," Sarah said. "It's beautiful."

"Isn't it?" Maggie said. "What's amazing is that the glass is handmade, so every tabletop is just a slightly different color. You'll never find another that looks just like this one. I got this at an estate sale over in Jefferson. They had some beautiful jewelry too." She pulled the lid back from a cardboard box to reveal a treasure chest of paste jewelry, all nestled carefully in bright turquoise tissue paper.

"Wonderful," Sarah said.

"And this," Maggie said, pulling the sheet away from a piece of furniture that towered over her head. The fabric fell to reveal a magnificent mahogany buffet decorated with elaborately carved grapes and cherubim. "I'm not sure what the grapes have to do with the cherubim," Maggie said. "But I love it. It's so strange and funny."

"And beautiful, in its own way," Sarah added.

"It really is," Maggie said, gazing at her new acquisition. "Oh!" She turned away and began to rummage through a wooden crate. She pulled a toy soldier and a transistor radio out, still searching. Finally she lifted an old bottle of some kind in the air, triumphant.

"This is for you," she said.

"Thank you," Sarah said, somewhat taken aback. She was interested in old quilts, but she didn't really collect glass. She would have thought Maggie would know that by now.

"It's from the Genie Syrup Company," Maggie explained, handing the bottle to her. "I thought you might like it because of the Collins quilt project."

"Oh!" Sarah said, examining the bottle with interest. It looked very much like the standard maple syrup bottles in stores today, with a narrow mouth and a small glass handle, but it had a distinctive label: a blue Genie swirling up against a background of maple trees. Sarah gave Maggie a quick hug. "This was so thoughtful of you!" she said. "Thank you. It means a lot."

"Well, it means a lot to me that you're willing to come look at this old junk," Maggie said. "I know Jason thinks it's just a silly hobby."

"Oh, Maggie," Sarah said. "He may have had his reservations about opening the store, but he knows how much it means to you. Why do you think he stayed up all night trying to keep your inventory dry in the basement when the pipes burst?"

"I felt terrible about that," Maggie said. "He wouldn't have had so much to do if I didn't have so many things down there. And he never liked the idea of the store in the first place."

"That's not how he told it to me," Sarah told her. "He wasn't irritated about the work at all. He just wanted to make sure your things were safe. He said he'd feel terrible if anything happened to them, because he knows how much they mean to you."

Tears sprang to Maggie's eyes. "Really?" she said.

Sarah nodded.

Maggie enfolded her tightly in another hug. "Thanks, Sarah," she whispered. "I know how much Jason and I love each other, but with the store and the kids and the pipes breaking, it's easy to forget what matters. I needed to hear that."

"Well, I'm happy to tell you," Sarah said, when Maggie released her. "But you should tell him yourself."

Maggie smiled and wiped a tear from her eye. "I will," she said. "Don't you worry."

When Sarah got home, she was still thinking about Maggie and Jason, interspersed with little prayers that the two of them would grow in their relationship and keep finding ways to make each other happy, despite their misunderstandings. She'd already had a full day, and it was only midafternoon. She thought about returning to her sewing room to take another look at the quilt, but she just didn't have the energy for it. She had spent the last two days researching, and now she had more questions than she had when she started. And the quilt's story had begun to seem so dark, with Emily's distress and Annie's story. She needed to let her thoughts and feelings settle for a bit. She'd look at it in the morning, when she was fresh.

Instead, she went into the kitchen, where she'd left the Genie Maple Syrup bottle on the counter. Whenever she did solve the riddle of the quilt and its letters, the bottle could be a happy memento of her current project. It might make a pretty vase for a few stems of flowers. But it was grimy with age. Before she did anything with it, it needed to be cleaned.

She didn't want to simply dunk it in a tub of soapy water for fear of damaging the bright colors of the label. The old paper had survived intact this long, and she didn't want to be the one who did it in. Instead, she pulled a bottle of alcohol from underneath the sink, and went to work with a cotton swab, rubbing away the gray mist that time had cast over the glass.

I wonder if I'll release a real genie, with all this rubbing, she thought, and smiled.

Half an hour later, the glass was as clean and sparkling as it must have been on the day it was filled with maple syrup and packed off to the shelf of a nearby store. Sarah set the bottle on the counter and stepped back to admire her work. Against the shining glass, the label looked even more vivid. It was really a beautiful image: the swirling tail of the genie, with the brown trunks of the maple grove behind it. Most of the leaves of the trees were green, but some were starting to turn red and orange as they had this autumn.

Suddenly, Sarah snatched up the bottle, gazing intently at the label. The genie's blue curves. The brown tree trunks. The green leaves with the few traces of red and orange. Could it be…?

An instant later, she found herself standing at her sewing table after all, spreading the neat stacks of Genie's quilt pieces out over the wide surface. The brown swaths did branch like the limbs of trees. The curves of blue mirrored the genie on the bottle. But she wanted to be sure.

She picked out one of the few pieces with a hint of red and orange sewn into it. She laid it down in front of her and stood the bottle beside it, scanning between the two for comparison. The similarity was undeniable. The square exactly mirrored a flash of red in the forest on the label, just below the genie's outstretched arm.

Just when she had meant to take a break from the mystery of the quilt's pattern, she had solved it.

Moments later, Sarah was scattering all the quilt pieces across her sewing table in a loose six by seven pattern. Then, using the bottle as a guide, she began to trade the pieces into their proper places, grouping the blues down the center, where the genie rose in front of the forest, building a dense swath of greens at the top where the forest was thickest, turning pieces this way and that even after she'd put them in the proper spot, to make sure they were right side up.

Even in pieces, the result was breathtaking. A gorgeous mosaic of branches and leaves, the genie's tail swirling through the tree trunks and rising over the crowns of the trees, a mysterious smile on his lips.

"Genie," Sarah murmured, both to Genie Collins, wherever she was, and to the figure on the quilt. "This is beautiful."

Then she noticed something else. The quilting stitches, which had seemed to be haphazard to her at first, were actually true and perfect. Sarah hadn't been able to see it without understanding the pattern of the quilt, but now that the pieces lay side to side, in the right order, she could see that the quilting on the individual squares lined up exactly, with seemingly effortless leaps from square to square.

She had just opened a container full of pins and begun to pin two corner pieces together when the doorbell rang.

Belle stood on the porch, a big smile on her face, a suitcase in each hand, and a floppy beach hat on her head.

"Welcome home," Sarah said, swinging the door wide for her.

Belle stepped in. "I know this hat is ridiculous," she said. "And I know I won't wear it all winter. But I couldn't bear to leave it in storage. It reminds me that summer's coming again, even if fall is setting in." She set the suitcases down in the foyer. "I hope I didn't interrupt anything," she said. "I just didn't have the key." She doffed the beach hat and set it on one of the suitcases.

"Well, we can fix that," Sarah said. "I've got extra keys in my office. I'll give you one now."

Belle followed her down the hall and into her sewing room.

"I've never seen an office that looks quite like this," she said.

Sarah rummaged through her desk drawers until she found the small manila envelope where she kept keys for her boarders. She pulled one out, dangling from a keychain with a bright giant dahlia pattern emblazoned on it. When she turned around, she found Belle gazing down at the quilt pieces arranged on the table, transfixed.

"It's so beautiful!" Belle whispered, as if she were in an art museum. "How did you ever figure it out so fast?"

It hadn't seemed fast to Sarah. She felt as though she'd been stuck on the mystery of the quilt pattern forever. But at Belle's question, she realized that just this morning the quilt had been an unbroken code. Now it was spread out on her sewing table, solved. Of course, now there were mysteries she was even more worried about. What had happened to poor Genie Collins? Why had Emily been so frightened in the park? But even so, here was the quilt, laid out in the right way for the first time in decades. Maybe she was making more progress than she thought.

Sarah tapped on the maple syrup bottle. "My daughter-in-law found this for me. She's an antiques dealer."

"They're the same!" Belle exclaimed. "Look at that!" She looked closely at the label, then set the bottle down and glanced over the quilt. "It's so intricate," she said. "I don't know how anybody would have the patience. And how did they get the pattern to match up like this?"

"Not only that," Sarah said. "Let me show you the quilting." She trailed her finger along the green lines of quilting, showing Belle how they ran in even lines from piece to piece.

"Amazing," Belle said.

"I'll bet we can see it better on the back," said Sarah, and turned the piece over to show Belle the bright stitches outlined on the pale backing.

As soon as she did, she remembered the letters. She had been so focused on the beautiful mosaic pattern that she'd forgotten the code stitched into the back.

"Is that a P?" Belle asked. "Is it some sort of message?"

"Let's see," Sarah said. She began to turn over the squares, careful not to get them out of order. Belle caught on quickly to what Sarah was doing and began to turn squares in place herself. In no time, all the pieces lay face down, their backing showing.

Sarah flipped her quilting light on to see the pale tan stitching better against the brown backing. She leaned over the table to read the top line. "Help me…" she said.

"…escape," Belle finished, reading the line below. "You are my…"

" … only hope," finished Sarah.

The two women looked at each other.

"Where did you get this quilt?" Belle asked, her voice quieter than it had been, as if afraid someone might overhear them.

"I'm restoring it as a favor for one of my previous boarders," Sarah said. A sense of danger began to creep over her, even though she knew she was safe in her own house. But the person who had stitched this message into the quilt clearly didn't feel safe.

"Is this the kind of message you usually find?" Belle asked. "In a quilt?"

Sarah shook her head. "No," she said. "It isn't."

"Huh," Belle said. She folded her arms over her belly and stepped away from the quilt and the sewing table.

Help me escape, the quilt pleaded. *You are my only hope.*

"Will you excuse me, Belle?" Sarah said. "I need to make a phone call."

Belle seemed glad for an excuse to leave the room. "Oh, of course," she said. "I'll just go upstairs and get situated." She turned back at the door. "Also, I meant to tell you," she said. "I'll be spending the weekend back in Jefferson tomorrow night and the next, just tying up a few loose ends. I didn't want you to worry."

"Oh, thank you," Sarah said.

Belle smiled and slipped out.

"Let me know if you need anything at all," Sarah called after her.

Before Sarah dialed Emily's number, she bowed her head. *Lord,* she prayed. *Please protect Emily, and show me how to help her. Make your truth known in this situation.*

Then she picked up the phone and dialed.

After several rings, the call went to voice mail. "Hello!" Emily's voice said. "This is Emily Collins." There was just the slightest hesitation before she said Collins, and she said it with a thrill of excitement, as if she'd recorded the message just after she'd gotten married, maybe even on her honeymoon. "I'm so glad you called. Just leave a message, and I'll get back to you as soon as I can!"

The phone beeped.

"Emily," Sarah said. "I have some news. I've been able to put the quilt together, and I'd love to show it to you. So just give me a call whenever you're free, and we'll find a time for you to come over." She paused for just a moment, then added, "And please let me know if there's anything else I can do for you."

After she set the phone down, she went back to the sewing table and looked down at the message inscribed with faint thread on the backing. Emily's happy voice on the recording rang in her ears. That was the Emily she had known, not the frightened girl who'd avoided her at the library and dissolved into tears at the park. She and Tad had only been married for a few months. What could possibly have made such a serious change in such a short time?

Sarah leaned over the quilt again. This time she noticed the monogram piece, "EPC." It was set at the end of the message, almost as if it were a signature. Genie didn't start with E, and she didn't know what Genie's middle name had been. But she knew someone whose name did fit the monogram: Emily Price Collins. Suddenly she wondered if it was really Genie who'd sewn the beautiful quilt. In one way or another, Emily seemed to have been making cries for help ever since she asked Sarah to take on this project. Did Emily and Tad's problems go deeper than typical newlywed squabbles? Was something much darker than she'd thought happening at the Collins house?

CHAPTER FOURTEEN

The phone rang again.

Still foggy with sleep, Sarah pushed her covers away and reached for the telephone next to her bed. Who would be calling this early in the morning? Were the kids all right? Then an image of the quilt flashed in her mind, and she remembered the message stitched on the back. *Could it be Emily?* she wondered. If so, thank God. It would be the first time Emily had really spoken with her since Sarah had taken on the project.

"Hello?" she said.

"Sarah!" Martha exclaimed, her voice full of excitement.

"Yes?"

Martha's voice dropped. "Oh," she said. "I didn't wake you up, did I? I'm so sorry."

Sarah glanced at the clock. It was already eight thirty in the morning. On a normal day, she would have been up and about by now.

"Don't worry about it," she said. "I just had a late night with the quilt."

"Is that a good thing or a bad thing?" Martha asked.

Sarah considered this for a moment. She'd solved the puzzle of the quilt's pattern, but she wasn't sure she'd call the message stitched into it good news. She settled by just telling Martha what had happened. "I figured out the pattern," she said.

"Oh my gosh!" Martha exclaimed. "Congratulations! I wasn't sure anyone could figure that out. Those pieces are unlike anything I've ever seen. But if anyone could, it would be you. What is it?"

"It's based on the old label they used to put on Genie Maple Syrup," Sarah said.

"I remember that," Martha said. "When I was a little girl, I used to rub it while I was eating my pancakes, and make wishes. They never seemed to come true, but that's probably a good thing. If they had, I'd have long blonde hair and wear party dresses all the time, and I'd be married to the postman."

Sarah laughed. "How is Ernie doing?" she asked.

Martha sighed. "He's all right. His occupational therapy seems to be helping. But that's not what I called to talk about."

"Right," Sarah said, brushing her hair away from her forehead. "Is everything all right?"

"It's better than all right," Martha said. "It's wonderful. When I took Ian home after our visit to the syrup factory, he told me how sorry he was for all the trouble he's caused. So I said, let's do something about that. And we sat down and wrote letters together to the people whose buildings he painted on, apologizing for disrespecting their property."

"That's great," Sarah said.

"But that's not all!" Martha said. "First thing this morning, I went down to the police station to see Chief Webber. I took him copies of the letters Ian had sent, to show that he really has learned his lesson. And Chief Webber told me that a woman from the railroad had called him yesterday afternoon. It turns out they actually love the painting Ian did on the train trestle. I haven't been out there, but I guess he painted giant morning glories, climbing all the way up from the water to the bridge. I don't know how he painted all that without falling in the river. I probably don't want to know," she said. "But the railroad has been getting calls and letters from people who love the art ever since. When they found out Ian was the artist, they decided to ask him to do a mural on the warehouses by the depot downtown."

"Oh, Martha," Sarah said. "That's amazing. Talk about God making good things out of bad."

"Amen," Martha said. "They were willing to pay him for the project, but in light of the fact that Ian's original projects weren't cleared with the owners of the property, Chief Webber suggested that he do it as community service."

"Perfect," Sarah said.

"If all the property owners agree, Chief Webber is willing to let the case drop," Martha went on. "It won't have to go to court at all. So it won't be any kind of mark on Ian's record. I'm going out to talk to Will Percy about the barn this morning. I can't think he'll object. He wasn't too upset to begin with. Chief Webber says the maple syrup company hasn't agreed to drop the charges yet, but they want the mural removed from their property. So Ian will also need to go out there and strip that old place back to the original wood."

"That's too bad," Sarah said. "It's a beautiful mural."

"I know," said Martha. "But he's got to learn his lesson."

"Well, that's all great news," Sarah said. "Tell Ian when he's a famous artist, I'll be proud to say I knew him when."

"If we can just keep that boy out of trouble until that happens," Martha said. "Gotta run. I'll see you later."

"See you," Sarah said and hung up the phone.

Thank you, Lord, she prayed. *Please bless Martha's conversations today.*

She had replaced the receiver in its cradle, but she hadn't taken her hand away yet from the warm plastic. After a moment, she picked it up again and dialed Emily's cell number, which she still remembered from the months she and Emily had shared the house together. It might be a little early to call somebody, but most businesses were open by now, and maybe she'd catch Emily before she went out and got distracted by the pressures of the day.

But after several rings, her call again went to voice mail. Emily's voice came on, filled with the hope and excitement of a new bride on a honeymoon. Again, the difference between the message and Emily's recent demeanor tugged at Sarah's heart.

"Emily," Sarah said when the beep sounded for her to leave a message. "It's Sarah again. I've got some news about the quilt, and I'm also starting to get a little worried not to have heard from you. Would you just give me a call when you get this to let me know you're all right? Take care."

She set the phone back in its cradle. Then she pulled out the phone book, ran her finger down a list of business names, and called the main number for the Genie Maple Syrup Company.

"Genie Maple Syrup," the operator answered.

"I'm trying to reach Tad Collins," Sarah said.

"Please hold."

A moment later, the phone began to ring again, this time the bell-like ring of the company's internal phone system. Then a ring broke off.

"Hello?" Tad said.

Relief washed over Sarah at the sound of his familiar voice. Tad had been in her house countless times, courting Emily. She couldn't imagine him wanting to harm his new bride. He'd probably be able to give her a simple explanation for his wife's erratic behavior over the past few days. "Tad," she said. "This is Sarah Hart. I'm calling about Emily."

Tad's normally friendly voice suddenly sounded wary. "Oh," he said. "All right. What can I do for you?"

"Well, I've been working on the quilt," she said. "I've tried to talk with her about some questions I have about it, but now the topic seems to upset her. I've called her several times, but she hasn't returned my calls. It just doesn't seem like her. I only wanted to make sure everything was all right with her."

There was a long pause on the other end of the line.

"Tad?" Sarah asked. "Are you still there?"

"Sure, sure," Tad said. His attempt at his usual easygoing style felt forced to Sarah. "You know what? Emily just hasn't been feeling well these past few days. So she might have seemed upset, but I think she was probably just getting sick. She felt really bad this morning, so I told her to stay home from work. She's there now, just resting up. When she feels better, I'll ask her to give you a call."

Sarah gave a sigh of relief. There it was: her simple explanation. Anyone might seem a little off when they were coming down with something. And she couldn't expect Emily to call her right back if she was fighting some kind of sickness.

"I'm glad I called," Sarah said. "It sounds like I was worried about nothing."

"I guess so," Tad said. His voice was hearty, but something in it sounded strange to Sarah, almost as if he was trying to convince himself as much as her.

"You can tell her I have some good news for her as soon as she feels up to it," Sarah said.

"I sure will," Tad said.

Sarah hung the phone up again.

Downstairs, while pulling a carton of yogurt out of the refrigerator for breakfast, Sarah spied a glass dish of the chicken soup she'd made for dinner earlier that week. Emily had always loved that soup, and Sarah had always whipped a bowl of it up for her when she was under the weather, even though feeding her tenants wasn't officially part of their rental agreement.

A plan crystallized in her mind. It was too bad that Emily was sick, but at least now Sarah knew where she could find her. And despite Tad's assurances, Sarah still wasn't convinced that all of Emily's strange actions over the past few days were due to her coming down with something. Maybe Sarah could take Emily a bowl of soup and offer her some comfort—but also have a real talk with her, the first one since Emily had asked her to take on the quilt project in the first place.

Half an hour later, she hurried out of the house, carrying a steaming covered dish of chicken soup tied up in a thick towel to keep it warm, with a bag of fresh blueberry muffins dangling from one arm. It was one of Maple Hill's bright, clear autumn mornings, and even though Tad's simple explanation for Emily's moodiness over the past several days seemed to make sense, Sarah still couldn't shake a sense of urgency.

The drive to Emily and Tad's little bungalow didn't take long. Sarah parked at the curb, collected the food from the front passenger seat, and went up the walk. At the door, she rang the bell and listened as faint chimes echoed inside.

No one answered.

Sarah shifted the pot of soup in her arms. If Emily was dozing, maybe she'd missed the sound of the gentle chimes. And Sarah didn't want to disturb her rest. Maybe she'd just slip inside and leave the soup in the kitchen for her.

She tried the door. The knob turned easily under her hand, and she went in. The kitchen was just to the left of the door, a small galley-style room that would have felt crowded to Sarah but was perfect for a young couple just starting out. Sarah set the chicken soup and the muffins on the counter, picked up a scrap piece of paper from beside the phone, and scrawled a quick note: *Emily, I hear you're under the weather. Know you love this soup, and hope it'll help you get well. Let me know if there's anything I can do. Sarah.*

She sighed and stepped quietly back into the front hall. From there she could see that the door to the front bedroom stood open. Inside, the bed was neatly made. Nobody was in it.

Sarah frowned. There was only one bedroom in the house, along with a tiny square of an office. She knew the layout from helping Emily think about decorating the rooms and moving her things during the weeks before the wedding. Where was Emily if she wasn't there? Had she fainted or fallen somewhere in the house?

Sarah stood in the door of the bedroom and surveyed the room. Emily was nowhere to be seen, and the bed looked as if it might not even have been slept in. Quickly, she surveyed the other rooms of the house: the dining and living room just off the kitchen, and the small office in the back. Emily wasn't in any of them, but a plaid blanket lay crumpled on the couch, as if someone might have spent the night there, then not bothered to fold the blanket up in the morning.

"Emily?" Sarah called.

Again, no answer.

She's not here, Sarah thought. *If she's that sick and out wandering by herself, Tad should know.*

She reached for her phone, but when her hand closed around the smooth metal case, something stopped her. Tad's strange pauses and nervous explanations. The crumpled blanket on the couch. Emily's frightened face and her tears. Sarah had wanted to believe Tad's simple explanation, but it didn't stand up. Emily hadn't been acting like a girl who was sick. She had been acting like a girl who was scared.

So why had Tad told Sarah that Emily was sick? Had Emily lied to him or was he lying to Sarah?

CHAPTER FIFTEEN

S arah let go of her phone. There was still a chance that the young couple was just going through some kind of problem that was none of Sarah's business. But if Emily really was in trouble and Tad was trying to hide that fact from Sarah, there was no reason for Sarah to tell Tad everything she knew, until she knew better whether to trust him or not.

She went back into Tad and Emily's kitchen and collected her soup, note, and muffins. Moments later, she was out of the house and back in her own car.

As she mulled it over on the way home, her mind kept returning to the quilt. It was the missing piece, she realized. Tad's story that Emily was sick might explain why Emily had been acting so strangely and hadn't returned Sarah's calls. But it didn't explain the message stitched into the back of the quilt that Emily had given Sarah: *Help me escape. You are my only hope. EPC. It didn't explain the message,* Sarah thought, *because Tad didn't know the message existed.*

But who had written the message? The initials were undeniably Emily's, but in all the time they'd lived together, Sarah had never seen Emily sew, although Emily had watched the progress of all Sarah's projects enthusiastically. Was the young girl capable of such intricate work? Or the challenge of blending the two unusual techniques, mosaic quilting and quilt-as-you-go? It still seemed more likely that the quilt had been made by a seasoned quilter like Genie Collins.

But that brought Sarah to another mystery. Was Genie Collins really still living, as the missing obituary and gravestone, and Annie's hints, suggested? And if so, where was she? As Sarah carried the soup back up her own front walk, she pondered over all the clues she'd found in the historical society documents, but what kept coming back to her was Genie's melancholy face at all those fancy parties, and even in the portrait Ward Collins had gazed up at on the first day Sarah had seen the quilt.

As she set the soup back on a refrigerator shelf and closed the door, a new thought broke in on her. Ward Collins. That very first day, he had insisted that he went to see Genie every Saturday. At the time, it had seemed like the wistful ramblings of an old man whose mind had begun to wander. But Tad had confirmed at least part of the story: that his grandfather made a trip to Genie's grave each weekend.

And now Sarah knew that Genie didn't have a grave.

So where did Ward go each week? Sarah leaned back against her counter and crossed her arms. She still didn't know whether or not she could trust Tad about Emily's illness, but he had seemed sincere when he explained that his grandfather visited the cemetery. So the visits to Genie, wherever she was, must have been brief enough that they could be kept secret even within the family—although Sarah supposed that perhaps Tad was just so well schooled in keeping the family secrets himself that a lie about his grandmother's whereabouts might come easily to him. But in any case, Genie couldn't be far away, if Ward and Samuel were able to get there and back in the space of an afternoon.

In fact, Sarah thought, she might even be right here in town. And if she was, there was only one place in Maple Hill where an older woman could stay anonymous for long: Bradford Manor, the local nursing home.

A minute later, Sarah was stacking cookies onto a pair of paper plates. She hadn't seen her father, who lived at Bradford Manor, in several days. He'd be glad for a visit, and maybe she'd be able to find something else out along the way.

At the nursing home, before she went down the long hall to her father's room, Sarah stopped at the desk. Tiffany Henderson, one of her father's favorite nurses, smiled up at her. Sarah smiled back. Over the years, she'd seen Tiffany do all sorts of small kindnesses for her father. Her affection for him went beyond just the demands of duty in her job. Sarah knew it was genuine, and she was grateful that her father had people like Tiffany taking care of him.

"Well, hello Sarah!" Tiffany said. "Those cookies look delicious. William will be delighted to see you."

Sarah put one of the plastic-wrapped trays on the counter. "They're not all for him," she said. "I packed a plate for the nursing station too."

Tiffany retrieved the plate immediately, peeled the wrap back, selected a cookie and bit into it. "Bless you," she said. "They taste as good as they look."

"It's a small thank-you, for all the things you do for us," Sarah said.

"Oh, William makes it easy," Tiffany said. "I know we're not supposed to have favorite patients, but I've always had a soft spot for him. He may not remember a lot of things, but you can still see the kind of man he is."

"I'm wondering if you can help me with something else," Sarah said.

Tiffany nodded. "Anything I can do," she said. "What is it?"

"It's a quilt I'm working on," Sarah said. "It was made by a local woman, years ago, and as I've begun to restore it, I've started to wonder if she might still be in the area. Of course, she'd be very old now, so I thought there was a chance she might be here."

"Do you know her name?" Tiffany asked.

Sarah hesitated. The Collins name was too famous in town for her to mention it. And if Genie was hidden at Bradford Manor, chances were she was here under some kind of assumed name. But maybe she'd kept her first name. And giving that wouldn't compromise the Collins family in any way. "Genie," she said.

Tiffany thought for a minute, then shook her head. "Officially, I can't give you any information about our patients," she said. "But I think it'd be all right just to say I've worked in most of these wards over the years, and that name doesn't sound familiar to me."

Sarah tapped thoughtfully on the counter between them. Maybe Genie really had taken a completely different name. But if she'd been here since she disappeared, certainly the staff would know her. "She'd have been here quite a while," she tried. "Since around 1963?"

Now Tiffany shook her head. "That isn't possible," she said. "We only opened up in 1965."

"Ah," Sarah said. She remembered that construction had begun on the sprawling complex sometime during her late high school years, but she hadn't been sure of the date. And now that she thought about it, Genie would have been too young in 1963 to fit in easily at a nursing home. But that didn't mean that she hadn't been moved here at some later date. And if Sarah saw her again today, she thought she might recognize her.

"I'd love to just take a look around some of the other wings," she said. "And see."

Tiffany shook her head again. "I'm sorry, Sarah," she said. "We're not able to let you do that. You come on and off this ward freely because we know you're here to see your dad, but the other wings are limited to approved guests and family."

Sarah sighed. "Well, it was worth asking," she said.

"I'm sorry I couldn't help you more," said Tiffany.

"Oh, you're always a great help," Sarah said. "Thank you." She turned down the hall to her father's room.

"Cinnamon-raisin bars!" Sarah's father exclaimed when she appeared in the door. "Well, this is a red-letter day."

Sarah smiled.

Sarah pulled the plastic wrap back from the paper plate and held the cookies out to her father. He chose one and took an enthusiastic bite.

"These are delicious, sweetheart," he said. "You've outdone yourself."

Sarah smiled. Visiting her father in the nursing home could be difficult, because she was never sure how much he would remember about her or his life. Sometimes he confused her with her mother, and sometimes he didn't remember ever having been married at all. But he never lost his enthusiasm for her cookies.

Today seemed to be one of his good days. He was in high spirits and relatively clear. The two of them had a nice conversation about the mountain lake where he used to take Sarah fishing when she was a girl. Sarah had loved those long quiet days, just her and her brother and her father, and her father still remembered the biggest catch they'd ever made: a largemouth bass about half as long as Sarah had been tall. She'd hooked it, and her father had reeled it in for her. When they'd gotten home, her mother had filleted it, fried it up, and invited the neighbors on both sides to come over and enjoy the catch with them.

Sarah loved going over these old reminiscences with her father, especially since his memory had become so spotty that each recollection he did have had begun to seem like a special gift. But she could see that he was getting tired, and she was getting a little anxious about Emily and the quilt. *What kind of trouble was Emily in?* she kept wondering. And what should she do about it? Confront Tad, who she wasn't sure she could trust now? Go to see Alex, who had seemed so angry at the park, or Samuel, who had been buying the mysterious rope? How serious was it? Should she even talk with Chief Webber about her concerns?

Her father popped the last bit of the raisin bar in his mouth and looked up at her, his eyes twinkling.

She held the plate out again. "Do you want another one?" she said.

"Cinnamon-raisin bars!" her father exclaimed. "Well, this is a red-letter day."

Sarah smiled. Often, his failing memory caused her real pangs. But sometimes his waning memory meant that he approached the world with a child's fresh eyes because of what he'd forgotten. Like now: he'd forgotten about the cookies she'd given him when she first arrived, so he was just as excited as he had been when she first offered them to him.

"I'll leave them here on the nightstand for you," Sarah said. "You can finish them up anytime you want."

"Is that right?" her father asked.

Sarah glanced at him. This was a favorite catchphrase of his, and when he started using it, she knew that his mind had begun to wander and he was starting to lose the thread of a conversation. She wrapped the plate carefully back up in the plastic and set it near his bed, where he could catch sight of it easily, even if he'd forgotten it was there.

Her father watched her as she straightened up. "I don't know why you take such good care of me." From the way he said it, Sarah had the sense that he wasn't sure who she was now. He sounded as if he were wondering why a stranger would go to such trouble for him.

Sarah bent down to kiss her father's cheek. "Because you took such good care of me," she said.

"Well," her father said. "I did my best."

"You did great, Dad," Sarah said, and kissed him again. "Are you getting a little tired out now?"

Her father considered this for a minute. "Well, I guess I am," he said.

"That's what I thought," said Sarah. "I'm going to go, and let you get some rest."

"That sounds good," her father said. "I could use a little rest."

"All right," Sarah said, squeezing his hand. "I'll see you soon."

"Is that right?" her father said.

Sarah squeezed his hand again, and went out.

Just outside the lobby on her father's floor was a beautiful courtyard garden, planted with purple, orange, and yellow mums. The day was unusually warm for autumn, one of the last beautiful days of Indian summer they'd have before the winter really began to set in. Sarah paused as the automatic door slid shut behind her and pulled her phone out of her purse. She dialed Emily again. Again it went to voice mail. This time Sarah didn't leave a message.

She slid the phone back into her purse and sighed.

"Well," Olive Cavanaugh said from behind her. "That's quite a sigh, Sarah Hart. What have you got on your mind?"

Sarah turned around. Olive sat in a wheelchair in one of the nooks of the courtyard, bundled up in a pair of sweaters and what looked to be several layers of afghans on her lap. Her blue eyes were hidden behind a pair of aviator sunglasses, and she wore a Yankees baseball cap.

"Olive." Sarah said. "I didn't even see you there. I'm so sorry."

Olive waved a thin hand. "Oh," she said. "I thought you just didn't recognize me with the sunglasses. I have to wear them when I go out, you know. Otherwise the paparazzi are terrible."

Sarah smiled. She knew from taking her father out on walks around the grounds how important it was for older people to protect their skin and eyes from the sun, but she'd always enjoyed Olive's playful jokes. Olive had been Jason's Sunday school teacher through all of middle school, and she and Jason had developed an unlikely friendship. Sarah would never have expected her boisterous son to gravitate toward the older woman, but the two of them enjoyed playing small pranks on each other, and even after he went to high school, Jason would hang around Olive's Sunday school classes after they ended, waiting for a chance to talk with her. The conversations sometimes lasted so long that he'd tell Sarah and Gerry not to wait for him; he'd just walk home. "What do you talk with her about?" Sarah asked him once. "Just things," Jason had told her. Like many teenage boys, he was trying not to tell his mother too much, but that answer actually told her everything she needed to know. It meant that he was talking over things that really mattered to him with Olive, and that thought gave Sarah a lot of comfort.

Olive's mind was still sharp, so she wasn't in the same memory-care ward as Sarah's father, and despite the fact that she was wheelchair bound, Olive made it a point to get around. Sarah often crossed paths with her on visits to see her dad.

"Oh, I'd recognize you anywhere," Sarah said. "I was just so distracted I didn't realize there was anyone else out here."

"Well, and down here in this chair, I'm not exactly in your line of sight," Olive said. "I'm easy to miss, so I hear a lot of interesting conversations. I don't eavesdrop on purpose, it just happens. But I think the government is missing a real opportunity with us old ladies in wheelchairs. We'd make great spies. You just put us anywhere, and nobody thinks twice about it. I could hide a camera under this afghan."

Sarah laughed. "Well, I wouldn't want to cross you, I know that much," she said.

"That's right!" Olive said. She made an attempt at looking stern and mysterious, then lapsed into giggles. "But how are you doing?" she asked when she'd collected herself. "I don't usually see you looking so serious. Is everything all right? Jason and Maggie and the girls are fine?"

"Yes, they are," Sarah said, adding a silent prayer of thanks. "It's not them I'm worried about. It's this quilt I've been working on."

"A quilt?" Olive said. "But you looked pretty worried. It must be some quilt."

"It is," Sarah said. "And it's not just the quilt I'm worried about. It's the girl who asked me to take on the project, Emily Collins. She's an old boarder of mine, and she's a lovely girl, but ever since I started working on this quilt for her, she's acted so strange. Almost as if she's in some kind of trouble. I've never seen her act this way. She's nothing like the Emily I know."

"How odd," said Olive.

It was a relief to talk about her worries with Olive. Olive seemed just as concerned as Sarah was, and somehow problems seemed more manageable when she shared them with someone. Emily's behavior had been so different in the past week that Sarah was starting to doubt her own memories. But when she told the story out loud, she became more sure of herself.

"And then the quilt itself is full of mysteries," Sarah said. "While I was repairing it, I discovered that all the newspapers the quilter had used to stabilize the squares were about the same thing, some old land dispute. But the newspaper articles are all so vague. It's as if nobody really understood what the dispute was about, even at the time."

"Well, I know all about that," Olive said.

"And then—" Sarah said. She had gotten so wrapped up in telling the story of the quilt that it took her a moment to realize what Olive had said. Then the full import of Olive's words dawned on her.

"You do?" Sarah asked.

CHAPTER SIXTEEN

O live nodded.

"But I'm getting chilly out here," she said. "Would you mind taking me in?"

"Of course not," Sarah said.

Olive tucked her thin hands under her afghan and Sarah kicked off the parking brake on the wheelchair and navigated her through the entrance. She followed Olive's directions through the maze of the nursing home's hallways until they arrived at the door of Olive's small apartment. Olive pulled a key from the afghans on her lap and unlocked it.

"Welcome to my humble abode," she said.

Sarah wheeled her in. "Do you have a favorite place to sit?" she asked.

"Right here is fine," Olive said, indicating a space near a table piled high with books and magazines. "You can see it's my lair by the mess I've made of it."

Sarah brought the chair to a stop where Olive had asked.

"Can I offer you anything to drink?" Olive said.

Sarah shook her head. "Would you like me to get you anything?"

"I'm just fine, thanks," Olive said. "Have a seat."

Sarah found a place on a small love seat near Olive.

"So, the Peters-Collins scandal," Olive said. "You're right. They never did print much of it in the papers. By then I think everybody was pretty well fed up with John Peters. We'd all gotten an earful from him at one time or another, and we didn't have the stomach for much more of his opinions. And Ward Collins was a nice boy. He came up hard, but he was always respectful with everybody, always trying to better himself. So I don't imagine we really had much appetite for dragging that story out for everybody to see. John Peters was never going to do anything with that land except drink it away. And as soon as Ward Collins got hold of it, he started making improvements and hiring local men. So I guess we were as glad to see him get hold of it as anyone."

Sarah listened with dimming hope. This was an interesting insight into the mood of the town at the time of the scandal, and it explained why there was so little information to be found about it. But Sarah wanted the facts. She had thought Olive might know something the papers hadn't printed. But this didn't sound like much more of the story, only more small town gossip.

"So it sounds like everybody must have known the story at the time?" Sarah prompted Olive.

Olive shook her head decisively. "No, they did not," she said. "You see, it wasn't in either party's interest to make the whole truth known. But I knew."

"How did you know?" Sarah asked.

"Well, a young lady like you is probably too young to remember this," Olive said. "But my daddy used to own the Red Hawk Tavern."

"The Red Hawk?" Sarah said. "You're right. I don't remember that."

Olive nodded. "It probably closed up before you were born," she said. "Partly because of stories like this one. My daddy got tired of seeing the kinds of things that happen in a tavern. When he retired, he just shut it down and sold the building."

Sarah wasn't sure what the Red Hawk Tavern had to do with the Peters-Collins dispute, but it didn't seem like Olive was likely to take the most direct route through any conversation. So Sarah played along, hoping they'd arrive at something that had to do with her quilt soon. "I didn't know we had a tavern by that name," she said.

"Yep," Olive said. "It was on the same street where The Spotted Dog is now. Seems like people are always naming their stores after one creature or another. But I used to work at the Red Hawk when I was a girl, some nights, helping my daddy. So I knew John Peters real well."

So this was how John Peters fit in. Sarah jumped to make sure Olive stayed on this topic. "He was a customer?" Sarah guessed.

"Not just a customer," Olive said. "He thought he owned the back booth."

"So he came in a lot?" Sarah said.

Olive nodded vigorously. "Every night. That back booth was the only one with a round table, and he'd sit back there and play cards and hold court. If he came in and anyone else was sitting there, he'd fuss and pout. He kept asking my daddy why he wouldn't just reserve the table, since he knew he'd be there every night. My daddy always told him he was still hoping one day he'd come to his senses and find something better to do than sit all night at a tavern. John Peters would tell him he wasn't a very good businessman, and my father would tell John Peters there were things in life that mattered more than business. Not that it ever took. Every night, there was John Peters again, in his same corner booth. It got so he didn't need a reservation after all. Everyone was so tired of him fussing and pacing if they took his table that they just left it for him."

It sounded like Olive really had known John Peters better than the rest of the town did. Sarah leaned forward, propelled by the excitement she always felt in getting a glimpse into history. But had Olive known Ward Collins as well? She would have been only a girl at the time. What could she have known about the dispute between the two men?

"Did Ward come into the tavern too?" Sarah asked.

Olive shook her head. "Not often," she said. "He had better things to do with his time. And his money. I never knew a boy to save so much. Even when he did come in, he always ordered the cheapest drink in the place. I was real surprised to see him spend as much money as he did on that house on the hill. I didn't think he had it in him. But I guess he built it for love, and that makes men do all kinds of things you'd never expect of them."

Sarah couldn't argue with this bit of wisdom, but she was itching with impatience to hear the rest of the story. If Ward didn't spend much time in the tavern, how could Olive have learned the truth of the dispute over the maple grove?

"Do you remember Ward Collins and John Peters talking much?" Sarah asked. "Those nights Ward was there?"

"Never," Olive said. "Ward wasn't interested in those games, and John wasn't interested in anyone who wasn't interested in those games. I never saw them speak a word to each other. Until one night."

"What night was that?" Sarah asked.

"A dark and stormy one," Olive said with an impish grin. "Straight out of a gothic novel."

Sarah broke in with another question before Olive could begin a disquisition on her thoughts about literature. "And what did they say?"

"Nothing," Olive said. "They didn't speak all night. But I remember Ward left just after John Peters went out. He couldn't have been more than two minutes behind him. Twenty minutes after that, John Peters stumbled back in, white as a sheet, wanting to use our phone. When my father pulled the phone out from behind the bar, he saw blood on John's hands."

"Blood?" Sarah repeated.

Olive nodded. "John said it was his own, from a cut on his face after he ran his car off the road. My father tried to get him to go to the hospital, but John wouldn't do it. He was dead set on calling up a servant to come get him and take him home."

"What about Ward?" Sarah asked. "Did he come back in too?"

"Not that night," Olive said. "But he came in the night after that, which was strange for him. And John Peters wasn't there, which was even stranger."

"Did John ever come back in?" Sarah asked. "And did Ward come back again?"

"John Peters didn't come back to the bar for four whole days," Olive said. "I think it was the longest time he ever stayed away until he left town for good. And every night until he came back, Ward Collins came in, all alone, and checked the booth in the back. When he didn't find John there, he'd go right back out. I told Ward we'd give John a message, but Ward said he needed to talk with him himself."

"He didn't say anything about what it was about?"

"Not a word," Olive said. "But he didn't have to. Because on the fourth day, when John was there, he said it all to John. And I was right there, wiping down the tables and filling up the salt shakers. I stood there for that whole conversation, just doing this and that, and listening, and I swear neither of them even noticed I was there. The government's missing the mark with all these secret agents in dark suits and camouflage gear, I'm telling you. They ought to hire old ladies and young girls. No one even thinks to look at us, no matter how long we're standing there."

Sarah smiled, but her curiosity still wasn't satisfied. "So what did they say?" she asked, trying to lead Olive back from this rabbit trail.

"John seemed real nervous," Olive said. "He could barely look Ward in the eye when Ward sat down. And then he asked him how it went."

"How what went?" Sarah said.

"That's what I wondered," Olive said. "So I just stayed there, wiping down the booth next to them. And then Ward said, 'he's dead.'"

"Dead?" Sarah repeated.

Olive nodded. "And John let out with a string of curses that I won't repeat for you here."

"And did Ward leave after that?" Sarah guessed.

Olive shook her head. "No," she said. "He told John a story. From what I could piece together, it sounded like John hadn't gotten very far from the bar that rainy night when he came up on a stranger, walking down the side of the road. He tried to swerve, but he hit him."

The words "he's dead" flashed again in Sarah's mind. "Did he just leave him there?" she exclaimed. "And walk back to the bar?"

"To his credit," Olive said, "he did pull over to help the man. And like I said, Ward was just a few minutes behind him."

"So he must have come across the accident," Sarah said.

"It would have been hard to miss," Olive said. "John Peters' big fancy car, pulled off the road like that. When Ward saw it, he stopped to make sure everything was all right. Of course, John had been in the bar all night, so he was in no shape to be driving."

But there was a third person in the story, Sarah realized. "What about the man he hit?" she asked.

"He was still alive," Olive said. "But with John driving in that state, there was no guarantee either of them would make it to the hospital in one piece. So Ward offered to take him. That's what John Peters was interested in when they talked that night. He wanted to know what Ward had told the doctors, about how he found the man."

"And what had he told them?" Sarah asked.

"He said that he'd just picked the man up in his head-lights and decided to stop. He told John Peters he hadn't said anything about John or any other car. John Peters was real relieved to hear that."

"I guess so," Sarah said.

"But then Ward Collins told him that the man had died."

Sarah sat back against the love seat, stunned. Again, this mystery had gone deeper than she ever dreamed. She'd thought it was a simple land dispute. But now it sounded like a matter of life and death.

"What did John Peters say to that?" she asked.

"When Ward was finished telling the story," Olive said, "John just sat back in the booth, shaking his head. He told Ward, 'I guess I owe you.' And Ward said, 'I guess you do.'"

"Do you know what he meant by that?" Sarah asked.

Olive nodded again. "Ward went right ahead and told him," she said. "He wanted to buy the Peters family land, with that maple grove on it. He told John Peters he'd give him everything he'd saved for it. It was an impressive amount for a young man like Ward to have saved, but it wasn't nearly enough for that land, even back then."

"What did John Peters say?" Sarah said.

"John asked Ward if Ward thought he was crazy. He told him the land was worth a hundred times what Ward was offering. Ward just told him, 'You can think of it that way, or you can think of it as paying back what you owe me.'"

Olive glanced at Sarah to see what effect her story was having.

Sarah just shook her head. "So what you're telling me," she said, "is that Ward Collins bought the Peters family land in exchange for covering up a murder?"

"That's what I thought at first," Olive said. "I even went and told my father about it. He'd seen enough that night to be suspicious himself, so he called up the police chief, and the chief checked with the hospital about deaths on that date. But there weren't any."

"I wonder if Ward took him to another hospital," Sarah said. "Maybe Jefferson or Dexter."

"That's what the police chief wondered," Olive said. "He didn't take the idea that a man had died in Maple Hill lightly. So he called every hospital in a sixty-mile radius. There hadn't been any deaths anywhere else either."

Sarah thought back to her recent meeting with Ward Collins, a sweet old man looking up longingly at a portrait of his young bride. A chill came over her. "He didn't just leave him somewhere to die, did he?" she asked.

"I had terrible dreams about that," Olive said. "For weeks. I'd dream I was walking along the side of the road, and suddenly headlights would shine out of the mist…"

"But did you ever find out for sure?" Sarah broke in.

"We did," Olive said, nodding. "We actually found out at the same time John Peters did, right there in the bar."

"Did Ward tell him?" Sarah asked.

"Ward never came back that I saw," Olive said. "John sold him the land a few days after he came in that last time, and I guess Ward was busy making his improvements to it. No, this was months later."

"Who else knew? Did Ward tell someone?" Sarah asked.

"Ward didn't tell anyone," Olive said. "But Doc Watson knew."

"He was at the hospital that night," Sarah guessed.

Olive nodded. "That's right. And he came into the bar a few months later to play a round of cards at that game John always had going on."

"But John would never have mentioned it," Sarah said. "If he thought he had killed someone."

"He didn't," Olive said. "It was Doc Watson who brought it up. Near the end of the night, one of the other fellows in the game got up to leave, and he could barely stand. He was just weaving and staggering. Doc Watson was real sharp with him. He told him to sit back down or call his wife to come over. That fellow tried to make a joke of it, but the doctor said he'd just released a man that some drunk had run down in a hit-and-run. Ward Collins had found him and brought him in, and it had taken the doctor six weeks just to patch him up to where he could walk out of the hospital under his own power."

Sarah's mind raced, putting the pieces together. "So John Peters never killed anyone after all," Sarah said.

"I'm not sure if that's to his credit or not," Olive said. "He sure thought he had. But there he was, just playing cards in his booth at the tavern."

"But he'd already sold Ward all that land. What did he do when he heard the man hadn't died after all?"

"He started swearing to beat the band," Olive said. "The doctor threw his cards down and said he didn't have to listen to that kind of language, and the party broke up. And John Peters went storming out, shouting for Ward Collins."

"But by then it would have been too late," Sarah said. "Ward owned the land."

"Yep," Olive said. "They said he was out there the day after the sale with a thousand tin buckets, tapping those trees himself."

"So that must have been when John Peters brought the fraud case against Ward," Sarah reasoned.

"It was around that time," said Olive. "But like I said, it never seemed very much of a case to any of us."

"The reports in the paper are so vague," Sarah said. "He must have been afraid to explain what actually happened."

"That's what I always thought," Olive said. "He sure had some fancy lawyers, but they never seemed to get anywhere. And as soon as the suit was dismissed, Ward got a loan from the bank and started hiring. He had that first factory building built by the end of spring. And he finally got old Woltherstorf's permission to marry his daughter Genie."

"Had they been together for a long time?" Sarah asked.

"They'd been trying," Olive said.

"But Ward hadn't had the money until then," Sarah said, thinking back on the articles about Genie's privileged upbringing.

"I was just a kid, and even I knew that," Olive said. "Old Woltherstorf wasn't about to let Ward Collins run off with Genie if he wasn't going to be able to support her."

"Do you think money really mattered that much to her?" Sarah said. Genie had always been dressed in nice things in the photographs Sarah had seen, but she'd never seemed fussy or showy. And given how happy Genie had looked in her engagement announcement, Sarah couldn't imagine her choosing money over Ward.

"I don't think it was just about that," Olive said. "Genie was always different, you know. Things had to be just a certain way, or she got upset. She didn't get angry or complain, she just got...strange. So her family always tried to keep things the way she liked them."

"It sounds like it might have been hard for her to manage a house on her own," Sarah said. "Especially on a newlywed's budget."

"I know it was hard for me." Olive said. "The first year Jim and I were married, we ate rice every night for a whole winter. Sometimes I cooked it with beans, and sometimes with milk and a hint of sugar. But we had meat only once a week. But I remember him bringing home a block of ice cream that Christmas. Nothing else ever tasted better! We'd have a spoonful each night, and it lasted until Valentine's Day."

"So maybe her father was more worried about how she'd do without his support than he was about the money," Sarah said, trying to bring Olive back to the topic. "He wanted her to have a home that felt safe to her."

"Well, Ward gave her that, too, in the end," Olive said. "And he sure worked hard for it. The money he paid for that land might not have seemed like much to John Peters, but Ward sure worked for it. He'd work all day at the livery, then take Genie for a drink at the soda fountain. You could see them there every afternoon, like clockwork. And then he'd take her home and go work another six hours at the grocery store, restocking shelves, until he got to go home at midnight."

"You can see how he might start to resent someone like John Peters, who never had to work at all," Sarah said thoughtfully.

"He wouldn't have been the first one in town to feel like that," Olive agreed. "Or the last."

Sarah settled back into the curve of the love seat again, letting Olive's words sink in. So Ward Collins hadn't helped cover up a murder, but he had lied about a man's death. Maybe it wasn't honorable, but it was certainly understandable. But if he was capable of lying about one person's death, would he be capable of lying about another's? "Olive," she said. "Do you remember anything about Genie Collins' death?"

"No more than anyone," Olive said. "It was a shame they didn't have a funeral for her. People in this town loved her. We would have liked a chance to say good-bye. And we would have tried to help Ward and that boy, if Ward had let us."

Sarah thought back to her original suspicion, that Genie might be right here in Bradford Manor. "I talked to someone who told me Genie Collins may not have died," she told Olive. "Someone who worked with the family."

Olive raised her eyebrows. "That would explain a lot of things," she said. "And it wouldn't be the only secret that family has kept."

"Is there any chance she might be here?" Sarah said, and leaned forward. "Some kind of private ward, under another name?"

Olive thought for a moment, then shook her head. "I don't believe so," she said. "For one thing, people knew Genie in town. Too many people on staff would have recognized her. And you can't keep a secret like that in a place like Maple Hill. Plus they've given me pretty much full run of this place. I guess I talk to just about everybody who's willing to talk with me, and the rest of them I know by sight. If she were here, I'd have recognized her. And so would about a hundred other people. If that family did put her away somewhere, I don't think it could have been in this town."

Sarah sighed and nodded. "Well, Olive," she said. "Thanks for taking the time to talk with me. You've been a real help."

"Oh, thanks for bringing me inside, and for listening to an old woman go on and on," Olive said. "These days nobody seems to care much about the things that happened way back then."

"Well, that's the interesting thing about this quilt," Sarah told her. "Whatever happened back then, it feels like it still matters today. Maybe even more than a lot of things that have happened since."

CHAPTER SEVENTEEN

When Sarah stepped out of the nursing home's main entrance into the circle drive where she'd parked her car, she raised her hand against the bright sun, and frowned. Every bit of information she seemed to get about this quilt only led to more questions. She finally understood the story behind the articles sewn into the quilt, but she still didn't know who had sewn them there. Had Genie collected the clippings as the events unfolded? Had Emily somehow discovered them in the past months and built them into the quilt as some kind of a message? And what about the other message, stitched on the back of the quilt? Who had left it? Genie? Emily? Someone else altogether?

Not only did Sarah have more questions than ever, the questions she had seemed to be growing more troubling with every passing hour. What had begun as a simple quilting puzzle had become a tangled web of family secrets, with Emily at the center. What was Emily frightened of? Where was she? Did Tad know? And if he did, why would he lie to Sarah about it? Sarah didn't even know how to guess at the answers to these questions, but a growing sense of unease was building in her as she found out more details about the Collins family and their secrets.

Again, her mind returned to the quilt. Who had made it? If it was Genie, the cry for help stitched in the back echoed out over the decades, about a danger that might be long past. But if it was Emily, the threat was recent and urgent. There might still be something Sarah could do to help her. But first she needed to know who had made the quilt.

Tad wouldn't be any help, she reasoned. He'd been sincerely surprised when he saw Emily with the quilt the day she delivered it to Sarah. If Emily had made it in recent months, she'd done it in secret. But what if Genie had made the quilt? Who could tell Sarah that? Only one person, she realized: Samuel. Tad had been clear that he didn't want Sarah to talk with his father about the project, but it seemed to Sarah that they were beyond that point now. She'd discovered a cry for help in the quilt. Emily's behavior had veered from erratic to inexplicable. And Tad was obviously keeping some kind of secrets of his own.

Sarah pulled her keys from her purse and started for her car. It was time to find out what Samuel knew about the quilt. And maybe she'd learn something about what had happened to Genie, or Emily, as well.

She pulled into the drive to the new maple syrup plant a few minutes later. It was long and full of twists and turns, like the shady road out to the abandoned factory, but instead of being surrounded by giant maples, it wandered through low rolling hills, covered with carefully manicured lawns. Here and there the landscapers had planted young saplings or small gardens where red or yellow mums provided bright splashes of color. Beyond, perched on a hill, much like the old Collins house itself, was the factory, a gleaming complex of modern glass and steel.

Sarah parked near the door and went past a small forest of snapping flags to the main entrance. The glass doors opened into an atrium with a ceiling that soared several stories overhead. Beside the door was a kidney-bean-shaped black desk. Behind the desk was a slim, efficient-looking young woman, her blonde hair pulled back severely from her face. "Can I help you?" she said. She spoke as if Sarah had just interrupted her in the midst of an important conversation, although as far as Sarah could tell the young woman hadn't been doing anything when Sarah arrived.

"I hope so," Sarah said. "I'm here to see Samuel Collins."

The girl's expression changed from annoyance to bemused pity. "Mr. Collins is a very busy man," she said. "Let me see if he's available. Can I tell him what your visit concerns?"

"Please tell him I've just got some questions about Genie," Sarah said.

"You mean the company?" the girl said.

Sarah shook her head. "No," she said. "Just tell him they're questions about Genie."

The girl arched her eyebrows, then picked up the phone as if she might as well, since she couldn't think of anything more interesting to do. "Yes, I have a visitor for Mr. Collins," she said. "She says she has some questions about Genie."

A woman's voice spoke on the other end.

"No, not the company," the blonde girl said with an air of mockery. "Just Genie. Sure, I'll hold."

Sarah looked around at the imposing atrium. Giant black-and-white photographs of maple trees dotted the walls, along with a metal icon of the genie mascot Sarah recognized from the old bottle. A modern designer had done his own take on the old drawing: This genie was sleeker and less jolly than the original. It was clear that the company had come up in the world since the days when Ward had built his first factory, now drowsing empty in the woods. But despite the magnificence of the surroundings, Sarah had a sense that something had been lost in the move from the original location. This place was more impressive, but it lacked the warmth and character of the first factory.

"Yes," the blonde girl said. "Oh! It's—" she looked up at Sarah and hissed, "What's your name?"

"Sarah," Sarah said. When the girl nodded impatiently, she added: "Sarah Hart."

"Sarah Hart," the girl told the woman on the other line. Then she gave another "Oh!" of surprise. When she had settled the phone back onto its cradle, she looked at Sarah with a new expression. Not exactly respect, but something closer to it. And curiosity. "She says you can go up," she said. "The elevators are over there. You'll go up to the fifth floor and ask at the desk. You can't miss it."

"Thank you," Sarah said.

She walked to the bank of elevators, hit the call button, and boarded the elevator when it arrived. When the doors slid wide again, they opened on a plush receiving area. Thick navy carpet ran from wall to wall, and watercolor paintings of old-fashioned ships hung over the substantial furniture.

"Sarah Hart?" said a woman behind an imposing mahogany desk.

Sarah nodded.

The woman smiled. "You can go right in. He's expecting you."

Samuel Collins sat behind a mahogany desk that was even more massive than the one his receptionist presided over in the waiting area. Shelves of leather bound volumes lined the wall behind him. He rose when she came in.

"Oh, please," Sarah said, waving for him to take his seat again. "There's no need."

"Well," Samuel said. "Will you take a seat?"

The other day in the park, Samuel had seemed like a sad old man. But now, something in his face made him look like a scared little boy. From Tad's reaction to the idea of telling Samuel about the quilt, Sarah had thought Samuel might be angry when she arrived. Instead, he seemed wary, and even a little helpless. He sat back down, and she took the seat across from him.

"Thanks so much for seeing me," Sarah said. "I know it's short notice, and I'm sure you're busy."

"What brings you here?" Samuel asked.

"Well, I don't know if you've heard this around town, but I do quilt restorations," Sarah told him.

Samuel looked slightly puzzled.

"People keep quilts in their family for generations," Sarah explained. "And sometimes they're damaged over time. I repair faded or torn pieces, and bring a quilt as close as I can to its original state. Most of the work is done by hand, and I use antique techniques and vintage fabrics, so it's as authentic as possible." She could see that Samuel was confused, trying to understand what this had to do with him, so she added. "And right now, I'm working on a quilt that belongs to your family."

"My family?" Samuel repeated, as if he wasn't quite sure what the words meant.

Sarah nodded. "When I took the project, I was told that it had been made by your mother, Genie," she said gently. "But as I've worked on it, I'm not so certain. I'm at a place in the project where that's starting to become important. So I was hoping you might be able to help me establish who really made the quilt. Your mother was known in town as an accomplished quilter."

Samuel nodded uncertainly, as if he were worried that he might be stepping into some kind of trap. "Yes," he said. "She was."

Sarah leaned forward. "Were you ever involved with her quilting?"

"Oh," Samuel said. "She always had something in her hands. I can't say I ever helped her much."

"Would you remember any of the designs she worked on?" Sarah pressed.

Samuel shrugged reluctantly. "I might," he said.

"What about a design based on the old Genie Maple Syrup Company label?" she asked. "Did you ever see anything like that?"

Samuel seemed to search his memory for a long moment. Then he shook his head. "I don't believe so," he said.

Sarah decided to make one last try. "What about her sewing things?" she asked. "Her materials and patterns. Do you know what happened to those when she passed away? If I could look through them, I might be able to confirm whether she created this quilt or not."

Until this point, Samuel seemed to have been feeling Sarah out, trying to understand why she had come. But now his face hardened. "I'm sorry," he said. "I'm afraid that would be impossible."

"I'm very careful with everything relating to the quilts," Sarah said. "My techniques are all archival."

Samuel didn't seem to be moved by this at all. In fact, his brows drew together after he spoke, as if his mind had just taken off down a completely different track. "I'm sorry," he said. "Can you tell me how you came into possession of my mother's quilt?"

Sarah hesitated. Tad hadn't wanted his father to know about Emily's involvement with his grandmother's quilt. Sarah didn't want to lie, but she also didn't want to betray Tad's and Emily's trust. On the other hand, Samuel and Emily had clearly had an emotional conversation at the park. If she mentioned Emily, maybe she could learn more about what had happened there, whether Emily was in trouble, and if Sarah could help.

Before she could answer, a knock sounded on the door.

"What is it?" Samuel called.

The heavy oak swung open and Alex Crane entered. "I've just got another one of these documents for you to sign," he said, glancing down at the thick sheaf of papers in his hand as he crossed the room. He had extended the papers to Samuel over the desk before he realized that Samuel wasn't alone.

"Oh," he said, letting the papers sag. "Hello."

"Alex, you remember Sarah Hart," Samuel said.

"Of course," Alex said. He set the papers on Samuel's desk and reached for Sarah's hand. His grip was tight and decisive. "What brings you here, Sarah?"

He looked at Sarah with more interest than the casual question would normally stir. Sarah thought she might even have caught a glint of anxiety in his eye. Did this have something to do with his evasiveness when they'd met at the library?

"I'm working on a quilt," Sarah said.

"A quilt from my family," Samuel elaborated. "But this is the first time I've heard about it. She was just going to tell me how she came to be working on the project."

Both of the men turned now and looked at her intently. Sarah wasn't sure she'd ever seen two men giving such rapt attention to a quilting question before. And she still didn't want to betray Tad's and Emily's confidence, but these were the same two men who had confronted Emily in the park. Maybe if she mentioned Emily, she could surprise them into revealing something that might help Sarah learn the truth about what was going on.

"Well, Emily asked me to work on it," she said.

Immediately, Samuel's face darkened and Alex's eyes narrowed.

"Where did Emily get this quilt?" Samuel demanded.

That was a good question, Sarah realized. Emily hadn't told her. Sarah had assumed she'd found it somewhere in the Collins house, maybe while she was helping clean or organize some old things. Or even when she went looking for Genie Collins' wedding dress to have it refitted for her. "I'm not sure," Sarah said. "But she was interested in having it repaired for Tad so he'd have a connection with his grandmother."

"What is that supposed to mean?" Samuel asked, his voice rising. "His grandmother has been gone for years. How could he be more connected with her?"

Sarah could see she'd hit some kind of a nerve. Samuel's passionate response wasn't just the result of old grief. He acted like a man still struggling with a deep loss—or a current threat.

"Well, I think that was the idea," she said gently. "To give Tad something of his grandmother's, since he never really had a chance to get to know her."

"Plenty of children lose their grandparents before they get to know them," Samuel said. "It's not the worst thing that happens in this world." But his voice sounded false, as if he were trying to convince himself.

"Well, I know she was only hoping to help," Sarah said, still trying to smooth the waters.

Samuel laughed. The sound was ugly and rude. Sarah straightened up in her chair. She wasn't used to this kind of disrespect.

Alex gave her a measuring glance. "You haven't told her, have you?" he asked.

"Told me what?" Sarah said.

"I don't see that it's anybody's business but ours," Samuel said.

"Well, the fact that she's gone will come out, one way or another. Mrs. Hart might as well know, before she gets too much further on this ... project," said Alex.

"What are you talking about?" Sarah asked. "Is Emily all right?"

"I guess she got what she wanted, at least," Samuel said bitterly.

Alex composed his face into a compassionate mask. "I know you're friendly with Emily," he said. "So this may come as a surprise. But we discovered a few days ago that she's been stealing from the company." His features were arranged in an expression of sadness, but in his eyes, Sarah thought she caught a glint of glee.

"I'm sorry, I can't believe that," Sarah said.

Alex tilted his head. "I couldn't have either," he said. "Until I saw the numbers in black and white."

Sarah glanced at Samuel. He was gazing down at his desk with the same defeated expression she'd seen in the park.

"Well, have you talked with her about it?" Sarah said. "Maybe there's some explanation."

"Of course, she denies everything," Alex said. "She'd have to. The amount of money she's siphoned off makes it a federal offense. But the evidence is undeniable."

"He's right," Samuel said, looking up. "I've been over the numbers myself. And over them, and over them. That's what they prove."

Sarah shook her head. The men seemed to believe what they were saying, but Sarah just couldn't make it match with what she knew of Emily. She thought back on Jason's warnings to be more careful about checking references for her tenants. Was she really such a bad judge of character? But she had lived with Emily for almost a year. She'd seen her happy and sad, tired, sick—and overjoyed when she shared the news of her and Tad's engagement. Sarah couldn't imagine that Emily had kept such a dark secret from her all that time, or betrayed Tad's love so quickly. Maybe she was just naive, but she didn't believe it. There must be some other explanation.

A red file lay on the right side of Samuel's desk. He pulled it to him, and flipped the cover open to reveal column after column of numbers. When he did, a single envelope remained on the shining wood beside him. Sarah glanced at it. Unlike the other business correspondence scattered over the surface, this letter was addressed by hand, but with a return address stamped in the upper left-hand corner: Blue Mountain Haven. Sarah's heart skipped a beat. It sounded like a rest home, but not one she'd ever heard of. Before she could turn this thought over, Samuel spoke again.

"We didn't have any choice," he said, as if he were talking to himself again, and not to the other people in the room.

A spasm of fear ran through Sarah. "What do you mean?" she asked.

"We had to ask her to leave," Alex said matter of factly.

"The company?" Sarah said. That only made sense. If Emily was under any suspicion, of course she'd have to give up her accounting duties until she cleared herself.

But Samuel shook his head slowly. "No," he said. "Maple Hill."

"Leave town?" Sarah repeated. "But what about Tad?"

"He's the reason we asked her to leave," Samuel said. His eyes flashed as he looked up at Sarah. The sad old man was gone now, replaced by a protective father. "I didn't want Tad to find out the truth. It would have broken his heart."

"But Emily leaving town wouldn't?" Sarah said.

"That might hurt him," Samuel said. "But at least he can start again."

"If we gave her a chance to stay, she might have convinced him to believe her lies," Alex explained.

"He loved her so much," Samuel added. "I didn't want him to live his whole life with someone who could betray him that way."

The argument in the park was starting to crystallize in Sarah's mind. She remembered the manila envelope that Samuel had offered Emily. "So you offered her money to go?" she guessed.

"That was all she seemed to want, anyway," Samuel said with bitterness. "At first she pretended to refuse it, but she called later and told Alex to bring it to her. We haven't heard from her since."

"She's left town," Alex said. "She got what she wanted."

"But what are you going to tell Tad?" Sarah exclaimed.

"We're not going to tell him anything," Samuel said decisively.

"Don't you think he deserves to know the truth?" she asked.

"People are sentimental about the truth," Samuel said. "But the fact is some things are better kept secret."

Sarah shook her head slowly.

"So I don't suppose you'll need to work any further on this...quilt project," Samuel said. "In fact, as it's our family property, I'd appreciate it if you'd return whatever you have to us as soon as possible."

Despite the story she'd just heard, Sarah didn't like the idea of giving up on a quilt halfway through. And now she was less sure than ever that Genie Collins had sewed the plea for help herself. Maybe Genie had made the original pieces

—but was it possible that Emily had stitched the letters in the back as a plea to Sarah herself? "Well, I've just now discovered what the pattern is," she said. "It's a beautiful image of the original Genie Maple Syrup label. It could be absolutely beautiful on display in your lobby. I'd love to finish it for you, if you don't mind."

"Actually, I do," Samuel said. "Just return it to us, please. As soon as you're able."

Sarah sighed.

"I'm sorry I wasn't able to be more of a help with your project," Samuel said. "But at least you won't be investing any more wasted time in it, now that you know the situation."

Sarah rose and glanced down at the envelope on his desk again to remind herself of the name. *Blue Mountain Haven.* "Thank you for seeing me," she said.

Alex Crane watched her closely.

"Alex," she said. "Good to see you."

He nodded, and Sarah went out.

As she drove down the syrup company's long lane, she tried to fit the new pieces she'd just learned together. No matter how she thought about it, she couldn't take Alex's and Samuel's accusations of Emily at face value, at least not without hearing Emily's side of the story.

But there was another piece that didn't fit: Tad. Alex and Samuel seemed to believe that Emily had left town already. But Tad had told Sarah that Emily was home sick, just as if nothing had happened. Was it possible that he knew more than Samuel and Alex thought? Had he learned about their suspicions about Emily despite their efforts to keep them secret? Did he know where his wife was? Or had he, God forbid, done something to her?

Sarah reached for her cell phone and dialed the syrup company's main number.

"Genie Maple Syrup," the operator chirped.

"I'm trying to reach Tad Collins," Sarah said.

"I'm sorry," the operator said. "He's out for the day."

"Thank you," Sarah said, and ended the call. She thought for a moment. Maybe it was Emily who was keeping secrets from Tad. Maybe he truly believed that she was home sick, and had gone home early to check on her.

Sarah dialed Emily and Tad's home number. It rang several times, and then voice mail picked up. The message began with faint giggling. "Hello, this is Tad!" came Tad's voice. "And this is Emily..." Emily said. "Collins!" she added, with the same giddy emphasis Sarah had heard on Emily's personal voice message. "Leave us a message," she continued. "And we'll get back to you as soon as possible," Tad finished. The line beeped.

"Hello," Sarah said. "This is Sarah Hart. I'm actually trying to reach Tad. Tad, if you're able, would you give me a call? I'd like to talk with you about something. Thanks so much. Bye."

She ended that call, and dialed Emily's number.

"We're sorry," a computerized voice announced. "The mailbox belonging to—"

"Emily Collins," Emily's voice broke in, full of newlywed hope.

"—is full. Please try again later."

Sarah set the phone back in her purse. She'd done everything she could think of to reach Emily. Now all she could do was wait.

CHAPTER EIGHTEEN

W hen Sarah got home, she headed straight for her sewing room. Samuel Collins might not want her to continue working on the project, but Samuel Collins hadn't given her the job. And until she heard from Emily that Emily wanted her to stop working, she was going to continue doing the job she'd been given.

Besides, working on a quilt always calmed her nerves and gave her a chance to collect her thoughts. And when nothing else in the world was going right, it was one thing that she could always do, and do well. She might not know exactly what to say to her grandchildren when they were upset, or how to track down a worried young bride, but she could make even, perfect stitches all day long.

Sarah switched on the light over her sewing table with a sense of relief. She had come to roadblocks down every path she'd followed, tracing the mystery of Genie Collins' history. But nothing was stopping her, she realized, from doing the one thing she had really been hired to do: turn Genie's scattered pieces into a whole quilt. And she had at least solved enough of the mystery to do that.

She would never consider using a sewing machine for a project this delicate, especially not with the layers of fragile paper sandwiched between the fabrics, and the batting hanging loose, ready to gum up the machine's works. Also, although the squares were approximately the same size, they varied from piece to piece by as much as a quarter of an inch. To make sure that Genie's beautiful quilting didn't get sewn together askew, she'd need to finish the quilt the same way Genie had started it: by hand. But at the end, she knew she'd have a finished quilt, even if she still didn't have all the answers about its history.

She started to sew the pieces together one by one, first the intricate mosaic of the top of the quilt, then the simpler fabric and faintly stitched letters on the back. Strip by strip, the quilt began to come together. She worked from the bottom up, connecting the deep browns that represented the forest floor and the tree trunks that grew from it. Then she added on the rows that depicted the swirl of the genie's tail, and built up into the genie's barrel chest and out-flung arms, surrounded by a beautiful palette of green, orange, and red leaves.

The work was soothing and satisfying, but as she sewed the blocks into place with even stitches, she couldn't quite ignore the quilt's message as it emerged again on the back. "Help," it read. Then, "help me." And finally: "You are my only hope," still with that mysterious monogram, EPC.

Lord, Sarah prayed. *I want to help. Please show me who needs it.*

As she worked, the afternoon light died, and darkness gathered outside the windows. Long hours after she began, Sarah turned the quilt over to regard her handiwork—and Genie's. The intricate mosaic of vivid colors was breathtaking. And now that she knew what it was, it was hard to believe that she'd ever had trouble seeing the pattern of the genie and the trees. She wondered if looking down at the quilt was something like God looking down at our lives. Up close, it was easy to get lost in the details of the tiny pieces, and miss the larger shapes of the figures they created. Sometimes it seemed as if all the pieces would never come together in a way that made sense. But from God's perspective, everything had been part of a beautiful pattern all along. *Thank you, Lord, for helping me see this,* she prayed. *Please help me to keep believing in your pattern even when I can't see it.*

The quilt assembled, Sarah realized that she was hungry. She went to the kitchen and made herself a quick sandwich. Then she returned to the office, sat down at her computer, and shook the mouse to bring the monitor to life. The cursor in the search engine dialog box blinked invitingly.

"Genie Collins," Sarah murmured. "Where have you been?" On a whim, she typed in Genie's name. She found a singer from North Carolina on MySpace, and several teenagers and college students on Facebook. Further down the page, Linked In listed a real estate agent in Missouri.

A few articles came up by a reporter named Genie Collins in Ohio. None of them were anywhere near Genie's age. Sarah scrolled down further, and even flipped through several later pages, but after the first few items, the responses didn't relate to actual people, but to places where Genie's name appeared by accident in the chaos of the Internet, including a book about a genie written by a man named Collins Wentworthy. This search was just as much a dead end as the others had been.

Then her mind flashed back to the envelope she'd seen in Samuel Collins' office. She had forgotten it in her worry about Emily. What had that name been?

"Blue Mountain Haven," Sarah said, typing it in. She clicked the search button.

The first listing was for a bed and breakfast in Jamaica. The second included an address in a nearby town.

Sarah clicked on it.

The pictures showed a group of low buildings nestled under mature trees. But the focus of the text didn't seem to be about the elderly. In fact, although it was clear the facility had a medical angle, the information on the landing page seemed vague. It took Sarah a moment longer to realize something else. There were no pictures of the residents on the home page, just the buildings themselves. What kind of a nursing home was this?

She clicked on the "about us" tab. *Blue Mountain Haven is an elite sanctuary*, it read. *Where your loved one will receive cutting-edge treatment in an environment of beauty, caring, and hope.* Something stirred in the back of Sarah's mind.

Martha's description of Genie as seeming distant and pre-occupied. Annie saying that Genie had always been different. Olive's memories of Genie as easily excited, and having trouble dealing with life's details.

Sarah clicked on the "Treatments" tab. A list of mental health issues ran down the page. Depression. Bipolar illness. Schizophrenia.

Sarah sat back in her chair and tapped her fingers on the desk. Blue Mountain Haven wasn't a nursing home. It was a high-end facility for people struggling with mental illness.

Sarah stood up and went over to her sewing table, looking for some hint of Genie's troubles in the beautiful quilt. She gazed down at the mosaic of blues, greens, and browns, fingering the unfinished edge of the pieces that had sat uncompleted for so long.

The paper in the batting crinkled. She turned back a corner of the quilt face and looked down at the old newsprint. This square contained a scrap of the article describing John Peters' first accusations of fraud, and a thin slice of what must have been a much larger photograph of grainy black-and-white maple trees. Sarah read the partial column again. "Duress…improper dealing…significant damages…legal action…John Peters." Her finger lingered under John Peters' name. He was another loose thread in the pattern she was trying to see. Now she thought she knew where Genie might be, but where had John Peters gone after he left Maple

Hill? She'd studied the history of his family in the town, but John Peters could have lived for decades after he left it.

Where had he gone after he sold his inheritance at such a loss? What had he done after he vanished from Maple Hill?

She sat down at the computer and tapped out "John Peters." The search engine returned thousands of listings: Boy Scout leaders, financial advisors, aspiring actors, restaurant managers, even a teenager with dreams of becoming a professional ventriloquist. This was impossible. Almost none of the listings gave the kind of history she would need to identify the John Peters who had left Maple Hill so many years ago. She didn't even know what he looked like. Probably out of deference to his powerful family, the newspaper hadn't printed his picture along with the items noting the trouble he'd gotten into. If only she had some way to narrow it down.

Something stirred in Sarah's memory. She got up again and flipped open the notebook she had been using to record information about the quilt at the historical society. On the Peters page, she found it: John Peters' full name. Jonathan Abraham Peters. She carried the notebook to the computer, set it down beside her, and typed in the full name.

This time one of the first hits was on a genealogy site. The item contained the full name, "Jonathan Abraham Peters," and some mention of Maple Hill, but she couldn't tell from the listing if they were really connected on the page. Still, excitement pricked at the back of her neck. She clicked on the link.

It took her to a page of a genealogy site on the name Peters. She realized quickly that it was full of names she recognized: Abraham and Dolly. David, their son. Frederick, John Peters' father. And there was John himself, his name in red and underlined to indicate that he had more family information of his own on another page.

"So you did have a family," Sarah said as she clicked on the link. "I wonder where?"

The following page informed her that Jonathan Abraham Peters, born in Maple Hill, Massachusetts, had passed away about a decade ago in a town called Appleton, in Vermont. He'd married a Helen Avery in 1941, about five years after he left Maple Hill, and they'd had three children: Martha, David, and Ann. Martha had married a Pete Walker, and had one daughter, Jessica. Jessica had married a Robert Sharman and had twin girls, Kelly and Kristin. David had married a Jane Folch and had two sons, Mark and Chris. Ann had married a Steve Price and had three children, Miriam, Adam, and Emily.

Emily Price. Sarah's hand froze on the mouse. Could it be a coincidence? She stared at the name, trying to connect the cheerful young woman who had shared her home with the strange, dark history contained in the scraps of newspaper inside the quilt that lay on the table behind her. Emily's name was in red, and underlined, indicating a new family line would be visible with a click.

Lord, Sarah prayed. *What does this all mean?*

She clicked on the link. The next page contained only one more piece of information. Emily Price had married early that year. Her groom: Thaddeus Andrew Collins.

Sarah stared at the names on the screen. Could it be some kind of one-in-a-million coincidence that Emily had married the grandson of the man who had taken her grandfather's inheritance? That seemed too improbable to believe. But would John Peters have told the whole story to his children or grandchildren? That seemed improbable, too. The story didn't cast John Peters in a flattering light, and he'd been so reluctant for the details to come out that he hadn't even made them public in his suit to reclaim the land. It seemed even less likely that he'd pass them down through his family after making a fresh start in a new town. But still...

Sarah returned to the incredible coincidence of the connection between Emily's and Tad's families. It seemed that one of them, or somebody else, must have known about the relationship in the previous generations. Did Emily know the story of her grandfather's dealings with Tad's? Had she known about their families' strange history when they married? Did Emily want some kind of revenge? For the first time, Alex's and Samuel's accusations about Emily stealing from the company began to seem plausible. If Emily thought the land had been stolen from her family, she might not have had many scruples about taking the company's money for herself. Or was she innocent after all? Had Samuel or Alex

Crane somehow discovered the connection before Emily did, putting Emily in danger? Was Emily in fact the one who had sewn the old newspaper articles into the quilt, as some kind of cry for help?

None of these questions could be answered with simple research. Only the people themselves could explain what was going on in their own hearts. And Emily, the connection between all of them, hadn't answered Sarah's phone calls for days.

Sarah closed out the search engine and shut her computer down for the night. She stood over her sewing table and gazed down at the vivid colors that composed the intricate quilt. Then she switched that light off as well, plunging the room into darkness.

As she threaded her way by memory around the sewing table, heading for her room, her phone rang, deep in her bag.

Emily, Sarah thought. She'd left her purse on the floor by her chair, near the computer. Somehow, she found it in the dark, fumbled until she found the smooth body of her phone, pulled it out, and answered. In her hurry, she didn't check the caller ID.

"Hello?" she said, slightly breathless.

"Mrs. Hart?" The voice was a young man's, but Sarah didn't recognize it right away. She placed it just as he identified himself. "This is Tad Collins."

"Tad!" Sarah said. "I'm so glad to hear from you. I've been trying to reach you or Emily all day. Is she all right? Do you know where she is?"

"Well, that's why I'm calling," Tad said. "I was hoping I could come over and talk with you. Would you have time for that?"

"Of course," Sarah said. Tomorrow, she knew, her calendar was clear. "When do you think you'd like to come over?"

"Is it all right if I come now?"

CHAPTER NINETEEN

Ten minutes later, Tad stood in Sarah's kitchen, holding a cup of hot cider that she'd just heated up in the microwave. "Thank you so much," he said, cradling it in his hands. "You didn't have to do this. I didn't mean to put you out. I know it's late."

"It was no trouble at all," Sarah said, leaning back against her counter. "And I'm glad you're here. I've been worrying about Emily all day. Is she all right?"

Tad pressed his lips together just like Sarah's son Jason had done when he was a little boy, trying not to cry. "I wish I knew," he said. His voice rose and cracked with emotion. Then he broke off.

Sarah waited patiently for him to compose himself. A moment later he looked up.

"I haven't seen her since yesterday morning," he said.

"Yesterday morning?" Sarah said. "But this morning you told me she was at home, sick."

Tad shook his head. "I'm sorry," he said. "That was a lie."

"I know," Sarah said. "I went over there with some soup for her, and there was nobody home."

"Oh no," Tad said. "I never thought you'd go to that trouble. I was just so ashamed."

"Of what?" Sarah asked.

"That I didn't know where she was," Tad exclaimed, his voice rising again. "I felt like such a fool. Before we got married, Emily and I promised each other that we'd never go to bed angry. And we never have. She's acted strange recently but never mad. So I couldn't believe it when she didn't come home last night. And when you called, I didn't know how to tell you about it. I'd been up all night, worrying about her. And I was still hoping she might come to work this morning or come home and there would be a simple explanation. So I just told you the first thing I could think of." He looked at Sarah unhappily. "I'm sorry," he said. "That was so nice of you, to go over with the soup."

"You said she's been acting strange recently?" Sarah asked. "Because she's seemed strange to me too."

Tad nodded. "It all seemed to start around the time she gave you that quilt," he said. "Ever since then, she's been acting...different. She'd go out, and she wouldn't tell me where she was going. I know a wife doesn't have to report everything to her husband, but she's never done that before."

"It doesn't sound like her," Sarah said.

"I could tell something was wrong," Tad told her. "I kept asking her to let me help her, but she just told me everything was okay. If I pushed her too hard, she'd decide it was time to go out again for some reason. Then yesterday afternoon, I got a really strange phone call from her."

"What did she say?"

"She sounded so upset," Tad said. "Like she'd been crying. In fact, I think she was crying for some of it. I hate to hear her cry. I asked her if something had happened. She wouldn't answer me, but she said she wanted to talk. She had something she wanted to tell me."

"Did she say anything besides that?"

Tad shook his head. "I told her she could tell me anything, right then," Tad said. "But she wanted to see me face-to-face. I was up at the factory. I offered to go meet her at the house, but she said no, she was already in the car, and she'd come meet me there."

"But she never came," Sarah said.

"She never came," Tad repeated. "She told me she was only a few minutes away. I waited for half an hour, and when she didn't show up, I told my secretary to give me a call if Emily came in, and then I went out looking for her myself. She'd sounded so upset that I was afraid maybe she'd run off the road somewhere between the plant and the house. I drove around town for hours, checking every way she might have gone, but I never found her. And I called my secretary probably every five minutes. But Emily never went to the plant. And then she never came home."

"When was this?" Sarah asked, thinking back to the conversation she'd witnessed with Emily, Samuel, and Alex in the park.

"All day!" Tad exclaimed.

"But when did she call you?" Sarah said patiently.

"Oh," Tad said. He thought for a minute. "Around three o'clock. It was actually 3:08. I know because I started watching the clock when we hung up, because I was so worried about her."

Sarah had gotten to Maggie's for lunch around two thirty. So Emily's conversation with Tad had been about an hour after the scene in the park, Sarah calculated.

"I called the police last night," Tad said. "Around midnight. But they said they couldn't do anything about it until she'd been gone for twenty-four hours. The guy asked me how long we'd been married, and when I told him four months, he laughed, like this was all some kind of joke. He told me just to wait and she'd turn up. But she didn't come in to work this morning. And she didn't come home tonight."

Sarah took a deep breath and shook her head. So her intuition that Emily was in some sort of real trouble was right. But that didn't give her any comfort at all. Her mind raced, adding this new information about Emily's phone call to the pieces she already had. Emily's connection with the Peters family and her disappearance might seem to provide support for Samuel's and Alex's accusations that she had been stealing from the company. But this phone call she'd made didn't. Now it sounded more like she had tried to meet Tad to tell him some part of the story—but had she meant to tell him everything? Or just some piece of it? And should Sarah share the things she'd learned about his family with Tad?

"You're one of the people she knew best in town," Tad said. "I just thought maybe she told you something. Or maybe you know something about the quilt that could help."

Sarah looked into the young man's worried eyes. They were bloodshot and tired from lack of sleep, but mostly they were full of concern. If Emily had anything to fear in the Collins family, Sarah was pretty sure it wasn't from him. Sarah had wanted to talk with Emily about the quilt first, so that Emily could do the delicate work of introducing it to Tad. Sarah didn't like the idea of putting herself in the middle between the two newlyweds. More than anything, they needed to learn how to share their thoughts and feelings with each other. But now Emily was missing. Maybe one of the quilt's many mysteries would make more sense to Tad than it did to Sarah. And perhaps it would help him remember something that would help them find Emily.

"I want to show you something," Sarah told him.

She led him into her sewing room, where the quilt was spread out on the table, complete now, except for the border. The edges were still unfinished, and here and there crumpled newspaper peeked from between the layers of batting.

"I'm not sure how this quilt is connected with Emily's disappearance," Sarah said. "But you and I both noticed that she began to act strangely after she gave it to me. Maybe you'll see some clue in it that I haven't."

"Wow," Tad said, stopping just inside the door. "It's so big. And beautiful."

Sarah smoothed a wrinkle from one corner. "Your grandmother was an excellent quilter," she said. "Both these techniques are very unusual. They're hard to do separately, and even more difficult together. But she did it almost perfectly."

"It's the Genie Maple Syrup label," Tad said. "I remember it from when I was little. Mom used to make me clean my toys up and put them in an old crate that had the label on it."

Sarah nodded. "It took me a while, but when I saw an old bottle with the label, it all clicked," she said.

"She used so many different pieces," Tad said.

"She did," Sarah agreed. "And she did a few other things. Do you see this newsprint in the lining?" She lifted a corner of the quilt to reveal the yellowed paper underneath.

Tad nodded.

"It's an old technique," Sarah explained. "Usually a quilter chooses the paper at random, since it won't ever show. But all the paper in this quilt contains articles about a dispute between your grandfather and another man, over the land your maple grove stands on. Have you ever heard anything about that?"

Tad shook his head. "No," he said. His eyes were wide and a little confused. He waited for her to tell him more.

Sarah hesitated. She hated to tell him unpleasant family history, especially if his grandfather had never told anyone himself. But if she didn't tell Tad the story of the sale of the land, he wouldn't understand the significance of the fact that Emily was John Peters' granddaughter. "Your grandfather bought the land from a man named John Peters," she said. "But after he bought it, Peters accused him of fraud.

He claimed your grandfather misled him in order to buy the land."

"Did he?" Tad asked.

"I'm afraid he did," Sarah said. "It's a long story, and I can tell it all to you some other time, once we find Emily. But first, let me show you something else."

Carefully, she folded the quilt over and spread it out with the back side up, so that Tad could see the message stitched into the squares. "Do you see this?" she said, outlining the first letter for him with her finger.

"Help me..." Tad read, then scanned down to the next line. "Escape. You are my only hope." He turned to Sarah, his brow furrowed in concern. "Did my grandmother write this?"

"That's what I thought," Sarah said. "I certainly thought she made the quilt, especially with this period newsprint sewn inside. But I don't know how to explain this monogram here at the end."

"Where?" Tad asked.

Sarah pointed to the final block, with "EPC" sewn into it.

"Emily Price Collins," Tad said quickly.

"That's exactly what I thought," Sarah said. "And it made me wonder if I was wrong about who really made this quilt."

"I've never known Emily to sew before," Tad said.

"Neither have I," Sarah said. "Never in all the time she lived with me. She used to sit down here for hours, watching me work, but if she knew how to quilt herself, she never let on."

"So why would you think it was her?"

"Well, the initials match," Sarah said. "It's the first thing either you or I thought of. And you've never known her to just disappear before, have you?"

"No," Tad said reluctantly. Then he lifted his head to listen.

In the front of the house, a door had just slammed shut.

Sarah frowned. "That's strange," she said.

"Is it your new renter?" Tad asked.

Sarah shook her head. "Belle's spending the night in Jefferson," she said.

"Then who is it?" Tad asked.

Sarah raised her finger for quiet.

Outside the sewing room, they could hear footsteps echo on the creaky old floorboards as someone walked toward them, through the house.

Tad glanced quickly around the office, looking for some kind of weapon. As the steps grew closer, he settled on the thick plastic slab of a quilter's rule. He lifted it in the air, handling it like an unwieldy baseball bat.

"Well, there's no need for—" Sarah began.

"Get behind me!" Tad whispered. "I'll take care of this."

Now the footsteps crossed by the dining room table, just one room away. Despite herself, Sarah felt a chill of fear. She picked up a pair of scissors from the sewing table and slipped behind Tad's brawny figure just as the footsteps reached the sewing room's threshold.

CHAPTER TWENTY

A moment later Martha's familiar face peeked through the sewing room door. "Sarah," she said. "I'm so glad you're still up."

"Martha!" Sarah said, laying down the pair of scissors. "You scared me half to death!"

Tad lowered the ruler.

"Oh, I'm so sorry," Martha said. "I didn't even think. I saw your car was outside, so I just knocked, and when you didn't answer, I thought you were probably lost in thought back here so I'd better come in. I wouldn't bother you so late, but it's important. Hello, Tad."

"Should I go?" Tad said doubtfully.

"No, you should *not* go," Martha said. "In fact, I think it's very fitting that you should be here."

Sarah could feel Martha warming up to a theme, and she knew there was no stopping her. When she had a piece to say, Martha said it. It didn't matter who was there, or what they might think.

"I came over," Martha began, "because we've successfully negotiated with the railroad to drop charges in exchange for Ian painting a mural at the old depot. And the same with Will Percy."

Sarah suppressed a smile at Martha's use of the word "negotiate." That may have been what she did with the railroad company, but with old man Percy it was a lot more likely that he'd dismissed the event with a wave of his hand, then taken her on a friendly forced march to visit all six dozen of his fancy peafowl and exotic chickens.

"But this morning," Martha said, "I went to the Genie Maple Syrup Company." She accompanied this statement with a dark look at Tad. Tad's eyebrows drew together in confusion. He looked at Sarah. Sarah shrugged slightly and nodded back at Martha.

"I spoke to a young man there named Alex Crane." Martha said the name the way another person might have said "flu virus." "He claims there's no way the Genie Maple Syrup Company could drop the charges. He says it sets a dangerous precedent for all their properties. He said it was company policy to prosecute a case like this to the fullest extent of the law, and that he was sorry, but it was out of his hands."

"That doesn't make any sense," Tad said. "Alex *is* the legal department at the company. He makes all the legal decisions."

Martha raised her eyebrows archly, as if this was what she had suspected. "So I asked him who I might be able to speak to besides him. He said the only person in the company with the power to change the policy was Samuel. I asked to make an appointment, and he told me that Samuel's calendar was filled until after Thanksgiving."

"I'm sorry," Tad said. "I'm not sure I understand the problem you were meeting with him about."

"My grandson," Martha said, "painted a very beautiful work of art on your abandoned syrup factory. As well as on the railroad trestle where it crosses the river, and old man Percy's back barn. He didn't have permission for any of this, and now he understands that's a problem. But the railroad liked the mural so much, they'd like him to paint another on the depot in town. Chief Webber is willing to let that be his community service, to teach him a lesson, and so is old man Percy."

"Well, that makes a lot of sense to me," Tad said.

"Tell that to Alex Crane!" Martha exclaimed.

As Sarah watched, some of Tad's fatigue seemed to slip away. His shoulders straightened, and he took on an air of command. He seemed less like a confused boy, and more like a young businessman. This must be what it's like to see him at work, Sarah thought. One day, he was going to be a good leader for the company.

"I'll tell you what," he said. "I'll talk to him. Alex has been with us for years, and he always wants the best thing for the company. But sometimes he takes a little harder line than he needs to. It's something we've been talking about. This might be one of those places."

Martha's eyes widened. "Really?" she breathed. "Oh, that would be wonderful! Ian can be a knucklehead, but he's just a kid, and he's sorry. He really is. He was out there all day today, starting to clean the mural off the old factory building."

Tad nodded. "I saw what he did out there," he said. "Of course, I would have liked him to ask permission, but I can't deny he has talent."

"I know," Martha said. "It's beautiful. And he wasn't trying to hurt anything. Sometimes he just doesn't think."

"I'll see what I can do," Tad promised. But the anxiety was starting to creep into his eyes again. Business issues couldn't hold his attention for long, not with his wife missing. He glanced at Sarah.

"I'm interrupting, aren't I?" Martha asked.

"You're welcome at my house any time of the day or night," Sarah told her. "But Tad and I were having a conversation, yes."

"Then don't mind me," Martha said. "I'll go out the way I came."

"It was nice to see you, Mrs. Maplethorpe," Tad said.

"Oh, Tad," Martha said, gratitude still strong in her voice. "It was *very* nice to see you. You won't forget?"

Tad shook his head.

"Bless your heart!" Martha said, and slipped out.

"Alex," Tad said, shaking his head. "He's been with the company almost as long as I've been alive. Sometimes I think he worries about it more than we do."

Sarah thought back to Alex's angry face in the park. He had seemed even more agitated than Samuel. But why would that be, when it wasn't his money that had been stolen?

Then her conversation with Alex and Samuel earlier that day rose in her mind. They seemed to believe that they were the reason Emily was missing: She'd left town as they'd asked her to. But the call Emily had made to Tad threw all that into question. It was possible she had called to tell him she was coming over, then changed her mind. But it didn't seem as likely as a more upsetting possibility: that somebody or something had stopped her from reaching Tad after she made the call.

Tad gazed down at the quilt. "I wish I saw something in this," he said. "I just don't." He looked back up. "Do you know anything else at all that might help me find her?"

Again, Sarah hesitated over what information to share with Tad. If his concern about Emily was put on, he was one of the best actors she'd ever seen. And she could understand why he might make up the lie about Emily being sick if he was distraught and embarrassed. But she still wasn't sure who she could trust. On the other hand, he was the only person she knew who was in a position to verify or disprove his father's and Alex's charges about Emily.

"Well," she said. "I did speak to your father today."

"My father?" Tad said. His face grew even more pinched with worry. "Did you talk with him about the quilt?" he asked. "I thought I said—"

Sarah nodded. "I know. And believe me, I thought about it. But I couldn't get in touch with you or Emily. And I thought it was important to find out whether it was Emily or your grandmother who made this quilt, because of the message I'd found in it."

Tad nodded. "I see," he said.

"I just asked him if he had any memory of his mother working on a quilt of this kind," she said. "He didn't. But in the midst of our conversation, Alex Crane came in."

"He's in and out of Dad's office all the time," Tad said. "Sometimes Dad jokes that he should just move in."

"Well, Alex told me something about Emily," Sarah said.

"What?" Tad demanded, interrupting her before she could go on.

"It's not easy news," Sarah said. "And I don't know if it's true. But according to Alex Crane, Emily's been stealing from the company."

Tad shook his head vigorously. "No," he said. "No way. I've never met anybody who cares less about money than Emily. That's part of why I married her. I knew" His voice broke again, and he looked down. "I knew she really wanted me," he said, gazing down at his feet.

"That's what I remember about her too," Sarah said gently. "But Alex said he had proof. Your father had seen it too. And so he'd asked Emily..." she hesitated again, not wanting to cause Tad any more pain. But he looked up waiting for her answer. "He'd asked her to leave."

"Why?" Tad exploded. "There must have been some mistake. We'll look at the books and figure it out. I'm sure there's some kind of an explanation."

Sarah nodded, letting him run on.

"Why would he ask her to leave? What was he thinking?" Tad asked. He took a deep breath and let it out, trying to calm himself down.

"He was trying to protect you," Sarah said. "At least that's what he thought he was doing."

"So do you think that's what she did?" Tad asked, his voice anguished. "She just…left?"

"I didn't know," Sarah said. "She'd been so strange and evasive with me that I didn't know what to think. But I didn't know about this phone call she made to you. It sounds to me like maybe she didn't want to leave."

"Maybe she was coming to explain," Tad said.

Sarah nodded.

"I'm going over there right now," Tad said, taking a step toward the door. "I'll look up all of Alex's records. There must be something he missed. Maybe I'll find some clue to where she is." His bloodshot eyes were wild now, and his face was gray with fatigue.

Sarah shook her head. "Tad, go home," she said. "You've done everything you can tonight. And you haven't slept in forty-eight hours."

"But something must have happened to her!" he said. "I can't rest when I don't know where she is."

"You can't help her if you don't get some rest," Sarah said. "You can barely think."

Tad still shook his head but slower now.

"Besides," Sarah said. "If Emily does try to come back, the first place she'll go is home. You want to be there if that happens, not up at the office."

"Maybe you're right," Tad said. He ran his hand over his face. "I *am* tired."

"Go home," Sarah said again. "You'll be there in case Emily comes back, and you can go to the office first thing tomorrow morning."

"There must be some mistake," Tad said, his attention drifting to the question of the stolen money.

Sarah took his elbow and began to steer him toward the door. "You'll be in a lot better shape to find that out with a few good hours of sleep," she said.

Tad let her lead him, unprotesting, through the house to the front door. She opened it and he stepped out onto the welcome mat.

"I guess you're right," he said.

Sarah nodded.

Tad turned to go, then turned back. "Would you come out to the plant tomorrow?" he said. "To help me look through the records? I don't know who I can trust out there, but I know you're Emily's friend."

Sarah nodded again. "I'll be there first thing," she promised. "We'll take a look at those numbers in the morning."

CHAPTER TWENTY-ONE

The girl at the front desk at Genie Maple Syrup was no more excited to see Sarah on Saturday morning than she had been the day before. Her mood didn't seem to have been improved by the prospect of working on the weekend. But at least now she recognized Sarah.

"You're here for Mr. Collins?" she said, reaching for the phone.

"Yes, thank you," Sarah said. "But this time I'm looking for Tad."

"I haven't seen him yet this morning," the girl said. "But let me check." She reached for the phone slowly, as if this were just one more in a long line of futile tasks she'd grown used to enduring. "Hello?" she said when the person on the other line answered. "Tad? I have a visitor here for you. I'm sorry. I know it's early."

Again, her eyebrows raised in surprise. "Oh." She put her hand over the phone. "Are you Sarah Hart?"

Sarah nodded.

"Yes, it's her," the girl told the person on the other end. "I'll send her right up." She replaced the phone in its cradle. "He's expecting you," she said. "He must have gotten here early."

"Thank you," said Sarah.

"He's in the same executive suite as Samuel," the girl said. "Fifth floor. You remember where the elevators are?"

Sarah nodded. "Thanks," she said, and walked over to the elevator bank.

A few minutes later, the elevator doors slid open to release her onto the fifth floor. The friendly receptionist who had welcomed her yesterday wasn't at her desk yet, but Alex Crane stood behind it, sorting through a small stack of unopened mail.

He glanced up at the whisper of the elevator doors. When he saw Sarah, his eyes narrowed. He didn't offer a word in greeting.

"Hello," Sarah said pleasantly.

"What brings you here this morning?" Alex asked.

"Just stopping in to see Tad," Sarah said breezily.

"Seems early for a visit," Alex said.

"I like to get a good start on things," Sarah said. She stopped at the desk. "You know, it seems so strange to me that Emily would just leave the way she did. You worked with her for a year. Doesn't it seem strange to you?"

Alex met her eyes steadily. "Those figures that proved she'd been stealing seemed strange to me," he said. "After that, not much came as a surprise."

"But still," Sarah pressed. "Why would she go to all the trouble of marrying Tad if she was only here for the money? I don't understand that piece of the story. And once she'd married him, why would she need to steal from the company? She should have had access to anything she wanted. I can't imagine Tad would have refused her anything."

Alex shrugged. "The criminal mind," he said. "We don't understand it. Those people are different from you and me." He looked down at the sheaf of envelopes in his hand and sorted through a few more. It was clear he thought the conversation was over and he expected her to leave.

"What did she say?" Sarah asked. "When you took her the money?"

Alex looked up again, startled. "I'm sorry?" he said.

"The money," Sarah said. "At first she refused it, but Samuel said later she called and agreed to take it. I thought you had delivered it to her. I'm curious about what she said when you saw her then."

"Oh," Alex said. "She didn't have much to say for herself. I had the money in a briefcase, and I handed it to her. She just took it. I don't remember that she said much of anything."

"She didn't say anything at all?" Sarah asked. "Nothing about what her plans were? Where she was going?"

Alex shook his head. "I can't say I would have been that interested in her plans, to tell the truth. I was just glad to be rid of her. She's caused this company enough trouble."

He looked back down at the mail he was sorting, trying again to end the conversation. Sarah took a few steps toward the glass doors that led into the executive suite. Then she turned back. "I just have one more question, if you don't mind," she said.

"All right," Alex said, although the impatience in his voice suggested it wasn't.

"I'm sure you remember that I saw you and Emily at the library the other day," Sarah said. "I understand you and Samuel met with her to ask her to leave town to protect Tad, but you didn't mention meeting with her alone." Sarah wasn't sure what question she even wanted to ask, so she left it at that. Sometimes, she had found, you got more interesting information when you presented someone with an uncomfortable fact and didn't try to direct them with a question.

Alex's brows drew together. Sarah saw anxiety in his eyes, and perhaps a hint of anger. "I had just discovered that she was stealing," he said. "I asked her to meet with me to discuss it, before I brought anything to Samuel. At that point, I still had some hope that there might have been a mistake."

Sarah had to admit that this story would explain Emily's emotional exit from the library. But it didn't explain the meeting place. "But why at the library?" Sarah pressed. "Wouldn't it have been simpler just to discuss it here, in one of your offices?"

Now the anger in Alex's eyes was undisguised, although he kept his voice light. "Well, you've seen how our offices are around here," he said. "The whole team is always wandering in and out. This was a very sensitive matter. I didn't want to hurt the family by bringing up these concerns if they were false. So I asked her to meet me in a neutral place. The library is quiet and private. So we met there."

Sarah nodded. "I see."

"You were good friends with Emily, weren't you?" Alex asked.

"Yes," Sarah said simply.

"And you think maybe if you find her, there might be some kind of explanation." Alex's voice held a trace of mockery.

Sarah looked back at him steadily. "I'd just like to know that she's all right," she said. "This seems so out of character for her."

"Well, I can assure you she's all right," Alex said. "She was in perfect health when she took that money from me. Although I have to say, she was wise to leave town. If she'd stayed, I can't vouch for what Samuel might have done to her for hurting his son. Or what Tad might have done to her himself, if he'd found out how she robbed the company."

Sarah shifted uneasily. The same thought had occurred to her. She still wasn't sure whether she believed Emily was guilty as Samuel and Alex said, but if any of the Collins family thought the charges were true, they would have had a motive for Emily's disappearance. Even Tad. He seemed desperate to find her, but was it for love or revenge? Whatever his reasons, Sarah thought, the first order of business was to find Emily and make sure she was really all right. If she could team up with Tad to do that, she would do it. Without him, she didn't have access to the records that might contain hints about where Emily might have gone—and if Emily had gone there willingly.

"Do you have any other questions I can help you with this morning, Mrs. Hart?" Alex asked acidly. "If not, I've got some work to do."

"If you could just direct me to Tad's office," Sarah said.

Alex pointed with the sheaf of envelopes. "It's just across from his father's. You can't miss it."

"Thank you," Sarah said.

She found Tad behind a desk that was a mirror image of his father's. Now it was piled high with file boxes and scattered folders.

"Sarah," Tad said. "Thank you for coming. Can you shut the door behind you? We're on a skeleton crew for the weekend, but I don't want it to get around that I'm going through the company files like this. Usually you can't pay me enough to dig into the financials, so they'd know something is wrong."

Sarah settled into the seat across from him. "Have you found anything?"

Tad shook his head. "Not yet. But I've only been here a few hours."

"How can I help?" Sarah said.

"It's actually pretty simple, for now," Tad said. "I'm just comparing our books to our bank statements, month by month. It can get pretty complicated, because we try to give our various divisions autonomy, so we have separate accounts for the forestry team, the sap collection process, manufacturing, shipping, administration—you get the picture. But I figure if money really was flowing out of the company, you can hide it on the books, but it actually does have to flow through the bank at some point. I'm just trying to find any place where it looks like that might have happened." He laid a folder on the desk in front of her. "I'll start you out with a simple one. This is the shipping ledger for the year since Emily joined the company." He set another sheaf of papers on the shiny wood beside it. "These are the bank statements for the shipping account. I've just been going through and making sure they match up."

Sarah scooted her chair up to the desk, opened both folders, and placed the September ledger and statement side by side.

"So far I've only found one discrepancy," Tad said. "There's a big payment that goes out in October for the forestry division. Almost ten thousand dollars. It's not to one of the vendors I recognize, but sometimes we do have individual charges that big, for equipment repair or taking down diseased trees. I'm not sure this one means anything, but that's the kind of thing I'm flagging. It may just be a legitimate onetime charge, or it may be part of some kind of a pattern."

"I understand," Sarah said, looking down at the columns of numbers.

"And Sarah?" Tad said. "Thanks for doing this. I know it's not a very exciting way to spend your Saturday morning."

Sarah smiled at him. She was no stranger to painstaking work. Quilts were all about the tiny details. The jumble of boxes of records on his desk might intimidate someone else, but Sarah knew how they'd get through them—one by one, paying careful attention to each. It was just like hand-sewing individual squares together until they became a quilt.

In the shipping department, as far as Sarah could see, the September records were clean. Deposits and debits matched up closely, although sometimes charges appeared a few days later on the bank statements than they did on the Genie Maple Syrup ledgers. But in October, there was a charge that flowed out of the bank account without appearing in the Genie Maple Syrup ledger. A round red dot marked the number on the bank statement, as if someone had let their pen rest on the paper beside it as they looked over the numbers. The charge was for about eleven thousand dollars, and it didn't list a vendor, just an account number.

"Tad," Sarah said. "I don't know if this account looks familiar to you, but it doesn't match up with the internal ledger I've got."

"Let's see," Tad said, reaching for the papers.

Sarah handed the file to him. A minute later, he looked up at her, his eyes glinting. "It does," he said. "But today is the first time I've seen it."

He sorted quickly through the files at his own elbow, pulled out another bank statement, and pushed it across for Sarah to see. It was the strange charge he'd found in the forestry records—and the charge had flowed out to the same account number listed in the statement Sarah had just handed him.

When Sarah looked up, Tad was already dialing the phone. "Kevin!" he said, when the person on the other end picked up. "This is Tad, over at Genie Maple Syrup. Yeah, great to talk with you too. Listen, I've got a question. I'm going back over our financials for the past year, and I've got a couple of charges going out to an account I don't recognize. I just want to make sure I've got a handle on where everything is going. I wonder if you can give me any more detail you've got on it, other than this number here on the statement. Yeah, sure." He read the number off, slowly. "That ring any bells for you?"

He and Sarah locked eyes while he waited. Then the tinny sound of Kevin's voice came back over the line.

"An offshore account?" Tad said, with a nervous laugh. "Well, maybe Dad's been socking something away for retirement. Are you able to see who it's associated with? Great."

Another pause. Sarah watched Tad's face closely. A minute later, Kevin's voice sounded again. Tad frowned. "Are you sure?" he said. "Can you check again? Well, all right. Listen, thanks, man. I appreciate it."

He hung the phone up and looked at Sarah. "It's an offshore account," he told her. "In the name of Emily Collins."

Before Sarah could answer, the door swung open. She turned, expecting to see Alex Crane, but it was Tad's father

Samuel. When Samuel caught sight of the stacks of boxes and files on Tad's desk, he stopped in the doorway. Father and son stared at each other for a long moment. Samuel was the first to speak. "What's all this?" he asked.

"I'm trying to find Emily, Dad," Tad said. "She's been missing for two days. But I guess you already know that."

The same weariness that Sarah had first seen in Samuel's confrontation with Emily in the park seemed to settle on the older man's shoulders. "Son—" he said.

"Look, I know you were trying to protect me," Tad said. "But I'm a grown man. And Emily is my wife. You can't just send her away like you did."

"How far have you gone in these files?" Samuel said. "It won't take you long to see what I saw."

"I just found it," Tad said. "And I'm not sure I believe it. Did Emily admit she stole money when you confronted her?"

"Well, of course she denied it," Samuel began.

Tad shook his head. "And you didn't believe her?"

"I believe the numbers," Samuel said. "I know this must be hard for you, son. I'm sorry."

"Well, it's not over," Tad said. "Not until I find her."

"Are you sure that's a good idea?" Samuel said. "If she's gone, maybe she doesn't want to be found."

"I'll ask her that when I find her," Tad said. The two of them stared at each other again. Tad's face was determined. His father's fell into the same melancholy lines that Sarah recognized from Genie's photographs.

"Was that what you came in here to say?" Tad asked.

"No, no," Samuel said, as if remembering something. "I just stopped to pick something up. I was actually on my way out. I'm not used to seeing you working behind closed doors on a Saturday morning, so I thought I'd make sure everything was all right."

"Well, it's not," Tad said. "Not yet. Where are you going?"

"Oh," Samuel said vaguely. "Just an appointment. I'm sorry, but I need to be going."

Tad shrugged. "All right," he said.

"Sarah," Samuel said, nodding at her as he retreated. She gave him a weak smile in return.

"That was strange," Tad said as the door shut behind his father. "He doesn't usually work weekends. And he usually tells me where he's going, even if it isn't important."

Alex's warning rang in Sarah's mind, that he couldn't begin to imagine what lengths Samuel might go to in order to protect his son. "I can think of one reason he might not want you to know where he's going," she said.

Tad stared at her. "Do you think–?" he said.

A minute later, they were both on their feet, following Samuel Collins out of the building.

CHAPTER TWENTY-TWO

They waited inside the lobby doors for Samuel to get in his car and drive away. Then they sprinted out to the parking lot. Tad headed for his car.

"No," Sarah said. "He'll recognize yours. There's less chance of that with mine."

She popped the locks and they leapt in. As they zipped down the curving company lane, they could still catch glimpses of the Collins family's dignified black Lincoln taking the turns ahead of them. At the end of the lane, it turned right onto the country road, heading out of town, not back to it.

"That's really strange," Tad said. "There's nothing out this way."

"Well, that would make it a good place to hide, if you wanted to hide somebody," Sarah said.

"I just hope she's okay," said Tad.

For about fifteen minutes, Sarah followed the black sedan down a series of country roads, trying to keep far enough in the distance that she wouldn't be noticed, but not drop so far back that she'd lose him at a turn. After miles of winding country roads, they went through a small town, little more than a block of storefronts: a few restaurants, a bank, a flower store, and a post office. Just on the outskirts of town, Samuel's car slowed down.

Behind him, Sarah braked. Samuel's turn signal came on. Then the car made a left and disappeared into a wooded area just off the road.

"What the heck is this?" Tad said. "Has she been stuck out here in the woods?"

"We'll find out," Sarah said. As she turned after the black sedan, Tad read a small sign posted by the entrance.

"Blue Mountain Haven," he said.

A shock of recognition ran through Sarah. Samuel wasn't leading them to Emily, she realized. But was he leading them to Genie? At the same time, she realized that this was part of the story she hadn't shared yet with Tad. As far as he was concerned, his grandmother had passed away back in 1963, years before he was even born. If she was right about where they were going, Tad was in for a big shock.

"What do you think it is?" he asked.

Sarah steered her car down the winding drive under the canopy of trees that met above the road over their heads, trying to decide whether she should say something to him to try to prepare him for the shock he was about to receive. *Lord, please be with Tad in this time,* she prayed silently. *Let him know you're always here, even when his whole world seems to be changing.*

Before she could think of what to say, the canopy of trees broke open over their heads, and she pulled into a wide, shady parking area. It had been specially designed for lots of green space and shade. The strips of pavement only held one line of cars each, parked side by side, with islands of trees between them, connected by cement walking paths. At the far side was a group of low buildings under tall trees.

Samuel was just pulling into a spot near one of the buildings.

"There he is!" Tad exclaimed. "We've got to catch him before we lose him in the buildings."

Sarah wound her way through the lot, heading for Samuel's car. He was just passing through the double glass doors of the nearest building when she pulled up. Tad leapt out of the car and raced after him. Sarah turned the car off, got out, and followed.

When she stepped inside, both men's voices were already raised.

"Where is she?" Tad was shouting. "You can't hide her from me any longer! I don't care what she did! I still love her."

Samuel shook his head, his lips tight.

The reception area they stood in seemed more like the fancy spas Sarah had seen on TV than a waiting room. On one wall, a carved rock hung with a small fountain running down over its face. Beautiful orchids overlooked the carefully arranged magazines on the end tables. The desk was an elegant curve of brushed metal. A young woman with her dark hair pulled straight back from her face and cat's-eye glasses sat behind the desk, frowning at the ruckus the two Collins men were creating.

"I'm sorry," she said. "Could you please keep your voices down?"

"I apologize," Samuel said.

"You ought to," Tad said. "How could you do this to her? How could you do it to me? What is this place? Why are you keeping her here?"

Now Samuel's defeated look was gone, replaced by irritation. "You don't understand," he said.

"I don't!" Tad agreed vehemently. "So why don't you explain it to me?"

"Why don't—" Samuel began. Then his jaw hardened. "You're right," he said. "Why don't I?"

He turned his back and began to stride toward a set of brushed glass doors.

"Where are you going?" Tad demanded.

"You want to know?" Samuel said over his shoulder. "Then come with me."

For the first time, Tad glanced over at Sarah. Tad and Samuel were both upset, but somehow it seemed right to her. Finding out that his grandmother was alive would be a shock for Tad, but at least his father was finally telling him the truth. And Sarah was glad that she hadn't tried to tell him. The secret had come between Tad and his father. It was better that the truth should come from his father, as well. "Go ahead," she said.

Samuel disappeared between the doors.

"I want you to come with me," Tad said.

Sarah shook her head. "It's better if you go alone," she said.

Now Tad shook his head, stubbornly. "We got this far together," he said. "I'm not going without you."

Sarah still hung back reluctantly.

"*Please,*" Tad said. "What if we lose him again?"

Tad's pleas and her own curiosity finally overcame Sarah. She nodded and followed Tad through the glass doors.

The facility didn't look anything like what Sarah had expected. The halls were carpeted with dignified gray, the lighting was gentle, and the few doors that were open along the way revealed cozy apartments. She glimpsed only one resident, an older man dozing in a rocking chair. Halfway down the hall, Samuel made a sharp turn, and seemed to disappear into the wall.

When Tad and Sarah reached the spot, they discovered a glass breezeway that was attached to the brick wall of a building that had clearly predated the one they'd just left. Samuel had already vanished, but they followed the breezeway to the door on the far end. It was sheltered by the glass around it now, but it had clearly once been an outside entrance.

They slipped through it into what seemed like the hallway of an old Victorian house. Several rooms opened off a sitting room area decorated with antique furniture and paintings of country scenes. Samuel stood in the door of one of them, his back to Tad and Sarah.

A minute later, Tad had crossed the small sitting room to reach his father. "Emily!" he cried. "Where is she?"

A sweet-looking woman with curling, snow-white hair looked up from a plush velvet couch at the three of them. Her face had aged, but the lines were the same. Sarah would recognize them anywhere after all the pictures she'd seen.

"Genie," she whispered.

Genie ignored Sarah, but her face lit up when she saw Tad.

"Ward!" she said. "You came just like you promised! I knew you wouldn't leave me here alone."

"Ward?" Tad said. He looked at his father. "What is she talking about, Dad? Where's Emily?"

Sarah glanced at Samuel. His eyes were bright and his lip was trembling with emotion.

"Tad," she said gently. "This is your grandmother."

"Emily?" Genie said, her voice curious. "Is she coming?"

Tad's confusion was gone in an instant, replaced by a laser focus on the possibility of learning new information about his wife's disappearance. He leaned forward. "Do you know Emily?" he asked.

Genie didn't seem to want to meet his eyes, but she nodded with enthusiasm. "She comes to see me," she said. "She's the sweetest girl. We're making a quilt."

"A quilt?" Tad repeated. "The one with the Genie Maple Syrup label?"

Genie nodded again. "I started it a long time ago," she said. "When I first came here. But then I must have forgotten. But Emily found it. She said she'd help me finish it. She wanted to show it to someone."

Still keeping watch from the doorway, Samuel swallowed hard.

"You," Sarah said quietly to Tad. "She told me she wanted to show it to you."

Tad turned to his father. "Grandma Genie is alive?" he said. "And you told Emily, but you didn't tell me?"

Samuel shook his head. "I never told Emily," he said. "I had no idea she'd been here."

"Ward," Genie said. "Aren't you going to come sit with me?"

"Why does she keep calling me that?" Tad asked.

"You look like your grandfather did," Samuel told him. "Back when he and your grandmother were first married."

"Ward," Genie said, her voice rising in distress.

"We're upsetting her," Samuel said. "Come back outside."

Tad's eyes were still full of hurt and questions, but he followed his father. "We'll be right back," Samuel told his mother gently.

She nodded up at him.

In the sitting room outside, Tad faced off against his father. "She's been alive?" he said. "All these years? And you let me believe she was dead? What kind of person does a thing like that?"

"You don't understand," Samuel said.

"I guess I don't," Tad said. "I guess there's a lot I don't understand."

Sarah started for the breezeway that led back out of the maze of buildings. "I should go," she said.

"No," Tad said. "You're the only person who's told me the truth this whole time. I want you to stay."

Sarah shifted uncomfortably.

Samuel sighed. He looked tired again, and almost scared. Sarah had another glimpse of the boy he'd been fifty years ago, when the Collins family had told everyone that Genie had passed away. "I love my mother," he began. "More than anything." He stopped, overcome with emotion, and put his hand over his mouth.

Tad's face softened at this display of feeling. He reached out and touched his father's shoulder. "Okay," he said, more quietly. "But why didn't you ever tell me about her?"

Samuel composed himself and looked up, his eyes still bright. "She tried to be a good mother," he said. "She did everything she could for me. But sometimes she would get sad. For days at a time. Sometimes for weeks. I would try to help her then, but sometimes I wondered if she could even hear me. No matter what I said, she'd just lie there, staring at the wall or the ceiling."

Tad squeezed his father's arm again. Samuel nodded. "But we got through it. Me and dad. We did everything we could to make her happy. And she wasn't always sad. But every now and then, we had a scare. Once when I was little, she went out and didn't come back till after dark. When she came back, she didn't remember where she'd gone. After that, Dad hired a new maid, just to keep an eye on her. If she started wandering off, Maisie would call her back. It seemed like we were doing okay."

"So what happened?" Tad asked. "Why would you tell everyone she died?"

"The spring I was sixteen," Samuel said, "I woke up in the middle of the night, and my rug was on fire. Mom was just sitting there on the edge of my bed, watching me while it burned. She hadn't done anything to put it out, or to wake me up. If I hadn't woken up, we both might have died."

"Were you all right?" Tad asked.

Now that Samuel had begun to tell the story, the words spilled over each other like water breaking out of a dam. "I got up, and I started yelling at her to get out, so she would be safe, but she wouldn't go," he said. "There was a vase by my bed, and I threw the whole thing at the fire, the water and the flowers, and everything. It broke, and the flames died down enough that I could fold the rug in two. That kept the flames down until a servant came with a bucket of water. The whole time she just stood there, watching me." His eyes grew distant with the memory.

"Do you think she set the fire?" Tad asked, his voice low and serious.

Samuel shook his head. "I don't think so. I don't want to think so, anyway. I always thought she must have brought a cigarette into the room when she came to see me, and dropped it on the rug. It started the fire without her noticing."

"That's scary," Tad murmured.

"Yes," his father said. "It was."

Tad nodded. "I understand," he said. "You couldn't have her in the house. It wouldn't have been safe for anyone, even her. But why did you tell everyone she was dead? I could have had a grandmother."

Samuel shook his head. "I don't know if it will make any sense to you, today. But back then, people didn't understand mental illness the way they do now. It could poison a whole family's name. My father didn't want anybody talking about his bride that way. I think he might have been worried how it would affect the business. And I—" his voice broke again. "I guess I was afraid of what people would think of me too."

Tad wrapped his arms around his father. "I understand," he said. "It must have been hard."

"It was," Samuel said. "It still is."

When the father and son released each other, Tad looked at his father inquisitively. "I came out here looking for Emily," he said. "And she's still missing. She called me two days ago to say she was coming over, but she never showed up. I don't think she left town on her own. I think something's happened to her. Do you know anything about it, Dad? If you do, please tell me."

Samuel's eyes were still bright with tears, but at the mention of Emily's name, they hardened.

"You may not be able to see it now, Tad," he said. "But Emily's not good for you. I'm sorry, but it's for the best that she's gone."

"I won't believe that until she tells me herself," Tad said.

"I'm afraid she's already told you what you need to know, Tad," Samuel said. "By stealing from our company, and then leaving."

Tad took a half step forward, trembling with emotion, but then he checked himself. He turned to Sarah for the first time in the whole conversation.

"Come on, Sarah," he said. "Let's go."

CHAPTER TWENTY-THREE

T ad gave a long sigh and leaned back in his chair. He and Sarah had spent the better part of the day combing through bank statements and divisional ledgers, and the case against Emily had only seemed to worsen. Around four that afternoon, they'd had a bit of excitement when they came across the record of a large unexplained transfer in May, just after Tad and Emily were married. This transfer had landed in a different account from the offshore account they had found earlier, and Tad had immediately called his banker again—only to find that that account, as well, was registered in Emily's name. After that, the deposits flowed exclusively to the new account.

"That's it," Tad said, flipping the cover of the last folder closed. "We've looked at everything I can think of. It all points to her."

Sarah shook her head. "I still have trouble believing it," she said.

"I do too," Tad agreed. "But at least now I can see it from Dad's point of view." He pushed one of the Chinese food boxes he'd ordered in for dinner a few hours ago away from him on the desk. "I just wish I could talk to her," he said. "I want to know what she'd say about all of this."

Deep in Sarah's mind, a wheel began to turn. "Maybe that's where we should look next," she said.

"Where?" Tad asked.

"We've looked at all the company and bank documents," Sarah said. "But we haven't looked at Emily's personal files. There might be something there that would explain all this. Or give us some idea where she is. Is her office on this floor?"

Tad nodded. "She's just one door over," he said. "I'll show you."

He led the way down the darkened hallway, and flipped on the light in the office next door. It was smaller than Samuel's and Tad's, but more inviting, with watercolor paintings on the walls, and well-tended plants.

Tad went to a bank of file cabinets along the far wall and pulled one open. Sarah sat down at the computer and flipped it on. A welcome screen came up, requesting a username and password.

"Tad," she said. "Do you happen to know Emily's username and password?"

"Her username would be ecollins," he said. "That's the same throughout the company, first initial, last name."

Sarah typed it in. "What about the password?" she asked. Tad hesitated. She glanced over. For some reason, he seemed embarrassed.

"Um," he said, "try taddy bear."

"Teddy bear?" Sarah repeated.

"No," Tad said. "T-A-D-D—"

Sarah held back a smile. "I've got it," she said, and typed the password in. The monitor came to life with a close-up shot of a daisy in full bloom. The icon for the machine's hard drive appeared in the upper corner of the screen. Sarah clicked on it, and a dizzying list of drives came up.

"I've never seen anything like this," Sarah said. "You've got every letter of the alphabet here, and then some."

"Oh," Tad said. "Let me look at it. We've got all our divisions on different drives too. Emily had access to all of them, since she was in charge of centralized accounting. Why don't you trade with me? You'll never find it."

Sarah rose from the chair, and Tad took her place. As he began to tap at the keys, she pulled another file drawer out. The drawers were stuffed with thick files of financial reports, receipts, and bank statements. Sarah carefully pulled each file out and thumbed through it. The late hour and the long day were beginning to get to her. She did her best to scan through the numbers and text, but financial details had never been her strong suit. She began to worry that she might be looking right at the evidence they needed, and not even know it.

At the computer, Tad heaved another sigh. "Any luck over there?" he asked.

"Not yet," Sarah said. "I hope I recognize the right thing when I see it."

"It would sure help to know what we're looking for," Tad said.

"Any luck on your side?" Sarah asked.

Tad shook his head, and clicked to open another file.

Sarah carefully replaced the last file in the order she had found it, and pulled out the next one. It was labeled "Wedding Photos," in thick black marker. It was a strange place to keep wedding photos, Sarah thought, but thumbing through them would be a nice break from the endless columns of numbers she had been struggling to make sense of all day. She flipped the file open.

Inside was a single piece of paper, covered with Emily's handwriting. An account number like the ones they'd checked on with the bank was scrawled at the top. A single list of numbers ran down the page, accompanied by dates. From the long day of research she and Tad had just done, Sarah recognized several of the numbers. The ten thousand dollars in October. The large transfer to the new account in May. But these were all on one list, as if they were all part of the same account. At the bottom were three letters: AWC.

"Tad?" Sarah said. "Look at this."

"What have you got?" Tad said, swinging around in his chair.

She handed him the file.

"This looks like another offshore account," he said. "...And these look like the transfers we found today."

"What about those letters, at the bottom?" Sarah asked.

"Alex Wilson Crane," Tad said.

"I thought maybe that was it," Sarah said. "When I saw the A and the C."

"What do you think this means?" Tad said, picking up the single sheet from the manila folder.

"It looks like another account to me," Sarah said. "One that belongs to Alex Crane."

"So this is her side of the story," Tad said. "But what does it mean? Did she discover he was stealing from the company? But then why wouldn't she tell me?"

"Or were they working together?" Sarah added.

"But Alex is the one who told us she was stealing," Tad said. "Why would he do that if they were working together?"

"I guess it's too late to call your banker for information on that account," Sarah said.

Tad nodded. "And who knows if he'd even be able to tell? Most accounts have more privacy controls on them than Emily's, and even then I think he may have been bending the rules to tell me because Emily and I are married. Even if it *is* in Alex's name, I'm not sure we'd be able to find out."

"I can think of one way we might," Sarah said

"What?" Tad asked.

"Alex has been with your company for years," Sarah said. "If he's been stealing, there's a good chance he didn't just start last year, when Emily arrived. If we look back through the records and he's guilty, I bet we'll find evidence that shows he'd been making unauthorized transfers long before this."

Tad groaned. "Back to the files," he said.

Sarah glanced at the clock. It was almost midnight. She was more than ready to go home and get some rest, but she couldn't bear the thought of wasting any time while Emily was out there somewhere in the dark. "I'm game," she said, making an attempt to put some brightness in her voice.

Tad took a close look at her and shook his head. "You know what?" he said. "I think I can look for this on my own. Why don't you go home?"

"I'm just fine," Sarah insisted. "We'll work faster with the two of us."

"Remember what you told me last night?" Tad said. "When we get too tired, we can barely work at all. You've been a great help. I'll just spend a couple more hours here looking through a few more files. I'll call you first thing in the morning. Go home and get some sleep. Please."

Was Tad trying to get rid of her? Or was he just being kind? Sarah couldn't tell, but in either case, he was right. She was getting too tired to think clearly. She hated to leave, but she didn't know what else she'd be able to do to help Emily between now and morning. And if she got some sleep tonight, she'd be fresh to help tomorrow.

"Go on," Tad said. "You deserve a break. This has been a lot more than you bargained for when you took on that old quilt. I'll call you with any news tomorrow morning."

"All right," Sarah said, still somewhat reluctant. "But you'll let me know if you hear anything at all?"

"I promise," said Tad.

She hoped she could believe him.

CHAPTER TWENTY-FOUR

When Sarah woke up the next morning, it took her a moment to realize that it was Sunday. She sat up in bed and looked at the clock. She had slept well, and for quite a while. It was already eight fifteen. If she got ready now, she had plenty of time to make the nine o' clock service at church.

But worry about Emily tugged at her heart too. Could she really go to church when Emily was still missing? What if there was something else she could be doing to find her that morning? She didn't have to go to church every Sunday to know that God loved her. Maybe it would be better to skip this service.

By the time she was done getting up and getting dressed, though, she knew that church was where she needed to be. She'd been so tied up in the quilt and the search for Emily that she'd lost track of other things that were just as important. She didn't have to go to church to know that God loved her, but that wasn't the only reason she had for going to church. The weekly visit was a way to keep her in touch with what really mattered, no matter what was happening around her.

Lord, she prayed as she went out the door. *Please take care of Emily, wherever she is. I leave her in your hands. But if I can do anything to help her, please show me what it is.*

The familiar faces and sacred songs at church helped to calm her and ease her mind, but despite the good talking-to she'd given herself, Sarah had trouble concentrating through Pastor John's sermon. She found herself thinking about Emily and Tad, Samuel and Alex, turning over the details of the story in her mind to see if any of them seemed to fit together now any better than they had last night. By the time the last hymn was sung, she didn't have any new answers, but she was anxious to check her phone to see if Tad had called. But when she pulled it from her purse to turn the ringer back on, there were no messages.

Her heart sank. Could she really trust Tad? Had she helped him to find clues that allowed him to cover something up, or to learn something about Emily that Emily had wanted to keep hidden from him, with good reason?

She slipped her phone back into her purse and looked up to see Mavis Hoyt waving enthusiastically from the hospitality table in the narthex. Sarah had planned to slip out of church without doing much visiting, but Mavis's gestures were too broad for her to pretend she hadn't seen them. Sarah sighed and walked over.

"Sarah!" Mavis said. "I was hoping I'd see you here. I'm in charge of events for the women's circle this fall, and I was hoping you might be willing to come speak at one of our meetings."

Sarah nodded. She sometimes went to these events, and Mavis had a good heart, but she was famous for button-holing church members with long-winded stories. If she simply agreed with Mavis, Sarah thought, maybe she'd be able to slip away sooner. "That sounds fine," Sarah said.

"Wonderful!" Mavis exclaimed. "These teas have been really wonderful. The last one, we had Jane Carter in to tell us a bit about the history of the county fair. Have you heard that story? Maple Hill had their first fair back in 1882—"

This didn't sound promising. Sarah glanced around the room and saw Martha's grandson Ian, ladling lemonade into a plastic cup a few paces away.

"I'm so sorry, Mavis," Sarah said. "I need to go speak with Ian."

Mavis smiled understandingly. "Well, sure," she said. "But we'll be so glad to have you at the luncheon. I'll be in touch!"

"Great," Sarah said, moving away with relief.

"Hi, Mrs. Hart," Ian said when she came up. He set the ladle back in the bowl of lemonade, then remembered some of the manners his mother had spent years trying to teach him, and offered the full glass to Sarah. "Would you like some lemonade?"

"Oh, Ian," Sarah said. "That's sweet, but I'm on my way out. I just stopped by to see how you were doing."

"Okay," Ian said, nodding. "I was out at the abandoned syrup factory yesterday all day, stripping my mural off of it. It's a bad feeling, having to destroy your own artwork."

"Well," Sarah said. "That's one reason to be careful about where you put it."

Ian nodded again. "I guess so," he said. "It's funny. Kids love to talk about that place being haunted, and I never believed it. But that place sure makes a lot of noise for an empty building."

"What kind of noise?" Sarah asked, suddenly alert.

"All kinds of bangs and thumps," Ian said. "It must be the wind doing it, but the building's closed up so tight I can't really figure how. I thought about it all day while I was working. Sometimes you'd even think you heard voices. It's strange."

"Voices?" Sarah said. "What do they say?"

"Nothing you could really hear," he said. "Just like someone calling, far away." He shook his head and smiled. "You know," he said. "Ghost stuff."

"*Hmm*," Sarah said. Maybe it was wind, or a ghost. But maybe it was someone very much alive. Had she found a new clue to the case, just when she'd decided to leave it all in God's hands?

"But you're on your way somewhere," Ian said apologetically.

"That's right," Sarah said. "I am."

As she stepped outside, her phone began to ring. She opened it, walking quickly to her car.

"Mrs. Hart?" Tad said. "I'm so glad I caught you. I was up again last night, but I found what we were looking for. Those unexplained transfers go back years. And before Emily came to the company, they all flowed into one account: the one with the number we found in Emily's office."

"It sounds like Alex must have been stealing from the company for years," Sarah said.

"I got my lawyer on the phone this morning to confirm it," Tad said. "But just as we had feared, it's got better privacy protection than the ones in Emily's name. I told my dad everything this morning. He's up at the plant now with Chief Webber, showing him the books so that we can get a warrant for Alex's arrest."

"Have you been in touch with Alex?" Sarah asked.

"No," Tad said. "Dad and I have both tried him, but he doesn't answer. I'm hoping the police might be able to help us find him. And maybe he'll be able to lead us to Emily."

"Maybe," Sarah said. "But I've got another idea."

A few minutes later, Sarah turned into the rutted lane to the old abandoned syrup factory. Up ahead, she saw a flash of black. Samuel Collins' car. They must have arrived just ahead of her.

As she caught up, she realized that she was actually third in line. Captain Webber's familiar squad car led the eager procession to the old building. But the squad car wasn't the first car to get there that day. A golden Mercedes already gleamed on the gravel circle drive. The three other vehicles pulled up behind it, and stopped. Their passengers piled out.

"Emily!" Tad called. He ran to the closest door and pulled at it. It held fast. "Emily!" he shouted again.

Samuel Collins took a few steps toward his son. Chief Webber put his hands on his hips, watching the proceedings closely.

From inside came one of the thunks and thuds Ian had been talking about at church. Then one of the large front loading bay doors opened, and Alex Crane strode out. He carried a large blue athletic bag, and from the way he carried it, it seemed heavy. "Hey Tad," he said easily. "How are you doing?"

"What are you doing here?" Tad demanded. "Where's Emily?"

Alex glanced around at the assembly. "Well, that's why I came out here," he said. "I know how worried you've been, and I know the two of you used to come out here when you were first dating. I thought maybe I'd take a look for her."

Sarah watched as he rattled off these smooth lies, stunned but somewhat impressed by his brazenness.

"Alex," Samuel called quietly. "It's over. We know."

"The judge just called over," Chief Webber added. "I've got a warrant here for your arrest."

Alex's eyes darted from Tad, to Chief Webber, to Sarah. Then he made a break for it, dashing down the steps toward the gold Mercedes.

He didn't get far. Tad took a flying leap from the porch of the old factory, and tackled Alex to the ground before he'd taken more than a few steps. The athletic bag went flying. A flurry of green bills burst out of it.

"Money!" Tad said. "Didn't you take enough of it with all those transfers?"

Alex turned his face against the ground where Tad had him pinned.

Tad wrestled Alex's hands together and Chief Webber snapped a pair of handcuffs on them. Together, the two men pulled Alex to his feet. His shirt was stained with mud and grass.

"Where did all that come from?" Samuel said, watching the bills blow across the clearing. "You couldn't take that much out of any bank."

"I think I know," Sarah said. "There's a safe inside. He must have been hiding it away for months."

Samuel looked at his trusted employee. "Alex," he said quietly. "Why would you do this? Haven't we been good to you?"

Alex laughed. "Good!" he said. "I've worked with this company since before this little upstart was born! But did you ever offer me a piece of it? No! But the instant your son stumbles out of college, I'm supposed to work side by side with him. Take orders from some kid. Pretend his crazy ideas make sense."

"So you just took the money?"

"I created my own retirement plan." He nodded at the bills blowing into the trees. "I deserved it. This company wouldn't be anything without all the work I put into it."

"Alex Crane," Chief Webber said. "You are under arrest for felony embezzlement."

"You're a worse liar than you are a thief. You didn't start stealing because of Tad," Samuel said as the Chief led Alex to the car. "You'd been stealing from me for years before he joined the company. This is a simple case of greed."

"Maybe I just got tired of having all the responsibility of being family, and none of the money," Alex said.

"Money isn't what our family is about," Tad said. "It never has been."

"You should tell that to Emily," Alex said. "She's the one whose family you stole this land from."

"Where is she?" Tad demanded. "Do you know where she is?"

"I know she never loved you," Alex taunted. "I convinced her to come to Maple Hill. I found out about the John Peters story when I was researching family history, and it looked to me like he had a good case. A case that might still be valid today if any of his descendants cared to challenge the current ownership. So I tracked one of them down—Emily— and brought her up to speed on her family story." Alex tilted his head, raising his nose in the air. "Then I offered her a job with us so she could get to know the company your family stole from hers."

"There was no company here when this land was sold," Samuel said sharply. "My father built this business. In Peters's hands, it was never anything but trees."

"Maybe," Alex said. "But the company's still built on land that was acquired through theft. We'd have to take it to a jury to see. That was the plan. We were going to split it in half. I'd do the legal work, and win her the company. In return, she'd give half of it to me. It sure beat the tiny amounts I was able to siphon out every few months or so, with nobody noticing." Alex practically spit. "But then she figured out a way to betray me, and keep it all for herself. Marrying you."

"That's not true!" Tad shouted. "We were in love!"

"You were in love, maybe," Alex said. "Not Emily. She's as smooth an operator as I've ever seen. Naturally, I wasn't enthusiastic about keeping her around after she betrayed me. So I started drawing the money I wanted in her name. She never knew about it, but it sure looked bad when I showed the books to your father."

"So she didn't steal from the company!" Tad said, triumphantly.

Alex shrugged again. "She didn't have to," he said. "She already had the whole thing—she was married to you. Turns out that meant more to her than keeping her deal with me."

"But then why would she leave Tad?" Sarah broke in. "And where did she go?"

"Beats me," Alex said. "Maybe she got tired of the scam, or she got tired of him. Maybe it seemed like it was taking too long to pay off. You'd have to ask her yourself."

"Where is she?" Tad demanded again.

"Ah," Alex said. His grin was frightening. "That's the million dollar question, isn't it?"

Tad lunged at the lawyer. Chief Webber pulled Alex out of his way, and Samuel held Tad back.

"What did you do with her?" Tad shouted. "Where did you put her? If anything happens to her, I swear I'll–"

He froze in midsentence at the sound of an enormous, unearthly groan from the abandoned factory. It sounded like an old wooden boat ramming into the end of a dock. Everyone standing outside the factory turned to look.

"What in God's name—?" Chief Webber began.

Then a heavy pounding began to sound from somewhere on the second floor of the old building. It took Sarah only a moment to find the second-story door that shuddered with every blow. It was a wide door, probably used once for loading or unloading big shipments from the second floor. Inside the factory, someone or something kept hitting it with great force. The treetop that Ian had painted on it shivered each time a blow hit, as if some strange wind were blowing through its leaves.

Then the door swung open. Emily stood inside, looking down at them. Somehow, she had managed to kick the door free. Her hands were tied behind her back, and a bright red bandana had been tied around her mouth as a gag.

"Emily!" Tad cried. A moment later, he had disappeared into the building.

Again, the sound of a loud blow rang through the old factory. Then another, and another. Tad burst through the door of the room Emily stood in. As the small crowd below looked up, she whirled around on her ledge. Behind her back, her hands struggled against their restraints.

"It's okay," Tad told her. "It's okay. I've got you." He untied the bandana around her mouth first and let it fall to the floor.

"It's not true, Tad," she gasped. "None of what he said is true."

Tad was already at work on the thick rope that bound her hands. "I'm going to get you out of here," he said. He worked unsuccessfully at the knot. Then he pulled a pocketknife from his trousers and sawed at the rope. A moment later, her hands were free. The young couple threw their arms around each other.

A minute or two later, Tad and Emily emerged from the factory door, onto the wide porch. But they still had eyes only for each other. "I should have told you before we were married," Emily was saying. "But I loved you so much. I didn't want to lose you."

"So what Alex Crane said is true?" Sarah asked. "You knew about the family connection before you came to Maple Hill?"

"I did," said Emily. "But he didn't tell me anything about his plan to steal the company. He just called up one day and told me he'd discovered that my family had a connection with the family who owned Genie Maple Syrup. I told him I had just graduated with a degree in accounting, and he said you had a position open here that I should come apply for. So I did. I was lonely for family, especially after my parents died. I thought it would be nice to live in the place where my grandfather once lived.

"But when I got here, he kept saying I should own the company, that it would still be my family's land if Grandpa

Ward hadn't lied to my grandfather. I told him I really wasn't interested. My grandfather used to tell us himself that losing that land was probably the best thing that ever happened to him. He would never have made it into anything as valuable as the Genie Maple Syrup Company. And after he lost the land, he had to grow up. He had to get a real job, and to keep it, he had to stop drinking so much. Then he met my grandmother, and he found a reason to stay on the straight and narrow.

"My family knew the story about Ward Collins. We knew there wasn't something quite right about that deal. But my grandfather always said he hadn't done anything to deserve the land, and Ward took it and really made it into something. Ward might have lied to him, but my grandfather never bore Ward a grudge, not after he got straightened up and started his own family. And he might never have had one if it weren't for Ward."

"I doubt Alex liked hearing that," Sarah said.

"I didn't tell him all of that," Emily told her. "I realized pretty soon that I couldn't really trust him. So I just told him I liked my job at the company, and I wasn't really interested in much else. But that wasn't true," she said, looking up at Tad. "I was interested in you."

Tad put his arm around her shoulder.

"And he could see it!" Emily said. "So he decided to use that against me. Just before we got married, I found evidence in the books of the money he'd been siphoning away to different accounts. I confronted him about it, but he showed me how he'd used my employee codes to make the transfers. He told me that if I exposed him, he'd tell everyone my family's connection with your family, and claim that I was the embezzler. I was afraid of losing you, so I didn't come forward before our wedding. I'm so sorry," she said to Tad.

Tad just squeezed her hand again. "But that made him even bolder," Emily said. "When I checked the accounts again, I realized he had switched account numbers, and now he was taking even more. I couldn't live with that, so I told him I was going to tell the family."

"Is that what you were doing that day at the library?" Sarah asked.

Emily nodded. "But he went to Samuel before I could," she said. "And Samuel believed his story about me."

Samuel shook his head. "Emily," he said. "I'm so sorry. I think I'd lived with the lie about my mother so long that I was too willing to believe lies about other people."

Emily shook her head in return. "No, I'm the one who's sorry," she said. "I was keeping my own secrets. We all made mistakes here."

"I was just trying to protect Tad," Samuel broke in. "I couldn't stand the thought of anything hurting him so badly. That's why I offered you the money to disappear."

"And I didn't want it!" Emily cried. "There was nothing you could have paid me that would have made me leave him! That's what I decided after that day in the park. I was tired of lying to Tad, when I loved him so much. I just wanted to tell him the truth from then on. But when I got to the company, I started to go in the back way so that Alex wouldn't see me. But he was down at the loading docks. He forced me into one of the delivery trucks, and brought me out here. He was planning to leave this afternoon. He only came to clean out the safe."

"Well, Sarah and Tad found that evidence just in time," Samuel said. "Most of the money he stole is still frozen in his various accounts."

"I'm so glad," Emily said, breathing a sigh of relief.

"Even if it weren't, it would be worth it, to have you back," Tad said. Samuel nodded.

"And to finally get to tell the truth," Emily said. "I hated keeping secrets from you."

"Well, let's not make it a habit in the future," Tad said, kissing her cheek. Emily rested her head on his shoulder gratefully.

"I just have one question," Sarah said. "The quilt. How did you get it? When did you meet Genie?"

"I found out about Genie just after Tad and I got married, when I was promoted in the accounting department," Emily said. "I received one of the bills from Blue Mountain Haven, and because it was a big expense that I didn't recognize, I called to confirm it. The woman there told me it was for the care of Genie Collins. I could barely believe that she was still alive, so I went out there to see for myself. She was so sweet, and so lonely, that I just kept going back. Then one day, I found the bag of quilt squares in her apartment.

Genie didn't seem to remember them, but one of the older nurses said Genie had begun the project when she first arrived, and then had given up on it when she got used to living there. I couldn't tell what the pieces were, but they looked so beautiful I thought that the quilt would be beautiful too, if it were ever finished. And of course, I know a wonderful quilt restoration expert.

"I was still trying to think of a way to tell Tad everything I hadn't been able to tell him, about my family, and about the things Alex had tried to get me to do, and about Genie still being alive. I guess I thought maybe if the quilt were finished, it would be a way for me to tell him. And maybe even heal up the past, at the same time."

Sarah nodded. "There can be a lot of healing in repairing these old quilts," she said. "I think it's because they're made with so much love to begin with."

"She must have been so unhappy when she first arrived there," Tad said. "To sew that message into it."

"What message?" Samuel asked.

"It said, '*Help me escape. You are my only hope EPC,*'" Sarah said.

Samuel's face clouded again. "It sounds as though she was unhappy," he said.

"But not when I went to see her," Emily said. "They said she hadn't touched the bag in years. She was happy when I talked to her. She loved to see me, and then she liked to imagine what it would be like when you and Grandpa Ward came to visit next."

Samuel nodded thoughtfully. "It's interesting," he said. "Dad's always been a big donor to Blue Mountain Haven. He began putting money into a memory-care ward there about ten years ago, so now they've got a good facility for exactly what he's dealing with. I've been thinking for a while that he might be happier over there, with Mom. But I didn't know how I'd explain it to Tad, since he didn't know the truth about what had happened to his grandmother."

"Well, I do now," Tad said.

"So it's something we should think about," Samuel said.

"I'll tell you what I'd like to think about first," Tad said. "Taking my beautiful wife home, where she belongs."

"I'm so glad you still feel that way," Emily said. "Even now that you know the truth."

"Of course we do," Samuel said gruffly. "After all, this is your family land, in more ways than one."

CHAPTER TWENTY-FIVE

O h, Sarah!" Emily gasped. "It's beautiful!"

Sarah had just set the quilt on Genie Collins' lap. Now she was unfolding it, revealing the rich colors of the original fabric. Sarah had chosen a navy binding fabric to bring the vibrant blues, browns, and greens together, sewed the strips together on the machine, and then hand-stitched the binding to the quilt itself. It was her way of saying thank you to God for answering her prayers for the Collins family. They weren't the answers she had expected. They were even better.

I don't always know what to ask for, Lord, she'd prayed as she began to sew the binding to the original fabrics Genie had chosen so many years before. *But you answer anyway. So please take each of these stitches as a prayer for Emily and Tad, and Ward and Genie, and Samuel. And even for Ian.*

"I'll hang it over the back of the new chair Samuel brought me," Genie said quietly. Sarah's eyes drifted over to the wooden rocker in the corner of the room. A thick rope was coiled by one of the rungs. Sarah has seen it before. Recognition dawned. This was why Samuel had been buying a rope. To bring his mother a new chair.

Sarah smiled to herself, stepped back, and looked at the quilt that had been only a jumble of confusing squares a few days before. Now each of the scraps, too small and insignificant to be shapes on their own, came together in a dazzling picture. It was so much like the way God drew together the strands of many lives, even using the hard pieces, like illness and secrets, to make a wonderful story.

Thank you, Lord, she'd prayed.

"I wouldn't have thought I could like this quilt more than I did that first night you showed it to me," Tad said. "But I do."

"I think this is your best quilt ever, Mom," Samuel added.

Sarah nodded, and her eye caught on a small frame on an end table next to the new chair. It contained a scrap of yellowed newspaper. "Eugenie Pamela Woltherstorf weds Ward Collins." At last, an explanation for "EPC."

Seated beside Genie on her couch, Ward grinned as if all this came as no surprise to him. "They like your quilt, Genie," he said. "What do you think about that?"

Genie watched as the folds of her quilt spread out, fascinated. She looked up at Sarah. "Did you put this all together?" she said.

"You're the one who made this quilt, Genie," Sarah said. "I just helped put the pieces in order."

"I never thought I'd see it like this," Genie said, running her hand over the multicolored fabrics. "All put together, just the way it should be."

"And I didn't know if I'd ever see the family like this," Emily said in a low voice, beside Sarah. "Together the way they should be."

Sarah gave Emily a quick hug. "They have you to thank for that," she said.

"Well, you played your own part too, Sarah Hart," said Emily.

On the way back into town, Sarah pulled into a parking spot near The Spotted Dog to reward herself with one of her adored chai lattes.

"For here or to go?" Liam asked.

"To go," Sarah said. At the hint of disappointment in his face, she added, "But you know me. I'll be back soon enough."

"That's what I count on," Liam told her.

As she went out, she caught sight of Annie standing outside her store, untangling a pair of wind chimes. Sarah waved and walked toward her.

"You have any luck?" Annie asked. "With that quilt you were working on for the Collins family?"

"I did," Sarah said. "Thanks so much for all your help. It turned out really nicely."

"The Collins family always looked nice," Annie said. "From the outside."

Sarah turned to go, then stopped. "You know," Sarah said, turning back toward Annie, "I thought a lot about that curse you mentioned, on the Collins family."

Annie raised her eyebrows.

"I'm not sure if I believe in curses or not," Sarah said. "But if I did believe in them, I'd say this one is broken."

"Really?" Annie asked. Her voice had a trace of mockery in it, but she couldn't hide her interest. "And what do you think broke it?"

Sarah thought for a moment. She remembered the way Genie had smiled at Ward that morning: it was the same smile Sarah had seen in her engagement photograph, taken decades before. She remembered Tad and Emily, framed in the door of the old syrup factory. She smiled. "Love," she said.

"I've never heard of that breaking a curse before," Annie said. "But I guess I could believe it. Love," she repeated, as if she was trying the word out to see how it worked.

"That's right," Sarah said. She gave Annie a smile, got in her car, and headed home.

About the Author

Vera Dodge is a writer and avid sewer who is delighted to blend both her passions in the Patchwork Mysteries series. She grew up in small towns in the Midwest.

TIMELESS TREASURES

BY CARA PUTMAN

 CHAPTER ONE

Sarah hurried out onto her front porch, pulling her collar tight against the bite of the November wind. Her daughter-in-law Maggie stopped in her tracks on the sidewalk. "Eager to leave?" Maggie asked.

"I was hoping to keep you in the warmth of your truck," Sarah said, as she hurried down the steps. A sliver of wind trickled down her neck, and Sarah shivered. Maybe today wasn't the best day to head to an estate auction after all. A couple of days ago when Maggie had shown her the newspaper ad for the sale at the old Haber farm, the sun had been shining for five or six days straight and it seemed like a great idea. Now she hoped she had enough layers on, or there would be enough people around her, to block the wind. "Let me grab my bag from the trunk."

Maggie must have been excited about the auction, because she could barely stand still as Sarah walked toward her own car.

"Ready?"

"Be right there, Maggie."

Her daughter-in-law bounced on her toes beside her red SUV. Clearly she wanted to be on the road. Sarah pulled her bag out of her car, slammed the trunk, and hurried to the SUV. Maggie's cargo area could hold lots of great finds. Add in the trailer, and if Maggie had her way, they would overflow on the return trip.

As she pulled her seat belt on, she turned to Maggie. "Think you'll find anything special for the store today?"

"Hope so." Maggie shifted into drive and eased from the curb.

Sarah pasted a smile on her face as Maggie accelerated faster than necessary. "I'm sure we'll arrive with plenty of time to scan the collection before bidding starts." In fact, if they got there too early, they'd have to stand around awhile, and the cold November air could make that a bitter experience. But the weathercaster had suggested the wind would die late in the morning, leaving a perfect fall day in its wake. With Maggie's twins at school and her husband Jason at his office, Sarah and Maggie could enjoy the sale.

"I can't wait to find some good items today." Maggie slid to a stop at a light, and rubbed her hands together. Sarah smiled. Days like this gave her the perfect opportunity to spend time with Maggie and get to know her better. Sarah loved this town, its people, and the pace of life, but when her son Jason and his family moved from Los Angeles earlier in the year, Maple Hill had evolved into something even more perfect for Sarah.

Maggie hummed a tune and tapped the steering wheel in time as she guided the vehicle down Maple Hill's main street.

"Any special items you have your eye on?"

Maggie glanced at Sarah, before turning back to the road. "Why? You plan to outbid me?"

Sarah laughed. "My home is full enough. I just wondered if you had inside information."

Maggie shook her head. "Nothing that wasn't listed in the newspaper ad. Call it woman's intuition. This will be a special sale."

"Call it your finely honed skills." Maggie was an insatiable investigator when it came to antiques. The early success of Magpie's Antiques indicated others had noticed her ability to find treasures where some only saw trash.

"Maybe." The corners of Maggie's mouth tipped up in a small smile. "But if that's the case, anyone could develop a good eye."

Sarah studied her daughter-in-law's profile. Maggie had the glow you'd expect from someone who'd lived in Southern California for years. The faintest of crow's feet appeared at the corners of her turquoise eyes when she laughed.

"You knew Mr. Haber," she said. "Did he have anything worth snagging?"

Sarah shook her head. "Once Gerry died, I only saw him around town or at church. He seemed to live a confirmed bachelor's life. What I remember on the farm from before Gerry's death was pretty old and dated. Mr. Haber was closer to my dad's age than mine and maintained Depression-era sensibilities." Sarah couldn't imagine he had too much of value.

Maggie took the final turn listed in the directions. "We must be close. Look at all those cars."

Dented pickup trucks, minivans, SUVs, and luxury cars lined the country road. Sarah saw Martha Maplethorpe's car fifth in line. Her best friend hadn't told her she was going to the auction, and Sarah wondered why she hadn't. It didn't seem like Martha to forget. But now she could share the event with one of her favorite people while Maggie acquired inventory for her store.

"Come on, Sarah." Maggie threw her blue paisley Vera Bradley bag over her shoulder and hustled from the vehicle. As Sarah undid her seat belt, she mused that Maggie had more energy than any woman should. But of course she needed it, managing an active household and a growing business.

Sarah opened her door and hopped from the vehicle. Once on the ground she took a moment to absorb the atmosphere.

Tables were set up in the open space around the small farmhouse. Barn trestles and tabletops stretched in rows, back and forth across the area, covered with piles of mismatched goods, everything from table linens to stacks of ancient magazines. Behind the tables, furniture seemed haphazardly arranged, at least from what Sarah had come to expect at sales like this. It appeared the family and auctioneer had given little thought to the presentation of the items. The prices would probably suffer as a result—a good thing for Maggie. But Sarah had really expected more when she saw Bob Spencer listed as the auctioneer. He was a professional who ran estate auctions all over Massachusetts.

People milled among the tables. Sarah spotted several people she knew, but the area overflowed with strangers. There must have been about a hundred ambling about the farmyard. Some picked through the piles, while others opened and shut drawers in the furniture.

Maggie dashed ahead of Sarah, headed for the back tables and furniture. Sarah lagged behind to see what she could find on the first few tables, which were littered with boxes of miscellaneous items. She stopped at a table and rummaged through the first box: nothing but stained kitchen towels. Sarah pulled one out of the box and smiled at the dishwashing kitten embroidered on it.

"My mother used to have a towel like that in her kitchen."

Sarah startled at the rich baritone voice. Looking up, she saw an older gentleman who nodded at her and kept moving. He was dressed in pressed khakis and a tweed suit coat with a turtleneck beneath, looking out of place in a venue crowded with people in jeans and flannel shirts. He looked vaguely familiar, but she couldn't place him. Her gaze followed him for a second before she shook her head and turned to the next box.

If this sale had anything for her, it would likely come in a stack of muslin and cotton. At the moment Sarah didn't have a quilt to restore for a client—that meant she could work on a project of her own, but she didn't have anything waiting at home. Since these sales usually had stacks of antique family linens with at least a little more quality than the towels and rags she'd already found, maybe, just maybe, she'd find something that would catch her fancy.

She hoped so because her fingers itched to pick up a needle.

As she continued to pick through boxes, Sarah kept her eyes open for Martha, but couldn't see her. After examining a box that contained nothing more than a random assortment of silverware, Sarah strolled past the tables, getting a feel for how the sale was set up, but the best term she could think of was mishmash. The display lacked any organization. A stack of old records sat next to a box overflowing with old butter containers—every table was like this.

"Sarah Hart. What are you doing here?" Irene Stuart of the Maple Hill Historical Society approached Sarah, her purse tucked close to her side. Irene's fingers played with the charms on her bracelet as a smile curved her lips.

"Pecking through the piles."

"Isn't the search the fun part?" Irene surveyed the assembled people and tables calmly. "I haven't found much, not even a pile of old letters and family records for the society. But there's a stack of old quilts waiting for you."

"Where?"

"Over there by Martha." Irene pointed to the far corner of the tables. "In fact, she's doing a good job telling everyone how terrible the quilts are."

Sarah laughed. Martha was her dearest friend, but the woman had no sense for what made a good quilt. She knew enough to save them for Sarah's discerning eye though. Maybe Sarah should get over there and make sure the quilts were items she wanted to purchase. She'd hate for them not to sell because of Martha's overzealous defense.

"Well, I'm heading home. Keep my pocketbook happy. I'll see you the next time you have a puzzle to solve." Irene wandered off, leaving Sarah staring after her. Sure, Sarah had recently found her way into a few mysteries. But each time she'd accomplished good in the lives of people she cared about. She'd helped several friends and made new ones along the way. And when the puzzles involved quilts, she couldn't walk away from them, now, could she?

"Yoohoo! Sarah!"

She looked up to find Martha waving at her furiously. As Sarah approached, she overheard Martha shoo someone else away from the quilts.

"You really don't want anything to do with these. Have you seen the stains? Why, they're practically rags. I'm sure you can find something nicer and more usable somewhere else."

"Martha Maplethorpe, what are you up to?" Sarah crossed her arms across her chest and pretended to huff at her friend.

"Just keeping these jewels safe until you arrived."

Sarah shook her head, then stepped forward to hug Martha. "You're a good friend." She gave Martha a final squeeze and stepped toward the boxes. "Let me see what we've got here."

Martha stepped back from a large box. Sarah ran a hand down the side and saw five quilts stacked in it. "*Hmm*, I wonder what stories these quilts could tell."

Martha peeked into the box over Sarah's shoulder. "Those aren't ready to sell yet, are they?"

"I know, honey. But they should be easy to fix." One quilt in particular caught her eye. It seemed to be in good condition, only needing some seams reinforced, but it was a complete mismatch and hodgepodge of squares—a sampler quilt. "What's your story?"

Sarah looked up to find the distinguished older gentleman from earlier watching her again. His brows arched, and he nodded slightly. Who was he? She still couldn't place him.

Martha interrupted Sarah's thoughts. "That man seems fascinated by you."

Sarah blushed and shook her head. "You read too many novels."

"We'll see about that." Martha's grin got even bigger as the man stepped closer.

"Good day, ma'am." He tipped a slightly battered bowler-style hat toward her and then toward Martha. "I'm Chester Winslow, with *Country Cottage*, and you are…"

Sarah studied him, uncertain why his attention brought a flutter to her heart. "I'm Sarah Hart and this is my dear friend Martha Maplethorpe."

"It is a pleasure to meet you." He looked from her to the box of quilts. "Are you a quilt expert?"

"She certainly is." Martha strutted toward him, chest thrust out like a bantam hen's. "She's earned quite a reputation."

"Martha." Sarah felt heat flush her neck and cheeks. "She's a good friend."

"Enthusiastic." Chester smiled, a benevolent tilt to his lips.

"Have we met before?" Sarah studied him, bothered by a familiarity that she couldn't explain.

"I can't imagine we have. Well, I'll let you ladies continue with your shopping." He tipped his hat toward them and disappeared into a crowd of people pushing toward the stacks of chipped kitchenware.

"He seems taken with you." Martha stood on tiptoe watching Mr. Winslow leave.

"And you, my friend, see romance behind every bush."

"I just want you to find again what I have with Ernie." A contented smile crossed Martha's lips. "You know Gerry wouldn't want you to be alone for the rest of your life."

Sarah rolled her eyes.

"I'm quite content with my life." Martha's smile had a knowing edge, the hazard of a friend who knew you inside and out. "Well, now that I've seen the quilts, I think I'll keep looking. Maybe find something else others have overlooked."

"I have no doubt you will." Martha cocked her eyebrows in the way that said she'd return to the conversation later. "Well, I didn't see anything. Good luck sifting through the piles of junk." Martha squeezed Sarah in a quick hug and then hurried toward her car.

Sarah returned to wandering among the tables. She dug through a box here and sorted through a pile there, and had to agree with Martha's assessment. There wasn't much of value to be found in the sea of stuff. Maybe Willard Haber had focused on heavenly treasure instead of earthly treasures. From what she knew of the man, that seemed likely.

The pile of faded calicoes pulled her back toward the box of antique quilts. Sarah looked around. She pulled the first one from the box, but stopped when Maggie walked up.

Maggie's hands were shoved deep into the pockets of her down jacket. "Find anything interesting?"

Sarah pulled the quilt open, intrigued to confirm her suspicion that the quilt top was filled with a hodgepodge of patterns. Instead of precise rows of repeating patterns, this quilt had a random assortment, just like a sampler quilt that someone had pieced from a variety of practice patterns. "Maybe. This box contains five quilts. I can't believe the family isn't keeping them."

Maggie shrugged. "Maybe the quilts' stories have been lost."

"Maybe."

"Besides, if they hired an estate company like Bob's, the family probably didn't spend much time going through Mr. Haber's things."

"True." Though Sarah couldn't imagine not caring enough to sort through the items. "Anything catch your attention?"

Shuffling a half step closer, Maggie grinned. "There are a few promising pieces." She glanced at her watch. "Do you think they'll start on time?"

"Probably. Bob's a good auctioneer. Likes to run a tight ship." Sarah folded up the first quilt, pulling out a second. She brushed a separated seam. "This can be fixed."

Maggie shook her head. "But few people would know how."

"While it might not be perfect, it's still a beautiful quilt." We're all like it, Sarah mused. Marred pieces of humanity that the loving touch of God patches together. Maybe that's why she loved quilts so much. She could see the hidden beauty, just as God found in her.

Maggie nodded. "I'll stick to larger pieces. If I get them, they'll need some refinishing, but a few are ready for the store." She reached for a quilt toward the bottom of the stack. "Restore these, and I'll sell them in the store for you."

"If I can."

A speaker squealed as Bob turned on a microphone.

Maggie nudged her, and Sarah looked up to find Bob headed toward the raised platform. "Time for me to go guard the furniture."

Maggie zipped toward the front, but Sarah hung back. She'd let Maggie wage battle for the furniture. She'd wait with the other items, staying where she could see and hear but be out of the way. No need to give Bob a reason to tease her into a bid for something she didn't want.

It didn't take long for Bob to get the crowd warmed up on a couple of small pieces. Then he turned to the first piece that Maggie was interested in. It was a painted wooden Hoosier, one of those pieces that people used in the kitchen to store flour, sugar, and other essentials. Today, Sarah could envision someone using it to store craft items.

Bob got the bidding started, but a few minutes later pulled the microphone away from his mouth and shook his head. "Three hundred dollars? Come on, folks. That is entirely too low for a piece of this quality." The speakers screeched at the end of Bob's auctioneer prattle.

"Is there a reserve on it?" Maggie's voice cut across the distance, and Sarah tuned into the action to see if she'd get the piece.

"All right. Going once, going twice, sold to number forty-two. You've got yourself a steal of a deal, little lady."

Sarah caught a glimpse of Maggie's smile, the one that communicated how much she knew it.

Over the next fifteen minutes or so, the bidding heated up as Bob moved to other items, and Maggie focused on

Bob Spencer. The auctioneer had pushed up his barn jacket sleeves and tipped his ball cap back at an angle. He'd homed in on Maggie, cajoling others to bid against her.

"Come on, folks. You can't let this sweet gal from Southern California take all of the good pieces from this sale. I tell you, she has an eye."

Maggie waved him off. "No, I don't."

He snorted. "Next item is an antique wardrobe—looks like it could be the doorway to Narnia, doesn't it? Now, I expect some lively bidding for a piece of this quality. It would grace any of your homes. Don't let it go to a store. Of all things…

"One hundred dollars is the opening bid." Bob glanced at Maggie. "You gonna let it go for that?"

Maggie smiled. "Of course."

Bob cajoled a few more bids, but the price trickled up in twenty-five-dollar dribs and drabs.

"All right. Going…"

Maggie raised her hand. "Three hundred dollars."

And with that simple gesture the bidding on the item went crazy, and Maggie dropped out when it reached six hundred.

Maggie shook her head, and her shoulders drooped. Sarah wished she could reach her and give her a quick hug.

The next couple of items were old sofas, the kind from the sixties and seventies that wouldn't be a fit in Maggie's shop. She didn't bid, and the prices stayed low on the battered couches.

The auctioneer moved to his left and pointed at a bed frame. "All right. This fine piece was made in this area in the eighteen hundreds. Quality craftsmanship all the way."

It was a gorgeous frame decorated with intricate carvings of birds and ribbons. Sarah imagined it would be a beautiful piece in a bed-and-breakfast suite or the centerpiece of a master bedroom in a beautifully restored Victorian.

"Anyone ready to start the bidding at fifty dollars?"

Maggie nodded. In moments others jumped in and the price quickly climbed. Maggie finally grabbed the piece for seven hundred dollars.

When Bob finally worked his way to the box of quilts, most attendees had lost interest, and Sarah walked away with the box at a low price. She hefted the box, and Maggie came to stand with her in the payment line.

Maggie shook her head. "The one item you want, nobody buys out from under you."

With a shrug, Sarah shifted the box. "Guess Bob didn't recognize me from his post."

"You must have bribed him. Slipped him some coffee cake on the way in." Sarah sensed her disappointment even though Maggie was teasing.

"Not this time. But I'll file the idea away for next time."

The sound of a belabored automobile engine caught Sarah's attention. She looked around until she saw a rusted compact car pull into the parking area. The driver seemed to give no thought to others as he pulled behind two cars, parked, and jumped out. A slim woman stepped from the passenger side and followed closely behind.

"Who's that?"

Sarah shook her head. "I don't think I've seen them before. But they're late if they want to buy much."

The man stalked toward Bob, who continued to cajole bids out of folks from his position among the tables. The stranger waved his arms as he approached. "Sir, you need to stop this auction."

Bob looked at him, a frown creasing his face. "Excuse me?"

"I'm Willard Haber's next of kin, and I never gave my permission for this auction. I want it stopped now."

As the man's words bellowed across the area, everyone in the line around Sarah and Maggie shifted. A murmur rose as people talked to each other.

"Can he really do that?" A woman asked the man behind her.

He shrugged. "I don't know. Wonder if we'll still get to buy our items."

Sarah watched Bob, wondering what he would do in the face of the charge. What could he do? Stop an auction when many of the items had already been sold and some paid for? What else could he do?

A NOTE FROM THE EDITORS

Guideposts, a nonprofit organization, touches millions of lives every day through products and services that inspire, encourage and uplift. Our magazines, books, prayer network and outreach programs help people connect their faith-filled values to their daily lives. To learn more, visit www.guideposts. com or www.guidepostsfoundation.org.